THE LEGEND OF JOKTAN AND THE DAUGHTER OF THE
BLOOD GODDESS PART TWO

# THE FACE OF DEATH

BY

AZRIEL ST. MICHAEL

# THE FACE OF DEATH

SHEMYAZA PRESS

ᴀ A DIVISION OF THE SHEMYAZA SYNDICATE GROUP

# THE SAVAGE TRIBESLAND

HAWK

BEAR

THE NORTHERN DEFENSE

SABERTOOTH

FORT SULSTER

DURSTRY

XALTHAME

# STRALTONIA

PLAINS OF KABRIL

ALBANA

THE HAKON DESSERT

ZEBULON

TSARGUL RIVER

KEDDISHYAN PLAINS

# 1

Zebulon lay slumbering, shrouded peacefully in the darkness of the dead of night. The City Guards stood rigidly at their watches upon the massive, towering walls. As was the custom in most places, the city gates were closed and barred securely from within. Any late-night travelers would have to use a side entrance, a tiny narrow opening called the Needles Eye. Most men had to bed over to enter there, and camels were forced to crouch low upon their bellies and inch their way slowly through the forty-foot long passage. Such entrances were commonplace nowadays at larger cities throughout the lands of the Westermarch, but Zebulon had been the first city to utilize them, back during the reign of King Galba long ago.

Beyond the city wall stood the wizard Skeltar's forbidding keep, a black, obtrusive spike that jutted up ominously above the surrounding plains surrounded by a small dense grove of twisted oaks. It's heavy bronze gates were closed, the rusted iron bars which secured them drawn and locked from within. The surrounding wall was not nearly so impressive as that of the Capitol City of Straltonia nearby. Built of stone and mortar, in was scarcely four feet thick and only three times that height.

Birds shunned the shelter of the fruit trees in the gardens, an ancient grove that had been carefully tended by sacred virgins in an age now all but forgotten.

No guard stood watch upon the lip of the wall, no visible watchmen patrolled the sagging, tarnished gates, and there were no rabid hounds chained at the footsteps of the entrance. To the casual observer, the place was deserted and unprotected, easy prey to robbers and thieves.

Yet within the fortress courtyard moved fleeting, shifting forms. They darted swiftly along the walls, too quick for the naked eye to see in the light of day. In the black of the night, however, their presence could be felt like a silent, dreadful heaviness that sought to smother the life from anything that breathed.

Tonight the sky was darker than the foulest pit, the billowing clouds black and oppressive, strangling the pale glow of the moons eternally suspended in the endless heavens above. The air was still, but far from peaceful. The sense of impending doom gave birth and rise to fears that those who passed by quickly in the night had never felt before. They pulled their cloaks tighter about them, casting furtive, nervous glances toward the haunted keep, quickening their footsteps as frightful visions of terrible specters crept unbidden into their minds.

Few it was indeed who tread the road that led past the keep of Skeltar after the last light of the setting sun had faded from the skies. Fewer still who dared to scurry past in the bitter grip of the dead of night. There were many rumors about this place, all of them stories of horror and woe. No one seemed to remember how the keep had come to be, and of the dozen or more scrolls in which the tale had once been written, scarcely a handful yet remained.

High above in the brooding sky a black mass suddenly appeared. It's bat-like wings outstretched, it slowly circled, spiraling downwards toward the seemingly deserted keep of Skeltar. It blended deceptively with the darkness of the swirling clouds through which it descended, dropping silent as a phantom to alight before the entrance of the keep.

Clutched tightly in its talons, Sheba's pale skin contrasted starkly against the black hues of the creature, even in the darkness of the night. She lay limp and still as the saurg released its grip upon her, laying her scantily clad form upon the cold stones before the entrance of Skeltar's fortress.

A dozen or more such creatures followed closely behind, landing in the courtyard, then fanning out along the walls. They were not nearly the size of the first saurg, but they were frightful to look upon nonetheless. They watched intently, as the leader of the horde stood over her, waiting, his huge wings outstretched as if to shield her from their view.

Saurgs were creatures of little intelligence. An insatiable hunger for flesh and instinctive thirst for blood drove them constantly in search of prey. They usually kept to the darker places of the world, places where the blinding rays of the sun rarely shone. Their eyes were extremely sensitive to light of any kind, and their vision....which was poor at the best of times....was greatly diminished during the daylight hours.

Rarely seen in the civilized kingdoms, they would never have come into the world at all if it had not been for the melding sorcery of the ancient wizard Therion. Long ago, during the Ninth Age of Men, he had worked the foulest magick, conjuring demons and nameless devils from the dark regions that lay in smoldering chaos far below the blackest pits of Hell.

Few now knew of the existence of such realms, nor the unimaginable depths to which Therion had persistently delved within them. Saurgs were but only one of the lesser species of creatures the mage had discovered during the course of his investigations within those black, subterranean caverns. He had called them forth into the world of men, in legions too vast to number, and their black wings had blotted the very sun from the heavens above, plunging the world into a bitter war fueled by hate and necromantic malice.

Now that age was long forgotten, and with it the knowledge of where these vile beasts had once come. But there yet remained many cunning wizards who knew the arcane ways of controlling them, of manipulating the saurgs to do their bidding. Skeltar was one such mage.

The fearsome creatures began to grow impatient, sensing that dawn would be breaking upon the horizon within a few short hours, and they started to growl and pace anxiously about the courtyard. Their leader glared at them with sinister eyes, and like cowering jackals they retreated further into the shadows.

Presently the door of the keep swung open, and several cloaked and hooded figures appeared. Silhouetted by the flickering light of a single torch, they were armed with spears and crossbows. From within the entrance a woman's voice addressed the massive saurg, issuing a stern command, and hesitantly the creature drew back from the doorway and moved slowly down the steps. Two of the figures bent down hastily, grabbing Sheba by the wrists, and the heavy fortress doors slammed shut as they roughly dragged her in while the remaining forms stood guard outside.

The saurgs rose into the air, wings beating furiously. They flew up into the clouds from whence they had come, their mission fulfilled, while within, Sheba was carried down a long, narrow stairway of rotting stone that spiraled far below the keep. At the bottom of the stairs, a constricted passage led past rows of empty dungeons and tiny decrepit cells.

Cobwebs clung to the ceiling and covered the stone blocks of the walls as they hurried along, turning into a musty corridor on their right. It ended in another winding series of seemingly endless stairs before plummeting steeply down once more.

Finally, they reached a decrepit looking door that hung precariously on old, rusty hinges. Beyond the door was yet another cramped and dingy tunnel. It eventually brought them to an oval-shaped room that had been chiseled through solid stone. At the far side of this room was a dungeon, much smaller than any of the others they had passed previously along the way.

Sheba's limp body was tossed inside at the bidding of the shrouded woman. The iron-barred door closed with a metallic groan, and the lock clicked sharply, echoing eerily off of the walls outside the cell.

"Return to your quarters if you like," the woman told the cloaked man beside her. "I will send for you later."

The man who had spoken bowed slightly, and the woman withdrew a small leather pouch. She hefted it, appraising the weight of its contents. There was the metallic jingle of coins as she tossed it and he caught the small bag in the air.

"Fifty gold pieces," the woman informed him. "Just as we agreed."

The man bowed once more and hastily turned to leave. From his manner it was obvious that he was anxious to be on his way without further delay, but at the sound of the woman's cold and quiet laughter he froze abruptly.

"Sure you don't want to count it?"

"Have I some reason to mistrust you?" he asked lowly.

She smiled, not out of warmth, but rather calculation, in spite of the concealing hood that hid her features.

"Of course not, Gonar," she replied evenly. "Though it would be a shame if the trust we share at present were to become somehow.......lessened."

"My sentiments exactly," the other agreed. He bowed respectfully, but also out of fear. "I must leave now, my lady."

"So quickly?" she inquired. "Surely you will need a light to guide you on your way."

"Ah, yes, of course!" he exclaimed, feeling suddenly foolish. "That would be most helpful."

He hastily retrieved a torch from a brazen sconce, then waited while the woman lit it with the one she held in her hand. The added brightness caused shadows to dance strangely upon the cavern walls. They played upon his inner fears, and his feelings of impending doom grew considerably.

"Do be careful, Gonar," she warned. "Even I have no idea what manner of evil things lurk within this keep. But as long as you do not stray into places you don't belong, there should be nothing for you to fear."

His eyes grew wide beneath the hood of his cloak, and without another word the man took up the torch with a trembling hand and hurried off down the narrow passage through which they had first entered the chamber. His companions followed closely at his heels, dreading the thought of being left alone in such a frightening place.

After they had gone the woman moved quickly to the dungeon door to peer in upon Sheba's pale form. She was still lying there exactly as before, and for a moment the woman feared she might be dead. Then she noticed the gentle rise and fall of her generous bosoms, a reassuring sign that the captive yet lived. She instinctively breathed a sigh of relief.

"Sheba of Lothair," the woman spoke to no one save the shadows and the unconscious form upon the hard, stone floor. "After all it has taken to bring you here......," she reached through the grill to run her fingers over Sheba's long, fiery hair. "I expected so much more!" Her tone was malicious, her lips a sneer.

She rose fluidly and padded toward the entrance, then turned to look at the captive one last time. What horror will be hers, she thought, when she awakens and finds herself alone, with only Skeltar's demons to keep her company!

She climbed the precarious steps to the upper level, stopping from time to time, listening intently before continuing on. Reaching the main floor, she turned down an adjacent corridor. It veered sharply to the left before descending in yet another flight of crumbling stairs. At the bottom she paused to run her hand along the stone wall. Her fingers touched upon a familiar cleft, and she pressed her shoulder to the damp granite surface, pushing with all her weight against it. There was the grating sound of stone scraping on stone as a cleverly concealed door swung open into another narrow passageway beyond.

Gingerly she stepped forward, holding the torch out before her as she went. Roots grew down from somewhere above and dangled like hideous serpents from the ceiling.

The woman moved hurriedly down the tunnel, carefully side-stepping here and there as frightened rats scurried past, fleeing from the intruding glare of the flaming torch into the dank blackness ahead. Water dripped down from the ceiling and splashed upon the floor, and in places she was forced to lift up the hem of her cloak and wade through murky pools where snakes darted between her unprotected legs.

Presently she reached higher ground, and she continued on for some distance before arriving at another secret door. Extinguishing her torch, she opened it slowly and melted in behind a thick, woolen curtain that hung on the other side. Silent as a ghost, the woman slipped along between the heavy drape and the smooth stone wall. Her exertion in the passages had caused her breathing to become labored, and she stood still for several minutes, hidden from view, patiently composing herself. Then loosening the silken belt that wrapped around her slender waist, she slipped out of her cloak and stepped out softly around the curtain.

King Xalton lay sleeping upon his floating bed in the center of the pool, and as she moved toward the water's edge she casually surveyed the room. All was as it should be. Her presence failed to cause the slightest concern.

*Why should it?* she thought, *no one knew......!*

Those who did notice her entrance didn't seem to care; others smiled warmly in greeting as she slid into the cool depths of the pool. The water seemed to ease her doubts as it washed over her naked flesh. It felt soothing, even reassuring, and she closed her eyes, immersing herself completely. Holding her breath, she sank down until her feet touched the bottom, allowing the dirt and grime from the filthy passageways and tunnels to be cleansed away. *Where is that loathsome wizard?* She wondered suddenly. She hadn't seen him in the room. *Perhaps he's out performing one of his silly rituals or prayers....*

She pushed herself up toward the surface, throwing her hair back over her shoulders as she emerged with a splash.

"I am right here."

She started and nearly screamed at the unexpected intrusion of the wizard's voice. She looked about, attempting to see if her reaction had been noticed by the other women within the chamber.

"What did you say?" she demanded, turning warily to face him. The curious little mage was staring right through her, and she shivered involuntarily at the sight of him.

"I said that I am right here," he replied, and the smile that tugged at the corners of his lips was disturbing to behold. "That *is* the answer to the question you asked yourself, is it not?"

"Humph!" the woman snorted. "You flatter yourself, mage, if you think your whereabouts should concern me!"

"But clearly that seems to be the case," he responded icily.

"Perhaps," he said softly. "In any event, my only reason for being here is to protect the King from harm, regardless of where it might come from. Or from whom."

Her teeth clenched. "Are you threatening me?" she bristled, her eyes darting furtively about the chamber, aware that the others might have overheard and could be watching them now. Her eyes narrowed, gazing back at him like gleaming poisoned daggers. "Stay away from me, old man!" she hissed venomously. "I'm not so easily amused as the King."

"I may be old," Quan Chang Xu replied, "but my wisdom is greater than your guile, and my eyes see many secret things."

"And what do you see now?" the woman retorted snidely.

The wizard studied her thoughtfully. It felt as though his eyes were burning holes into her skin, and it was all she could do to look at him.

"I asked you a question, old man!" she insisted thinly, but his reply only fueled her barely constrained anger.

"Why, I see a snake!" the wizard smirked contemptuously.

"Is that so!" she retorted hotly.

"Most assuredly," the mage confirmed as he turned away, shaking his head as he went. "What an ugly serpent it is, too!"

# 2

With a heavy heart, Joktan stood for a moment, gazing back upon the blood soaked western bank of the Tsargul River, his face grim and haggard in the crimson light of dawn. It had taken several hours to retrieve and bury the mangled bodies of the valiant warriors who had died alongside of him during the battle with the saurgs.

His muscles were stiff and sore from the fight, and his thoughts were dark and dreadful as he surveyed the carnage along the opposite shoreline. He had fought many battles thus far in his relatively short life, but never had he become embroiled against such innumerable odds. During the struggle he'd doubted that he would live to see another day. It had been a fleeting thought, one that had entered his mind in the midst of the red madness, but it had been driven away into the night along with the black hordes that had assailed them so ferociously.

Now he uttered a silent curse at the bitter dawn as he mounted his horse and turned toward the north and east. They had suffered not only the loss of some good warriors. Several of their mounts had been torn to pieces by dark swarms of slavering saurgs, forcing them to double up on the remaining steeds. If the chaos of the night had been overwhelming for him and Chia's companions, it had been even more so for their horses. The beasts had defended their lives just as fervently as their owners, and even after the battle had ended their eyes remained wide with fright. Encountering such monsters was hard enough for human minds to comprehend, but to an animal whose mind had not the benefit of enlightenment, it must have been absolute terror.

None of them had slept. Joktan's body had received numerous cuts and wounds, some serious enough to warrant concern. The women had fared no better; four of them had survived, and each one bore wounds that would leave lasting scars. Yet their faces were set with determination, and Joktan marveled at their courage and resilience. They rode away leaving behind fallen friends and comrades, but in their eyes there was not the slightest hint of defeat. He'd met many men that would have fled at the mere sight of such ghastly creatures, but not only had these women stood their ground, they had fought bravely, without fearing the consequences, and had reaped countless lives. He knew beyond the shadow of a doubt that few men could equal them in combat, and his respect for these women had grown immensely during the course of the night.

They rode in silence for most of the day and well into the night, until at last they crossed over a small rise and came to a stand of trees that clustered around a pool of fresh, bubbling spring-water amid the gently sloping hills. Here they reined up their mounts, and Chia turned to him, her exotic features drawn with exhaustion and fatigue.

"We might as well rest up here for the night," she said, dropping wearily from the saddle. "Soon we will come to the southern reaches of the Hakon Desert, and from there it's a three-day ride to the next oasis."

Joktan nodded and joined her on the ground, his legs feeling numb from being in the saddle for so long without a chance to stretch.

"How far is it from there to Zebulon?" he asked, nearly stumbling to the water's edge for a sorely needed drink. All of their provisions had been destroyed during the battle, when saurgs had attacked the horses. His lips were cracked and swollen, his throat parched from thirst and exertion, for there had been nothing to stow water in since leaving the Tsargul River.

"That depends," Chia replied, splashing her face liberally with water as she knelt by the edge of the pool. "There is nothing but sand in the desert, unless you count the snakes and scorpions. Once we reach the next oasis we will still have another days travel before we reach grasslands again."

She drank deeply, bending down and putting her mouth into the water, then looked at him gravely. "After we're out of the desert, it will take perhaps six or seven days of hard riding to get to Zebulon. We cannot know what other tricks Skeltar has in store for us."

"Aye," he agreed. "Our mounts have suffered just as much as we have. I can keep going without rest, but they have been ridden hard for several days now. As much as I would like to keep moving, if they are played out right now, they will undoubtedly give out on us once we are in the desert. If that happens, we may end up dead before we get to the next oasis."

After watering his horse, Joktan rolled out his blankets beneath the spreading branches of the trees and laid down, stretched with a mighty yawn, and soon drifted quickly away into a deep but fitful sleep.

His dreams were dark and strange, crowded with dreadful monsters and hellish faces, images that taunted him relentlessly and leered at him with glowing, yellow eyes. He awoke countless times, his body shaking, chest drenched in sweat and forehead dripping perspiration, only to fall back into another cruel nightmare from which escape seemed impossible. He tossed and turned violently, as terrible demons gathered about him in the darkness, their deadly talons raking at his flesh, grinning teeth and fanged maws lunging from the shadows, only to awaken yet again and find it simply an illusion bent on robbing him of peace.

He fought the saurgs, an endless battle that seemed to last longer than it had the previous night, and watched in horror as he saw Sheba carried away into oblivion. And in the midst of it all he saw a face that looked like a skull, with skin that looked like parchment, and eyes that seethed like boiling oil.

Then he was back in the sacred circle of the Standing Stone, and Lamashtu stood before him, her long hair glowing like golden fire, her eyes gleaming like flaming jewels. She touched him gently, speaking words he didn't understand in a language that was unrecognizable. Somehow he knew it was more ancient than the stars that shimmered brilliantly in the heavens above. She moved her hands over his body, and the wounds he'd received in battle began to heal and disappear.

He could feel her power washing over him like refreshing ocean waves, sweeping into his very soul, driving away his worries and the anxiety caused by his previous nightmares. The radiance surrounding her was dazzling, and when she touched him it entered his body, coursed through his veins, filling him with new vitality and strength.

The dream was so vivid that it was impossible to discern if it was illusion of if he were actually standing right there with her, basking in the supernatural warmth of her splendor. Lamashtu spoke to him, telling him something that he couldn't seem to understand no matter how hard he tried. Then she smiled and kissed him deeply.

Suddenly he awoke to find Chia standing over him, shaking his shoulder firmly. He sat up instantly, feeling dazed and confused.

"It is just past mid-day," she said as he sat up shaking his head. "We've all slept much longer than we should have."

"It's all right," he told her groggily, wiping the sleep from his eyes with his fingers. "I know that I certainly needed the rest. I'm sure you did too."

"Aye," she agreed with a friendly smile, but her face showed concern as well. "At first my dreams were troubling. I tossed all night it seemed. It took hours before the nightmares ended, and then I must have slept like the dead."

"I too had disturbing dreams for a while," he replied, throwing aside his blankets and rising quickly to his feet. "It must have something to do with the wounds we sustained from the saurgs. Those were evil creatures." He frowned, his forehead furrowed in thought. "Perhaps it was their foul touch that made our weariness so intense."

Chia let out a startled gasp, and he wheeled. She was staring at him, her dark eyes wide, disbelieving.

"What is it?" he demanded.

"Your wounds!" she whispered. *"They're all gone!"*

He looked down at his body, and to his amazement, every scratch and cut had completely vanished. Some had been deep and painful, gashes that should have taken weeks to heal, but now there was not the slightest trace, and even the bruises had disappeared.

The others crowded around quickly to gape in wonder.

"How is it possible?" Liona asked, bewildered. "Not even a scratch remains!"

Joktan shrugged and shook his head, remembering his dream of Lamashtu. "I dreamed that a goddess came to me in the night and healed me," he said dryly.

"It would seem that your dream was not a dream at all," Fjora replied. "You are favored by the gods."

"I know nothing of gods and goddesses," Joktan admitted, "but perhaps you are right. At least one of them has taken an interest in me of late."

Sonya still stared at him strangely. "Never have I witnessed such a thing," she said, "but it is not only you that has been shown grace this night." She held up several leather water-skins. "I found these at the edge of the pool just before Chia woke you."

"We would have never made it through the desert without water," Chia said lowly. "I was worried about that last night before I went to sleep."

Fjora turned to Joktan, her golden locks shining in the sunlight, and her pale blue eyes sparkled with interest. "What goddess was it that touched you in your dreams?"

"Her name is Lamashtu," he replied. "She is an ancient goddess, now long forgotten by all but me, I suspect."

Fjora's expression was one of awe. "I will remember her at the temple when we come to Zebulon."

"As will I," Chia intoned, "although my respect would be more profound if she had healed our wounds as well...."

Joktan made no comment. He was secretly wondering if his wounds had been healed more on account of the blood he'd drank than by the touch of the goddess in his dreams. However, the ample supply of water-skins was no mere figment of the imagination. They were tangible and real, and he could not explain away their appearance so easily.

"We must prepare to leave," Chia's voice intruded upon his thoughts. "This place abounds with pomegranates, coconuts and many other fruits. Each of you stow away as much as can be reasonably carried. It will be only a few hours before we reach the Hakon Desert, and between there and the next oasis....three days of trackless sand. Our water supply will diminish rapidly, so be sure to fill your bellies with as much as you can drink before we leave."

Everyone set about the task of gathering fruit, while Sonya filled the water-skins and divided them up evenly amongst the horses. After tending to the mounts and drinking as much water as they could, the women stripped away their scant apparel and bathed in the cool depths of the pool.

Joktan watched with interest as they waded naked into the water, seemingly unconcerned that there was a man in their midst. Presently he decided to join them for a refreshing dip, trying hard to conceal his obvious erection.

As they started out toward the desert, a black speck appeared in the sky overhead. At first they all feared it to be another legion of saurgs, but soon their fears abated. It was an enormous raven, but as it approached it swooped down low to assail the riders with shrieking cries.

The bird proved to be relentless, circling above them, it's long black wings beating the air angrily as it came in for a closer look. Something about the creature's persistence made Joktan feel uneasy, and eventually he took up his bow and shot an arrow at feathered pest. His shaft flew wild, and he cursed bitterly, firing three more shots at the giant bird. None of them even came close to hitting their mark----and a stream of vulgarities and curses ensued. The noisome raven was not deterred, and Joktan begrudgingly put away his bow, urging his steed to pick up the pace.

The women, too, became quickly irritated by the bird's incessant caws and shrill cries, but having witnessed Joktan's futile attempts at bringing it down, decided against wasting their limited supply of bolts on the annoying creature. When they reached the fringes of the Hakon Desert, the raven still followed tenaciously. As they set out over the endless expanse of windswept dunes, the rogue bird stuck with them, swooping and diving at them from high above.

"Some sorcery guides that thing," Joktan growled to Sonya as they crested yet another dune. "What other reason would a bird have to follow so closely at our heel?"

The woman unwrapped one of her arms from around his waist and peered up at the lingering nuisance. "I think you are right," she agreed, her voice edged with irritation. "I suspect that Skeltar has set it upon us. I can think of no other person who could do such a thing, nor have reason to."

Several times Chia glared menacingly toward the bird and uttered profane threats of vengeance, and Liona eventually fired a bolt from her crossbow at it out of sheer frustration. But the raven maintained it's course overhead, and it's ceaseless calls continued, much to their dismay.

The scorching rays of the sun turned the desert into a veritable oven. Heat waves shimmered hazily over the sands, and the rider's skin--though already deeply tanned--began to slowly burn. The air was calm and dead, and by the time dusk had fallen and the night closed in about them, the only thing they had seen--other than sand and the occasional scorpion--was the whitened skeletal remains of an elephant. Its massive bones gleamed brightly, polished smooth as glass by winds that had blasted them with sand for countless years. How the huge beast had ended up out here in the barren desert was anyone's guess, but now it's glaring remains stood out like a silent sentinel of doom.

With nightfall the temperature dropped off surprisingly, and the small band of warriors took a much-needed break. Their dinner consisted of pomegranates, figs, and crisp, delicious apples, all of which wetted their parched throats and helped relieve their empty stomachs. They decided to save the coconuts for last, so that if they ran out of water before reaching the next oasis, the nutritious milk those fruits contained would help sustain them over the unforgiving sands.

The raven they had come to ignore, blocking it out of their minds with the passage of hours on end, and yet the accursed bird still screeched and mocked them just as relentlessly as it had from the start. As they feasted gratefully upon the fruits they had brought with them, the bird drew closer, enticed by the though of a bite to eat.

Joktan noticed it slowly working it's way in, and presently he tossed the creature a small piece of an apple core. It leapt away at first, then darted in swiftly to devour the fruit with ravenous lust. A few more such morsels and the bird abandoned it's wariness altogether, coming within inches of his outstretched hand to snatch up the meager samples he graciously offered.

The women watched him closely, and Fjora uttered a curse beneath her breath, but a harsh look from Joktan silenced her at once. She glared at him angrily, spiteful of the fact that he was feeding the very creature which had aggravated them all day long, but Joktan seemed not to care. He continued to coax the raven closer, making soft noises with his lips and offering it tiny portions of precious fruit.

Suddenly his hand flashed out, and in an instant he had the raven by the neck. His fingers closed like an iron vise about its slender, feathered neck. The bird struggled frantically, attempting to bite his fingers with it's long, hooked beak, and it's claws tore desperately at his flesh, but he gripped the bird even tighter, glaring at it with a triumphant grin.

"So you are the eyes of Skeltar!" he burst out loudly, taunting the frightened creature as it writhed within his fist. "Well, watch me now, wizard! See what I shall do to you!"

With a violent jerk he ripped the raven's head from it's body and tossed it into the sand. The beak opened and closed mutely, the eyes stared without blinking, as it lay there, and slowly the spasms of its dying body subsided. Joktan turned to Fjora with a smile that was hideous to see.

He thrust the headless neck into his mouth and gulped the raven's blood. It was warm and sticky, and the women regarded his actions with undisguised disgust.

"Care for some red meat?" he asked, holding up the raven's decapitated carcass.

She shook her head silently, staring at him like he was insane.

"Very well," he said, proudly admiring his prize, then turned to the other three who sat nearby. "Any one else want some? These things are very delicious!"

They too peered at him as if he'd gone mad, and Chia looked aghast. "Surely you're not going to eat the servant of Skeltar!" she exclaimed in horror. "It may be yet possessed by some fell sorcery."

Joktan's laughter roared into the surrounding darkness. "It is only a bird, my dear girl!" he replied with glee. "It was merely compelled to do the wizards bidding. Now that it is dead, it's just another bird." He studied it briefly. "And a big one too!"

"There is no wood for a fire," Chia responded with an abhorrent look, ignoring his reference to her as a girl. "I'm afraid you will not be able to cook it, no matter how hungry you may be."

"I have no need of fire," Joktan informed her, plucking the ravens feathers away in huge black fistfuls that drifted out over the sand and off into the night. "Freshly killed prey is best eaten when it is still warm. It's juicier, and far more tasty." He licked his lips with obvious relish, and Chia turned her head away in disgust.

Sonya watched him though with interest, and as he set about cutting strips of meat off of it with his dagger, she leaned forward.

"Is it really good like that?" she asked curiously.

Joktan answered her by skewering a large slab of flesh and thrusting it eagerly into his mouth. "It is most delicious," he replied after swallowing his mouthful. "Would you care for some?"

Her eyes shifted warily from his to the butchered bird. "I think so," she said at last with a coy smile. "I haven't had any meat for days now!"

"Sonya!" Chia gasped in dismay. "Surely you're not going to eat that......creature!"

Joktan chuckled and gave her a chunk of breast meat. She gingerly cut off a thin slice and bit into it, chewing slowly. Sonya paused a moment, as if waiting for some violent reaction to occur, but when nothing happened she shrugged her shoulders, cut herself a bigger strip and chewed hungrily. A smile spread across the beautiful features of her face, and upon seeing their companion eat the raven without vomiting, Liona and Fjora came closer.

Joktan offered each of them a generous portion, and soon the four of them set to, devouring the bloody meal hungrily. Chia watched them briefly with obvious disdain, preferring the sweeter taste of her figs and apples to the raw meat her companions now readily consumed.

The next day brought with it more scorching heat. In the afternoon a light breeze began to blow from the south, but it only served to further drive the fire of the desert into their flesh and make their thirst all the more intense, and by nightfall nearly two-thirds of their water supply was gone.

The apples the women had brought along were now fed to the horses. The poor beasts ate the tender fruit hungrily, then whinnied for more. With the arrival of dawn, the winds picked up speed. The small group choked on dust as sand swirled about them, and their sunburned skin was now rubbed raw from the grit that constantly pelted them, driven mercilessly by the wind.

The night should have been cool and refreshing, but the relentless wind made it a nightmare of blinding dust and sand that seemed to get into everything. Their eyes became swollen, their faces blistered, and their tongues clung dryly to the roofs of their mouths. The water was gone-- the last precious drops of it drank before noon--and now all that remained of their provisions was a handful of pomegranates and as many coconuts.

The pomegranates were shared equally, as well as the milk from the nuts, but the coconut meat they rationed out to the horses, hoping that the minuscule amount of moisture and nutrients it contained would give the steeds enough strength to last until they could get to the next oasis. There were only four horses left between five riders, and each one was desperately needed, but the following day one of them dropped to the ground, heaving heavily, it's sides caked in sand, it's mouth cracked and dry as the desert dunes.

It was done for, and with that knowledge in mind, Joktan pierced the main artery along the horse's neck and filled their water-skins with its blood.

If they must abandon the poor creature to the spiteful waste, then at least it's blood would provide them with life-sustaining nourishment. The steed had served them well in life, and even in death it would help preserve them. A merciful death was all they could offer it in the end.

Continuing onward, their faces crusted and blistered, their eyes glaring ahead from swollen sockets with unyielding determination, they peered hopefully over the crest of every dune, praying to see the welcome green of palm fronds and the glimmer of sparkling water. But all that greeted them were great gusts of sand borne on cruel winds, and white dunes stretching out into an endless horizon.

Even in her thirst-induced agony, Chia would not deign to drink of the horses blood, but the rest gulped it down feverishly, licking every last congealing drop from their crusty fingers. Joktan began to wonder if Chia had lost her way, for the oasis seemed nonexistent, and the endless expanse of dunes all looked exactly the same. Still they struggled onward, their horses staggering from exhaustion, and soon his mount collapsed beneath him, it's legs buckling and sending him sprawling headlong into the sand.

Once more he drained the beast's blood into their water-skins, his hands trembling uncontrollably as he sought to capture every drop. Much was spilled into the sand, and the desert drank it up greedily as his steed sighed its final breath and surrendered its life in the unforgiving heat.

Soon Chia began to falter, and Joktan forced a water-skin to her swollen lips, inducing her drink. She swallowed several mouthfuls, her face contorted in disgust, then handed it back to him and plodded on, cursing the saurgs that had attacked them and ruined their supplies.

Soon it seemed as though there were an oasis at every rise, and imaginary trees sprang up in the distance only to disappear into nothing as they staggered nearer. Three days had never lasted so long, though in fact it had been four since they had left the last oasis. Vultures began to fill the sky, flying lazy circles overhead, taunting them with piercing cries like messengers of certain death.

Chia fell to her knees, unable to rise and take another step, her supple body drained and unresponsive. Joktan slung her over his shoulder and continued on. He was determined to reach the oasis, knowing that every passing moment brought not only himself closer to death, but Sheba too. He stumbled like a drunkard, then regained his balance and lunged ahead, feeling his strength diminish with every advancing step.

It was nearly dark when he spied the tops of lush, green, swaying palms. At first he thought it to be another fleeting mirage, but as he drew nearer he realized that it was real! A glistening pool of water spread out before him, and the bulrushes that encircled it were no illusion. *They had reached the oasis!*

He fell heavily at the water's edge and helped Chia drink, then he submerged his face beneath the coolness of the water and let it wash the sun-baked sand from his face and eyes. He drank deeply, and never in all of his life had such a simple thing as water ever tasted so good! The others joined him, and for a long while they lay in the rushes at the edge of the pool, soaking in the soothing comfort of the water, letting it wash the burning heat of the desert from their chapped and blistered skin.

The night settled in around them, like a dark shroud, gleaming with a million sparkling jewels, and they drifted off into a deep, restful sleep, still lying by the water's edge. Snakes slithered past them unawares in the hours before dawn, and many other creatures that dwelled in the surrounding area passed by the sleeping travelers warily, then went about the business nature had prescribed for them without any further concern.

When morning came in brilliant hues of gold the five awoke, feeling greatly refreshed, their strength renewed, and ready to travel on. Yet they spent the remainder of the day in the shaded comfort of the surrounding trees, eating the fruits that grew there in abundance, and drinking deeply from the pool, allowing their weary bodies to recover more fully while the horses grazed nearby. Their mounts had truly suffered the worst of it, having made the trek with virtually no food and water to sustain them. Joktan knew from experience that their strength would return much slower than his own, and without horses to ride, their progress would be hampered tremendously.

From here the desert gradually surrendered to the fertile, grassy plains. It would be more prudent, they decided, to start out once more under cover of darkness, when the heat of the sun had died down and the air was much more cool. They would have to travel nearly half a day before the white sands of the Hakon were finally behind them, something Joktan looked forward to now with great anticipation.

As he sat with his back pressed against a coconut tree, gazing thoughtfully over the sand, his solitude was interrupted by a shadow that fell across his line of view. He looked up to see Chia standing nearby, and she moved closer to sit beside him in the grass.

"You are a strange man, Joktan," she said presently, a smile tugging at the corners of her full, sun burnt lips.

He returned her smile in a friendly manner, studying the feminine details of her lovely face. "Am I to take that as a compliment?" he asked jokingly.

"That you may," she replied, offering him a handful of plump figs. "I have watched you carefully ever since we met."

"I know," he responded truthfully, accepting the figs and stuffing two of them into his mouth.

"Honestly," she continued, "you are quite unique. There are many things about you that puzzle me."

"Like what?" he asked, seeming nonchalant.

"You get injured, then heal overnight," she said. "Even now, while the rest of us are burnt and blistered by the sun, your blisters are gone. Your skin was burned just as badly as ours, but now it has turned a deep bronze tan--even more so than before--and it will be at least a week until the redness has faded on the rest of us and our blisters heal."

Joktan shrugged. He had not really given it any thought, but now as he considered what she'd said, he realized it was true. His body normally recovered rather quickly, but lately it had been healing much faster than usual. So quickly, in fact, that it seemed almost impossible.

"I don't know what has happened to me," he confessed at last. "I have experienced many new things in the past few weeks. Some of them seem to be having a lasting effect upon me, although I must admit that I am certainly none the worse for it thus far."

"I'd say!" Chia remarked. "I can only dream of such abilities, yet you almost seem to take them for granted."

"I take nothing for granted," he replied darkly, his fangs gleaming brightly in the afternoon sun. Chia realized that she had offended him, and quickly apologized.

"I didn't mean it like that," she said softly. "What I meant was that you seem to be unconcerned about it."

"I am in many ways," he admitted, brushing his long blonde hair away from his azure eyes. "I don't waste my time pondering things I have no control of. And I guess that perhaps I might have considered it more if it were not for so many other, more urgent matters at hand."

"You saved my life in the desert," she said quickly, casting her eyes nervously at the ground. "I am indebted to you for that."

Joktan shrugged again. He wasn't used to having people thank him, and it made him feel uneasy and slightly embarrassed. "You would have done the same, if it had been me." he replied casually. "You owe me nothing."

"Don't be so sure," she objected. "I might have left you there."

He stared at her for a long moment, then smiled warmly. "I don't think so. It would be a dishonorable thing, and you seem to place great value upon your honor."

"Nonetheless," she replied. "I am indebted to you. I shall not forget it, of that you can be sure."

"Now let me ask you a question," he started.

"By all means," she replied, giving him a weird glance.

"Why do you serve King Xalton?"

She laughed softly. "You mean, why would I want to be his concubine?"

"That's not what I said".

"I know," Chia chuckled. "But that is what you were thinking."

"Fair enough."

She let out a long sigh. "I guess you could say that we all have our own reasons, but I like to think mine are more worthy. Be that as it may, my father is a powerful wizard."

"Let me guess," Joktan muttered. "His name is Skeltar."

"No!" Chia laughed even harder. "His name is Quan Chang Xu. He is nothing like Skeltar."

"Is your mother a witch, then?" Joktan wondered aloud.

She looked at him in astonishment. "You really *are* a savage, aren't you!"

Joktan shrugged. "I was just curious. My mother was a scathach."

"A what?"

Now it was his turn to laugh. "A witch."

Chia frowned. "You speak of her in past tense. Am I to assume that she is now….gone?"

"Aye," he replied. "She died several months ago."

"I am sorry for your loss," Chia said sincerely. "My mother died when I was just a child, and my father died before her, a soldier fighting in the border wars with Ramaya. Quan Chang Xu adopted me when I was scarcely four years old and raised me as his own. I have always considered him to be my father, for he has been the only one I have ever known. I am a very fortunate woman. The man I call father is the greatest wizard in all of the eastern lands. There is something very different about him too, for he is far older than he appears. Some say he is over one thousand years old, but I personally find that hard to believe."

"At any rate, five years ago he found an ancient scroll in the forgotten tomb of a long-dead priest. It contained a prophecy, and foretold of a wizard who would summon dark forces from the underworld and use them to unleash a terrible war."

"For months he poured over that scroll, rising before dawn and studying it into the long watches of the night, trying desperately to determine who that wizard might be, and if there was a way to stop him, before it was too late."

"He never did learn the sorcerer's name, but through various magickal methods, he managed at last to decipher where he would strike first."

Joktan already knew where her tale was headed. "Let me guess," he intoned. "The wizard is Skeltar, and the first battle will be in Straltonia."

"That is correct," she confirmed. "By now it would seem quite obvious, of course, but at the time it was merely guess work. To make a long story short, I came to Zebulon to be my father's eyes and ears in the Westermarch. What better place than in the King's palace, the very heart of the city at which the first strike would be aimed?"

"And did the scroll say how this wizard would go about summoning demons to fight his war?" Joktan asked curiously.

"It said only that he would piece together an ancient relic of evil," said Chia. "He never learned the name of it though, for that portion of the scroll had been destroyed long before he'd ever found it."

"The Black Scroll," Joktan muttered.

"Aye," she replied. "So you know of it too?"

"Of course," he grated. "That is why I intend to slay him....or at least part of it."

"If the Black Scroll is assembled, it will be the end of our world," Chia said gravely. "That is as much as I know of it."

Joktan chewed the last of the figs she'd given him. "Why is it that all the tales of evil wizards always seem to end so predictably?" he mussed aloud.

"What do you mean?"

"Think about it," he reasoned. "If our world ends, does not their world also end? It is the same place. Why would someone want to purposefully destroy their own world?"

"I believe it would be more correct to say that Skeltar will bring the world as we know it to an end," Chia offered. "He is on a quest for ultimate power. Mankind has little to offer him. It is the spirits from which he gains his knowledge, so I imagine that in return for their loyal service, he intends to offer them the lives of men, since we are of no use to him."

"Better to reign in hell than serve in heaven," Joktan quipped.

"Exactly."

They sat there silently for a while, looking out on the white sands of the desert that swept on into the distance. His thoughts turned to Sheba, and he wondered where she was, or even if she was still alive.

Suddenly the ground beneath them shook violently, and Chia nearly fell on top of him as she attempted to rise to her feet. She looked at him quickly, a look of startled surprise on her face, and instantly the earth quaked once more.

Joktan leapt to his feet and drew his sword, peering around in all directions, and Chia tore her own blade from the scabbard and stood beside him, shouting urgently for the other three women to join her.

"I see something moving in the sand over yonder," Joktan told her, pointing with his bared blade toward the opposite side of the pool in the oasis.

The sand was swelling, as if something moved beneath it, rising to the surface with tremendous speed.

"I see it too!" Chia confirmed. "But what the devil could it be?"

"I have a feeling we will find out soon enough!" he growled.

White sand spouted high into the air, and as the tremors beneath their feet intensified, a dark, monstrous shape could be seen as the sand broiled up around it. A pair of massive scaled wings burst up from the ground and spread out wide, a span of some fifty feet or more, and a terrible gray head rose up out of the desert.

It had dreadful elongated teeth and glowing, cat-like yellow eyes. Every inch of the behemoth's body was covered in thick, heavy scales that reflected the sun's rays with a dazzling shimmer of multicolored hues. It rushed up from the bowls of the earth amid a storm of white, dusty sand, to stand on four feet and tower high above the ground.

The creature let out a deafening roar that rent the heavens, then peered down at the five warriors clustered close together amid the trees, weapons gripped ready for battle.

"A sand dragon!" Liona gasped, cursing venomously. "Only a magician can conjure such monsters!"

"I see Skeltar has been keeping himself busy then!" Joktan muttered. "All the more reason to gut that lout when next we meet!"

"He must really want you dead," Chia noted sourly. "First a horde of saurgs, and now this! If we survive I will hate to see what he does for an encore."

"We must flee, quickly!" Fjora lamented. "This foe is far beyond us!"

"Do you see the legs on it?" Joktan shot back. "We'll never outrun that thing, and even if we could, take a closer look at those wings! Either way, we are all dead if we turn and run, and I have not crossed the desert to be foiled by this fiend without a fight."

"Listen to yourself!" Sonya objected. "No one can fight such a beast! If you intend to try then you are truly mad!"

"Do you have a better idea?" he snorted indignantly.

The woman shook her head derisively and armed her crossbow, reluctantly resigning herself to the impending struggle.

"Does it bleed?" Joktan demanded, staring intently at the monstrosity before them, his knuckles white upon the hilt of Avatare.

"Who knows!" Liona shrieked as the dragon bellowed ferociously. "No one I know has ever fought one and lived to tell of it!"

Joktan glared at the beast, his feet spread in a fighting stance, ready to spring in an instant.

"There's always a first time for everything," he grimaced horribly, "and by Lamashtu and the scales of Dagon, that time might as well be *now!*"

# 3

Sheba awoke with a start. At first she thought that perhaps she had died, and was now in the clutches of the Underworld, for everything about her was pitch black. The hard stone floor was cold and moist, and feeling her way on her hands and knees, she discovered an iron grill behind which she was imprisoned. She felt it's heavy lock on the other side, and could tell by the roughness of the bars that it was very old and rusted. A musty odor permeated the chill air, and somewhere nearby she heard the distinctive sound of water dripping, slashing on the floor.

How she had arrived here, and how long ago that had been, she did not know. The last thing she remembered was being lifted into the air in the talons of a massive saurg. She recalled how its claws had dug into her flesh mercilessly, and the beast's iron grip had forced the air out of her lungs. It had felt as if the saurg was going to crush her to death. Before she'd lost consciousness, the last thing that went through her mind was that the horrible creature might actually drop her from high up in the night sky, sending her plummeting to certain death upon the plains.

Slowly her eyes became more accustomed to the blackness in the dungeon, and she noticed that there was a larger chamber just outside the door. The air was frigid; she had the feeling that this place was ancient. Sheba ran her hands over her aching body to discern if there were some sort of bonds to keep her at bay, then breathed a sigh of relief when she discovered that there were none. This new knowledge gave her an instant surge of hope, for all that held her within the clammy closeness of the dungeon was the rusted, iron grill.

Her weapons had been taken away, but a hasty search revealed that her captors had somehow overlooked the dagger hidden in her boot. It was no tiny dirk, but a solid double-edged fighting blade twelve inches in length. The blade was tapered to a diamond point.

She closed her fist around the handle, and the touch of solid steel in her grasp felt comforting in the horrible darkness that prevailed about her. Putting her hands through the grill, she began working on the lock, but soon realized that the bronze mechanism which held her captive in the cell was not nearly as old as the bars to which it had been fastened. Her efforts were to no avail, for there was no way that her dagger could ever pry open the lock.

Next she moved to the edge of the door. If she couldn't free the lock, perhaps there was another part of the door that could be pried apart just enough to allow her to squeeze through.....

Her hands felt the hinges, and she felt her heart leap instantly within her breast. They were just as old as the rusted grill, fastened into the wall by ancient, decrepit iron pins. She set to work on them immediately with her blade, and as the hard steel scraped against rotted iron and crumbling stone, she caught a sudden movement out of the corner of her eye.

She stopped, sitting still for several moments, waiting and peering into the impenetrable darkness in the chamber beyond her cell. She saw nothing, but her keen senses detected that her eyes were betraying her, that something or someone lurked outside the heavy door, and her emerald eyes narrowed vengefully. She calmed herself, concentrating with her mind on the thing that waited just beyond, and gradually it came into focus.

It had an almost imperceptible glow about it, a sheen that could not be seen by naked eyes alone, but aided by the power her mother had recently awakened within her, the entity stood out in the blackness of the chamber so obviously that she wondered how she could not have noticed it sooner.

It was no human form that slunk along the carven stone walls without. It was shapeless, possessed profoundly of malice and hate, a faintly incandescent shadow that drifted eerily along the perimeter of the room. Against this silent, unearthly guardian her dagger would be of little use. She sensed that as long as she stayed within the confines of the dungeon, whatever it was that prowled the adjacent room would not attack. She also knew that should she break free of her tiny cell, she would surely be forced to deal with this minion from the depths of hell.

A cold shiver crept over her slender form.

Her mind raced as she sat there alone in the darkness, trying to decide what she should do. The idea of being intimidated by this supernatural spawn of the Underworld did not bode well with her in the least. She had no intention of waiting like a helpless victim for her captors to return and condemn her to some terrible death.

Sheba suddenly wished that her mother were here now. She would know how to deal with such a foe, or at the very least be able to give her some helpful advice! But the Goddess of Blood was far away, and this dilemma was hers, and hers alone.

She thought back to the battle against the priests of Dhampir on the plains of Gershom. By simply focusing her anger she'd caused them to burst into flames. Perhaps, if she concentrated hard enough, she could conjure the fire again. The chances that it would destroy the evil form that lurked outside her cell were slim indeed, but maybe it would be enough to scare it away temporarily, just long enough to give her time to escape….

Closing her eyes, Sheba remembered how she'd directed her rage at the attacking priests, and she mentally began to summon every awful feeling of hate within her soul. She encouraged it, allowing it to fester and grow within herself like the fury of a volcano. She imagined it as a tangible thing that she could touch and feel, a ball of molten, flaming malice she could hurl upon her adversary.

Sheba peered out into the chamber, glaring at the apparition with utter contempt and malicious intent, her green eyes burning pools of angry, seething fire. The entity sensed that something was wrong, that the captive in the dungeon had noticed it, and was preparing to attack. It began to move anxiously about the room, and whether it was out of fear or merely anticipation, no one will ever know.

With a terrible shriek Sheba screamed her wrath, and instantly a wall of fire burst within the chamber. It spread out over the stone floor and leapt up the walls, then billowed across the ceiling in brilliant hues of rolling red and yellow flame. The demon howled and squealed, it's shrill cries resounding deafeningly in the room, and Sheba was forced to cover her ears on account of the deafening noise. She watched as other entities--of which she had not been previously aware--now darted desperately about the chamber before becoming engulfed in flames. A triumphant gleam lit up the features of her comely face as they too screamed in panic and confusion, seeking futilely to escape the inferno ignited by her rage.

*It worked!* Sheba exalted. *It really, really worked!*

She snatched up her dagger once more. Aided by the fire's illumination, she worked quickly, prying the decaying hinges from the wall. She knew that the flames would soon fade, plunging the room into abysmal darkness, and she chipped at the rusted pins and rotted stone furiously. There were three in all, and it didn't take her long to free the ones at the top and middle of the grill, but the lowest hinge simply wouldn't yield. As the flickering light of the fire began to dim, her exasperation became too much to bear, and she stood back and kicked at the door with all her might.

It shook from the force of the blow, and she stepped back, delivering a flurry of punishing kicks that finally tore the remaining hinge out of the stone, sending one of the iron pins flying across the room. The grill, however, yet stood, and she moved to the very back of the cell, gathering her strength for one more mighty kick. She ran and leapt at the door, using the added momentum and her body weight to deliver the utmost force with the blow. There was the groan of rusted metal on crumbling stone, then the heavy grill gave way.

Sheba jumped through the opening, her dagger held firmly in her fist, fully expecting her efforts to have been noticed by now. She could no longer see the demons that had lurked outside her cell, but something inside of her feared that they would soon be back.

Still no one came to investigate the chamber, and her apprehension began to mount. *Surely they must have heard all the commotion,* she thought, but not wanting to wait and see, she went to the doorway and peered cautiously down the corridor. Finding an unused torch in an iron sconce upon the wall, she quickly held it into the last of the dying flames, and it flared up at once.

Then turning back to the narrow hall, she thrust it out before her and stepped out of the chamber. Reaching the spiral stairs, she fought the urge to run. Warily Sheba started up, torch in one hand, dagger in the other, while her heart pounded excitedly in her chest and one word filled her consciousness to the exclusion of everything else....*freedom!*

# 4

Skeltar jumped back from his mirror in disbelief. For the first time in countless years he felt the dreadful taste of fear. He grasped desperately at his throat, his breath coming in painful gasps as he struggled to fill his lungs with air. His head felt like it had been momentarily separated from his body, and it took several minuets before the disjointed feelings that overpowered his senses began to subside.

*Fool!* He fumed silently. *Soon you will wish you had never been born!*

His wrath was directed at none other than Joktan. A few days earlier he'd sent a raven, one of his many familiars, to spy upon the savage and his companions. It was an ancient method employed by sorcerers and witches, a way of keeping a close watch on someone at a distance, and it worked most effectively. Every now and then he could simply turn to his mirror and throw back the protective veil, and it was as though he was looking through the raven's very eyes. Whatever the bird saw, he saw, but while utilizing the familiar in such fashion, part of his consciousness had to enter into it.

When Joktan grabbed hold of the raven and ripped off it's head, he had unwittingly separated Skeltar's mind even more, causing the wizard's ethereal self to become splintered. The sudden agony had left the mage disoriented for several minutes, something he had never anticipated. Now one of his familiars was gone forever, eaten raw by an uncivilized savage!

Scarcely had his senses returned to normal when there was a solid rapping upon the door.

"What is it!" he demanded impatiently.

"We have secured the caravan," Brutus' voice responded. "We have taken all the horses and camels alive, as well as the women."

"None escaped you?" the wizard wanted to know.

"No. None at all. However, there were many slaves, apparently bound for Bezakzia. What shall we do with them?"

Skeltar opened the carriage door to peer out at Brutus. This was the fourth caravan they had captured since leaving Luxantia.

"How many are there?" he asked curiously.

"Looks like about fifty, sir, all men."

"Excellent!" he replied. "Take me to them at once!"

Brutus climbed aboard and instructed the driver to turn and take them down the dusty, hard packed road. They had not gone far when the carriage bumped to a halt and Skeltar emerged, his frail form concealed beneath his dark robes--over which he'd hastily thrown his usual hooded cloak--and Brutus led him to a half-dozen ox carts that had been drawn up in a row along the roadside. Each had been fitted with a heavy iron cage, over which a thick canvas tarp had been securely fastened, obscuring the occupants from view.

Slavers had been outlawed years ago in Straltonia. The owners of the carts had obviously sought to keep their illegal activities as secretive as possible.

Inside the carts there was little room for the prisoners to move about, but all were nonetheless shackled securely to the thick bars of the cage with iron manacles and heavy, rusted chains. The men were all from distant lands, a few as far away as Ramaya, Bashan, even Kish. They gazed back at him sullenly as he looked them over, disheveled and half starved, all of them covered with dust and filth. Skeltar saw no hope in those eyes, eyes which had doubtless seen a lifetime worth of sorrow and tragedy in the last few weeks. They wore only simple breechcloths.

Far from being filled with pity, the mage surveyed the slaves in silence. After several minutes, he addressed the occupants.

"My name is Skeltar," he intoned in a preternatural tone. "Perhaps some of you recognize the name, but if not, it presently makes little difference. You have all been captured to be sold as slaves, a most despicable enterprise indeed.....although I hardly need remind you I'm sure."

Most stared at him blankly, but those who had previously heard of him turned their heads with interest, and he continued without pausing for breath.

"During his rule, King Xalton has turned a blind eye to the activities of slave merchants. He has subjugated and taxed countless peoples, while living extravagantly and ignoring the woes of the common folk and peasants alike. If it were not for his blatant lack of responsibility and his unrestrained indulgences, men like you would not be stolen from their homelands and sold as slaves throughout the world. You should be living full lives, in happiness and contentment. Instead, you sit here, in chains in a slave wagon. Most of you are bound for galleys and merchant ships, to be chained to a bench and an oar for the rest of your life, which will be short at best."

He moved along the line of cages as he spoke, peering intently at the captives inside from time to time.

"This very night my soldiers, under my command, have slain the wretched swine who have held you in these cages like common dogs. Your lives have been spared, but for how long I cannot say, for that choice will be left up to you. Tonight I offer you freedom....for a price....but with generous reward!"

"What is your price, wizard?" one of the slaves rasped. "Well we know that freedom is never given freely." The man who had spoken was a large, well-muscled brute with ebony skin. His teeth were white as ivory, and his voice carried a thick, Ramayan accent.

"Well said!" Skeltar hissed. "Truly, you are a man after my own heart!"

He moved closer to the slave, seeming to glide rather than walk. "I am headed to Zebulon. It is my intention to overthrow King Xalton."

The slaves stared at him incredulously. "That is madness!" the large one ejaculated. "It would take an army of thousands to defeat that city, even if they had siege engines and catapults."

"Ah!" Skeltar boasted. "To you it would seem a great feat, but for someone such as myself….it is but child's play."

He held out a skeletal palm, and instantly the ox-cart of prisoners rose into the air, borne up by some unseen power. The men inside cried out in surprise, holding onto the iron bars of the cage as if their lives depended on it. With an arrogant sneer, Skeltar lowered his hand, and the cart of slaves gently settled back down onto the roadside. It was to him but a minor act of power, but nonetheless, it clearly had an impact upon the men inside the cage. Their eyes were now filled with fear and awe.

"I offer you the chance to fight for your freedom. Not only will you be able to return to your homelands, but you shall do so while carrying with you great wealth. Fight for me, for revenge upon the King who has allowed you to be forced into slavery, and whatever spoil you desire will be yours."

"And if we decide otherwise?"

Skeltar laughed. "Then you can rot in this cage, for all I care. Though personally, crucifixion sounds like a much better idea to me."

"Not much of a choice," noted a slave from Eridu.

"Yet it is far better than what any other passer-by can offer. Consider again where you are. Your situation could easily became much worse."

"I speak only for myself," the muscle-bound slave spoke. "But if it means a chance to slay King Xalton, then I will gladly join you. An army led by Skeltar the Great cannot fail!"

The mage peered at them. "Would you be men, or dogs! Slaves, or free men with a sword in your fist and a purse full of gold at your hip?" The wretches needed no further convincing. As one, they pledged their allegiance to the Skeltar.

The wizard turned back to his carriage, while Brutus had several of his men set the prisoners free. They would be given a hot meal, a flagon of wine, and a weapon, one that had been pilfered from the wares of merchants they had slaughtered earlier.

The mage disappeared, returning to the cramped comfort of his plush silk cushions. He now had an armed band of nearly three hundred, two thirds of which were slaves he'd coerced into his service. It wasn't much of an army; a motley horde at best. But it would be enough to cause the guards in Zebulon to seal up the city gates.........

# 5

The King gazed down upon the lifeless corpse of his only son. His eyes filled with tears, and a feeling of utter helplessness swept through him, like the cold chill winds of autumn heralding winter's frigid touch.

Normally the death of a king's son would be accompanied by endless processions of morning nobles, dukes, barons, courtiers, counselors, generals and servants. Criers would be sent throughout the city announcing the doleful news. At such times the Royal banner--a great golden eagle splayed proudly on crimson silk--would be flown at half-mast in honor of the deceased. But today such was not the case.

Instead of the usual ceremonies and rituals, he had elected to keep the details of his son's death a secret. There were already enough rumors beginning to surface as it was, whispers that told of a mysterious disease which slowly ate away at the king, an illness that no apothecary or physician could allay. According to some it had been brought on by the gods, as punishment for their ruler who had ascended to the throne with the blood of his own father still red and warm upon his hands.

Others postulated that it was due to the sexual indulgences of the King, and a few even went so far as to theorized that perhaps it was the work of a wizard in league with a foreign king, one who had devised a plan to weaken the kingdom from within before launching a full-scale invasion. Some said Perga, others Valdiva or Morava, but such speculation lacked the faintest shred of evidence. Nonetheless, the rumors persisted.

At any rate, now was not the time for the king to appear weak in the eyes of his subjects, a populous that lately had begun to view his rule with thinly veiled suspicion and uncertainty. A shadow seemed to be spreading quickly over Straltonia's most magnificent city, a dark portent of doubt and fear.

Xalton had always despised affairs of state. Listening to the endless tirades of pompous magistrates and the boring prattle of foreign ambassadors--while struggling to appear interested--was utter agony. He usually attended such formal meetings infrequently, having one of his trusted advisors fill him in on the pertinent details afterwards in the comfort of his chambers. But lately he had missed more official functions than usual, and his councilors were becoming alarmed. He could almost hear their guarded whispers behind closed doors, and he saw it in their eyes every time they looked at him. They knew their king was dying, and his only son was far too young to rule in his stead. He knew there would be a desperate rush for the throne the moment his last, rattled breath escaped his trembling lips. Perhaps it had already begun.....

Lately he had made a concerted effort to attend the official functions of the court with more regularity, to create an illusion of strength in spite of his rapidly deteriorating vitality. But nonetheless, the fact remained; he was weak, and his enemies sensed it instinctively like rabid wolves. He knew well that they were attending covert councils in anticipation of his death, and his situation grew more desperate with each passing day.

There were many barons, dukes and generals who wished to continue the bloody quest that his father had begun long years ago, to create an Empire that stretched from the borders of Perga to the shores of the Western Sea, and to the Tethys in the south. Such Imperialism had bankrupted the kingdom during his father's reign, creating unrest and dissension among the commoners while glutting the greed of the warring factions--many of whom were almost certainly plotting a return to power at this very moment.

In particular among them, he suspected General Namindi, the Chief Commander of Straltonia's northwestern defenses in the fortress city of Albana. He was the youngest man ever to have attained such a position, a fact that most people considered to be quite impressive, but his rapid ascent up the military ranks had not been accomplished without numerous bribes and favors, all of which he was rumored to have doled out in abundance to many of the kingdom's dissenting factions and nobility. Namindi was careful though. He was always courteous and humble in the King's presence--perhaps a little too courteous.

With the king's son dead, he and several others might now become impatient for king to die also, and it would only require a sudden bid for power--by merely one of his opponents--to inspire the rest of the circling vultures to follow suit. If Xalton wasn't killed outright, the warring factions and bloodthirsty generals would play their hand in the treachery, and Straltonia would be plunged headlong into civil war.

The king stared grimly at his lifeless heir. Never had his rule hung by such a precarious thread. Despite his efforts to keep it a secret, his son's death was already common knowledge within the palace, where intrigues and rivalries bred among the nobles like flies upon a rotting corpse. It was only a matter of time before news reached the commoners, and they were gullible at the best of times. A silver-tongued war-mongerer could play upon their superstitions with ease. It had been done countless times before--this he knew without a doubt--for had he not employed such tactics himself years before, when he'd seized control of the kingdom at the edge of a bloody dripping sword?

Such fears had been plaguing his mind of late. They clawed at his sanity like foul demons in the frantic hours of the night. But the bitter turmoil that convoluted his senses and robbed him of his sleep was nothing compared to the pain and sorrow he now felt.....the heart-wrenching agony which only a father who has lost his son can ever fathom.

He wanted to burst into tears.....tears of grief wrought by the untimely death of his only child.....and tears of anger for being cruelly robbed of the hopes and joys he'd dreamed of sharing with his future heir. *He would have been a strong, handsome man,* Xalton lamented inwardly. *And a good king....*

A commotion at the corner of the room broke in upon his thoughts, and he turned abruptly to see Elliasha moving toward him. She wore a long, black dress made of fine silk. It was close fitting about the waist and hips, but widened out near the bottom, trailing behind her along the floor as she walked. A sheer black veil faintly obscured the exotic features of her face.

*Strange to see her wearing clothes,* the king noted absently. Her usual attire within his chambers consisted of little more than a necklace. He did not seem to recall when she had left the room, and the young woman's sudden appearance caught him off guard. She stood beside him and in silence, and presently Xalton looked at her.

"This room has a heavy air about it," he intoned lowly. "I must retire to my chambers. Will you be so kind as to escort me?"

"Of course," she smiled weakly. "The sight of him pains me too much to bear."

Together the pair left the room, and those present watched them leave with a sympathetic stare. Few moved forward to offer the king and his concubine their condolences, and those who did manage to convey their regrets did so rather awkwardly.

Once in his chambers with the door barred securely, the king turned to his lithe companion.

"I didn't notice you leave the room earlier," he said casually. "Where did you go?"

"Alas!" she replied. "If it were not enough to be mourning the death of my firstborn, my moon time has come upon me also, and I had to steal away to attend it."

King Xalton looked away quickly, feeling somewhat embarrassed. "I didn't know...," he started, his voice trailing off faintly.

"No apology is required," said Elliasha. "It is the fate all women share. But enough of me. How are you feeling today, my Lord?"

"Old," he replied wistfully. "And helpless. So much darkness already surrounds me. Now it is compounded by our son's sudden death. It is a troubled time we witness this today."

"Aye," she lamented. "I should have liked to see him as a young man. He would have been a real lady killer!"

"Nothing is so hard as losing ones own child. Parents should never have to outlive the young. 'Tis but an omen of doom...."

Elliasha glanced hastily around the room. "Where is the old man?" she asked suddenly. "I've not seen him for hours."

"Nor have I," replied the king, "although I doubt that it troubles you too much."

"Why ever would you say such a thing?" Elliasha demanded sourly.

"I've seen the looks you give him," Xalton told her knowingly. "You look at him as though he were a rat, but the truth is, he has done much to keep me alive, and I am indebted to him. If not for his potions I might already be dead. He has been nothing but loyal to me thus far."

"But he has not cured you!" Elliasha ejected.

"Nor did he promise to," Xalton replied.

"Then what use is he?" she objected.

"Tea....potions....incense....he is nothing more than a common herbalist!"

King Xalton studied her quietly for a moment, and Elliasha began to inwardly feel uncomfortable beneath his thoughtful stare. "The old man has promised to aid me in defeating Skeltar, the most feared wizard in all of the Westermarch," he said at last. "That is why I keep him near. He has also kept me alive, something the best herbalists in my entire kingdom could not accomplish. Yes, my body has continued to grow weaker….a little more with every passing day….but nonetheless, my senses are just as keen as they were before my illness began. I am truly grateful for the efforts of Quan Chang Xu."

"Very well," Elliasha sighed. "Let him linger if you must. But just remember; it is I who love you, and because of my affection for you, I will yet regard him with suspicion until such time as you have been made whole."

"And that is one of the things I love so much about you!" he exclaimed, his eyes sparkling humorously.

She returned his smile coyly and slipped out of her clothes. He watched as her garments fluttered softly to the floor, his eyes feasting upon the young woman's supple form.

"I know other things that you love about me even more," she replied, pressing herself tightly against him. Her fingers quickly found their way beneath his robes, and her gentle, urging touch caused his stiffening manhood to become fully erect.

King Xalton yielded to her caress and sank to the floor as she plied him with long, wet kisses. He inhaled sharply when the hot moistness of her mouth engulfed the tip of his throbbing cock. Her tongue moved skillfully along the length of his aching shaft as it sank deeper between her full, dark lips, and she moaned enthusiastically, hearing him groan in response to her oral pleasure.

"Yes!" he managed breathlessly as Elliasha's fingers tightened around his hardness and her mouth moved expertly to the rhythm of his thrusting, pumping hips. "This is but one more thing I dearly love about you!"

The feelings mounted steadily; he could feel his orgasm yearning to explode. His fingers clenched tight, tangled up in her hair, and he closed his eyes and groaned.

"My sweet Elliasha! You remind me so much of my mother!"

# 6

Skeltar's forbidding keep rose imposingly against the gray sky as the cloaked figure of Quan Chang Xu moved cautiously forward. Beneath the thick hood that concealed his wizened features, the aging mage stared intently about the grounds of the deserted fortress. He stood perfectly still, a dark phantom amid the shadows, listening for any sounds of movement from within, his frail hands clasped together, hidden from view within the spacious sleeves of his robe.

He withdrew his right hand and held it out, and instantly his staff appeared within his grasp. The upper part of it was adorned with golden talons gripping a smooth, crystalline quartz ball. It shimmered with an ethereal glow, and his fingers wrapped around it as if it had been there all along.

At last he stepped silently up to the gates, and propelled by some unseen power they parted slightly without a sound, opening just enough for him to enter. At the prompting of an arcane command, uttered low and firm, the heavy gates closed behind him. He paused, peering deeply into the shadows that seemed to grow suddenly about him in the gloom. He shifted his grip upon his staff, holding it now firmly in both hands as he stepped forward, the faint light from the crystal illuminating the night. Instantly a shadow darted in. It was a shapeless form possessed of malice and contempt, and the animosity it exuded filled the darkness of the night like a living substance.

The wizard halted, bringing his staff to bear upon the soulless fiend. It swept toward him, red eyes glowing with hatred like burning embers of living fire, while from the blackness several more similar entities moved purposefully forward with ghastly speed.

Although they made no outward sound, the spectral guardians of Skeltar's keep shrieked at him mentally, and the volume of their telepathic assault would have been enough to deafen most men. For while it was seemingly inaudible, it resounded within the mind with an unearthly roar and unimaginable pitch. Innumerable hordes of angry, hellish voices screaming their rage, howling in unison, a cacophony of unspeakable madness that overwhelmed the senses and flooded the brain with images of atrocities and horrors that were vile beyond description. It drove away all reason and rational thought from the intellect and replaced it with insanity in the space of a heartbeat, a heartbeat that pounded so violently with terror that the victim would fall to his knees, clutching at his chest, and collapse lifeless upon the ground while his horrified screams still lingered upon his lips and echoed into the night.

But Quan Chang Xu was no ordinary man. Virtually unheard of in the west, his name was legend in the eastern kingdoms that lie beyond the mysterious waters of the Great Deep. Even in the dark jungles of Ramaya--were tribal headhunters and naked cannibals dance deliriously around midnight fires to the frenzied rhythms of beating drums fashioned of human skin--the name of this unassuming mage was regarded respectfully, and with great dread.

For eight generations, the Emperors in the golden palace of Zhenya had often sought the aid of his arcane wisdom and power. He was rumored to live in the Golden City, but a fortress of stone, built by the giants that dwell upon the mist-shrouded crags of Formoria, was his real abode. It was a land where no human dared to tread.

Now he stood before the keep of the mighty wizard Skeltar, and as the unearthly guardians that lurked there assailed him, the seemingly frail mage grew suddenly tall and imposing. The wrinkled folds of his aged skin became taught and smooth as massive muscles bulged and rippled powerfully. His eyes flashed like jewels, piercing the darkness that sought to blot out the radiant glow emitted by the crystal set upon his staff, and his voice....usually soft and gentle....now burst forth in a thunderous roar.

"Legions of darkness!" he cried, swinging his staff in a wide circle that cut a blazing ring of light in the oppressive blackness of the air about him. "Filthy spawn of Seth! I am Zaphkiel, bearer of the Light of Elyon! Hear my name and cower before me!"

The demons circled about him in a chaotic frenzy, a dark swirling mass of furious, shapeless shadows, but the wizard stood his ground and his voice boomed powerfully with an almost preternatural force.

"You shall not oppress me!" he bellowed wrathfully. "Go back to your abode, in the pits of fire and brimstone beyond the mighty river Nar Marratu!"

The demons shrieked audibly now, however their screams were not those of anger, but of terror. They sought desperately to avoid the piercing light that flashed before them, wailing hideously as Quan Chang Xu spoke arcane words that made the blinding illumination even brighter, and then they were gone.

The wizard muttered an incantation, and the light from his staff dimmed. It become a pale glow that shone only about his immediate vicinity, in contrast with the dazzling glare that had lit up his surroundings like the noon-day sun only moments before. His body shrank back to its usual form, and once more he was the tiny man from Zhenya as he moved up the stone steps that led to the heavy doors of Skeltar's fortress.

An unseen power caused the doors to swing open before him, and he stepped inside, his staff held firmly, his footsteps slow and deliberate. The Light of Elyon filled the foyer with an incandescent glow, and the mage studied the room carefully before venturing any further.

The walls were built of hewn stone, over which heavy hangings and tapestries were draped. Upon them numerous arcane symbols and mystical characters were boldly emblazoned, and Quan Chang Xu eyed them with mild interest before peering warily about his surroundings . Here and there, niches set into the walls held curious objects, all of which the wizard knew had a purpose that was far from mundane.

High overhead massive beams of cedar and oak arched, skillfully carved by ancient craftsmen into fearsome dragons and gargantuan serpents, supporting vaulted painted ceilings. The floor beneath his feet was made of polished black marble, and sculptures of intertwining onyx serpents framed each of the doorways, where various rooms and winding hallways branched off of the main entrance.

Directly in front of him, a spiral staircase rose on the right and descended to his left, leading to the upper and lower levels of the keep respectively. Along the sides of the steps, stone gargoyles stood like silent sentinels. They bulged with thick, corded muscles, and as the wizard began to move toward them, he got the distinct impression that he was being watched.

"I come in peace!" he declared loudly, his voice echoing down the corridors of the fortress eerily. "You may come up from the stairs, Sheba of Lothair. I mean you no harm."

From the shadows that darkened the stairwell on his left, a woman's husky voice answered.

"Oh, but I very much intend to harm you, Skeltar!," she growled venomously. "Sell your lies to someone else."

The wizard laughed good-naturedly. "I am not Skeltar, my Lady. I should take that as an insult, I suppose."

"Well you are obviously some sort of wizard," she retorted. "If not Skeltar, who then?"

"My name is Quan Chang Xu. Why don't you step into the light, so I can see your face?"

"Why don't you come a little closer so I can gut you, old man!" Sheba spat.

"Very well," the mage replied mirthfully. "I will come closer, but please sheath your dagger. I am unarmed."

Sheba warily peered out from around the corner down the descending spiral stairs.

"What do you want?"

"I have come to free you," the wizard informed her.

"As you can see, I am quite free," she replied.

"For the moment," he allowed. "But the fire you conjured against the wraiths in the dungeon will not protect you from the other evils that lurk in this place."

"How do you know about that?" she demanded suspiciously.

"I am a wizard. I know many things."

"So am I to assume that this place belongs to Skeltar?"

"Yes," he smiled. "It is his fortress. You were brought here by a saurg. It was acting in obedience to his bidding."

"And how do you profit by freeing me?" she inquired skeptically.

"I am not motivated by the desire to profit from this adventure," he chuckled humorously. "I am merely fulfilling my destiny."

"In what way?"

"I will lead you safely to King Xalton. The rest is up to you."

"And what do you expect me to do for him?"

"My, my! You ask a lot of questions!" the wizard mused.

"Does that bother you?" Sheba asked dryly.

"No," he replied. "But you have asked enough for the moment. We must get to the palace quickly." He started toward her. "I am coming over to you now."

"I'm watching you," she warned.

"Your eyes are not the ones which concern me," he replied ominously. "Stay where you are."

Sheba frowned, but made no comment. No sooner had the wizard spoken, than five of the granite gargoyles suddenly shuddered and came to life. Their gray shapes were no longer that of hewn stone, but now flesh and blood. The beasts shook their manes like a dog shakes water from its furry coat, and their thunderous roars reverberated off the walls and throughout the keep as they glared wickedly at the wizard. He jumped back instinctively, swinging his staff through the air, as one of the dreadful beasts leapt upon him, it's fanged mouth open in anticipation, dripping with slimy ooze.

The Light of Elyon responded to the attack, instantly bursting into a blinding brilliance that illuminated the hall intensely, and for a moment the gargoyles halted, attempting to shield their huge black eyes from the painful glare. But they were no demons of the Underworld, these monstrous creatures of horror, and they recovered swiftly.

The mage had only a few split seconds before the beasts sprang at him again.

His hands twisted upon the upper part of his staff, and instantly it separated into two pieces, one a hollow wooden sheath, the other a long, tapering blade nearly three feet long with a diamond point and razor edge. The Light of Elyon gleamed from the pommel like a flaming jewel, and Quan Chang Xu met his foes with a violent shout. His cry was filled with arcane power, and it carried such force that two of the gargoyles were bowled over backward. They flailed through the air and smashed into the granite wall, then crashed to the floor, snarling like rabid beasts, struggling to regain their feet.

A silvery flash of menacing steel clove the head from one creature in a single, mighty stroke, and it collapsed upon the marble floor in a pile of gray, shattered stone.

Sheba watched from the shadows, neither fleeing nor lending her aid. If the man was truly a wizard, he should be able to defend himself against the gargoyles. If not, at least there would be a few less for her to have to slay once he was torn to shreds.

But as soon as it had begun, the fight was ended, and the strange little man faced her, the gargoyles laying in dusty piles of rubble on the floor about him.

"I thought you said you we not armed," she observed wryly.

"Did you believe me?" he asked, his eyes twinkling with delight.

"No."

"Then it makes little difference." He replaced his sword in the staff and motioned for her to follow him. "There is one more room we must investigate before we leave," he informed her factually. "The king gave Skeltar a goblet full of his blood. I must find it and banish the spell he has placed upon it. Then I shall take it to the palace and return it to King Xalton. You may accompany me if you like, or you can wait here. I won't be long."

"Do you have an extra sword?" Sheba asked, peering hesitantly into the shadows.

"No."

"Then I'll come," she decided quickly. "This dagger won't be of much use to me if more of Skeltar's demons are wandering about these halls."

Quan Chang Xu turned and started up the stairs, and Sheba reluctantly followed close behind. The silence of the keep was unnerving, and their stealthy footsteps sounded loudly as they went.

As they circled endlessly higher, they passed dozens of doorways that opened into impenetrable blackness, and from many of them putrid stenches wafted sickeningly upon the close, musty air. At last the wizard halted before a heavy wooden door. It was unlocked, and swung open readily when he touched it, and the mage gave Sheba a wary glance before stepping through the doorway.

Suddenly they heard a familiar groan, as somewhere behind them in the darkness another door was being opened, and Sheba muttered a curse as something began to come toward them in the blackness of the hall. It moved with frightening speed, the sound of many legs and many claws, scraping and scratching as it rushed closer over the polished marble floor.

The sound brought back memories of the tree crabs both she and Joktan had battled in the Black Mountains, and a cold chill swept along her spine as the thing drew increasingly nearer.

The wizard muttered something unintelligible, and the light on his staff grew bright once more. In the shimmering illumination Sheba stared in horror at the creature scrambling toward them.

# 7

"Put away your weapons!" the dragon bellowed. "There is no need for them."

Joktan shot Chia a stunned look. *"It's talking,"* he growled. "Are they supposed to do that?"

"How should I know?" she ejected, equally shocked by the beast's ability to communicate verbally. Fjora stood frozen and astonished, her mouth agape as she stared at the monster in disbelief.

"Yes," the dragon replied, his annoyance only thinly disguised. "I can speak quite well, thank you. It is but one of the baser qualities I am possessed of. The race of dragons is far older than that of men, yet it never ceases to amaze me how superior you believe yourselves to be."

Joktan had recovered somewhat by this point, and now he studied the beast curiously. "What business do you have with us?" he demanded. "Are you just another minion of Skeltar's?"

The dragon looked genuinely insulted. He let loose a terrible roar that seemed to split the heavens in two, and Joktan raised his sword, preparing for a sudden attack.

*"Nice going!"* Fjora hissed sarcastically. "I don't think he liked that too much."

"I am no servant of Skeltar!" the dragon bellowed. "And cease speaking of me as though I am not here!"

"Do you have a name?" Joktan asked.

"Of course I do!" the dragon replied. "But that is none of your business. The important thing at this time is whether or not you are the companion of the daughter of the Blood Goddess."

"I am," Joktan declared. "What do you want with me?"

The dragon craned its massive neck about to peer at him intently.

"I am come at the request of an old friend, Quan Chang Xu. He has asked me to bring you and his daughter to Zebulon."

"My father sent you?" Chia gasped.

"Yes," the creature nodded, it's voice a low-pitched rumble. "Time is growing short now, for Skeltar will soon be there. He is bringing an army with him, a small one, but large enough when combined with the legions of evil he intends to summon against King Xalton. You must reach Zebulon before he does, and at your current pace, that will not happen."

He stared at them in silence for a moment, and Joktan was struck by the intelligence that seemed to emanate from the creature's emerald orbs, a feature that made him feel all the more distrusting of the massive beast.

"Your father has asked me to take you upon my back and bring you to the outskirts of the city this night," the beast informed Chia factually.

Joktan looked skeptical, and his companions seemed no less hesitant. It wasn't every day one saw a dragon. The few stories he had ever heard about them had been filled with dread and horror. Yet he was also aware that this creature somehow sensed his wariness, and it turned its head to peer at him intently.

"Ah!" the beast exclaimed suddenly. "Long has it been since I last looked upon the blade of Avatare! Whence came you by that sacred sword?"

"It was given to me by Lamashtu," Joktan replied thinly.

"Of course it was!" the giant beast mussed as if to himself. "Interesting."

Joktan frowned suspiciously, then, sensing that he was not in any immediate danger, he lowered his blade. "I, for one, will not be riding upon your back," he declared. "I'd sooner crawl to Zebulon on my hands and knees."

The dragon moved a few steps closer, and Joktan stood his ground, resolute and defiant. "If the circumstances were different I would most willingly oblige you," it said. "However, at this particular moment I am bound by an oath to a powerful wizard." He lowered his head to stare evenly into Joktan's narrowed eyes and motioned with a long, wicked looking talon.

"I must, therefore, insist."

Joktan raised his blade, pressing the point firmly against the monster's thick, scaled neck.

"Let's get one thing straight," he growled, baring his ivory fangs menacingly. "I have never met a wizard that I could trust. Therefore, I must also insist, for I'm certainly not about to start trusting their pets."

*"Pets!"* bellowed the dragon vehemently. "How dare you speak to me in such a way! I am no man's minion, least of all *a pet!"*

The great monster swung it's neck from side to side and blew a searing blast of fire into the air directly over Joktan's head. "I ought to incinerate you where you stand!" he roared fiercely.

Joktan stood unflinching, his sword now held ready to strike out against the dragon at any second, but Chia quickly stepped forward and placed her hand gently upon his blade, pushing it aside.

"If what you say is true," she told the dragon, "then surely my father must have given you some means whereby you can prove the validity of your words."

"Aye," the beast replied. "That he did."

"Then you had best present it now, before matters become….." She stared intently into the dragon's eyes, and there was not the slightest hint of warmth in her thoughtful, steady gaze-- *"unfriendly."*

The dragon returned her stare for a moment, then it almost seemed as if a faint smile began to tug at the corners of its huge, toothsome mouth.

"Women are always so much more pleasant to deal with than men," he muttered, holding out a giant hand. "Your father said I was to give you this."

Chia's eyes instantly lit up with both wonder and surprise. Joktan could hear the warrioress suck in her breath sharply.

*"The Heart of Tana!"* she exclaimed.

At the mention of the fabled jewel Joktan's ears pricked up and he stepped sideways a bit to afford himself a better view. If the gem which dragon now offered Chia was truly what she thought it was, it's value was incalculable.

"It is the only thing on earth your father swears by," the dragon confirmed.

"Surely you speak the truth!" she whispered, her voice filled with awe. She quickly scooped up the jewel and held it reverently in her hands. It was an oval-shaped blood ruby, nearly the size of a plum, about which a wreath of golden thorns had been skillfully crafted. It was attached to a golden chain, and Chia's fingers visibly trembled as she hastened to fasten the priceless jewel securely around her slender neck. The gem shone with a vibrant crimson glow that no ordinary ruby could posses.

"Please forgive me for doubting you."

"No apology is necessary," the dragon replied softly. "How your father managed to acquire such a treasure I cannot even begin to imagine. In truth, I myself thought the existence of the Heart of Tana to be nothing more than an ancient myth. However, I must remind you that time is very precious. We must be going."

Chia nodded, then turned to her companions. "We will ride to Zebulon upon the dragon," she declared. "I give you my word that he speaks the truth."

She looked at Joktan. "Will you also ride with us?"

He shook his head and spat into the sand, muttering an obscene curse in his native tongue. Chia was under orders to bring him to the palace in Zebulon, at any cost. So too, it seemed, was the dragon. Although he'd already decided to go there, he was getting the distinct feeling that he was being led like a lamb to the slaughter, a thought that made him uncomfortable to say the least. His options, however, had now grown few. Every hour wasted brought Sheba that much closer to death, if in fact she was even still alive.

"It is against my better judgment," he said bitterly at last. "But yes. I will come."

"Excellent!" Chia responded, obviously relieved by his decision.

"Quickly now!" the dragon bellowed to the other two warriors, urging them forward. They were moving slowly, unsure if their leader's choice to ride upon the back of a dragon had been made in wisdom or utter folly.

"Promise me you won't eat us," Chia demanded as she climbed onto the mammoth creature's back.

The dragon almost seemed amused. "Is that what they say of my kind?" he asked, his eyes sparkling with something very much akin to mirth. He lowered his head to the same height as that of the woman. "I assure you, I have no appetite for human flesh. It is an abominable thing for us, but I am also well aware that some of my kind have done such things in the past. Nevertheless, you have nothing to fear, my lady."

"So you say now," Joktan interrupted, "but it would be wise for you to bear in mind that while we ride upon your back, my sword will be unsheathed." He brandished the weapon threateningly. "Any foolishness on your part, and I shall flay the scales of your back like a fish. I'm betting that if Avatare can kill a god, it can certainly slay a dragon."

"As I said, you have my word," the dragon snorted in disgust. "You shall not be harmed."

# 8

"Get behind me!" the wizard commanded, his voice reverberating unnaturally in the closeness of the narrow hall. Sheba obeyed instantly. An excellent fighter she might be, but her small dagger would be useless against the creature that scrambled toward them. As the light held by the mage illuminated the darkness before them, the approaching fiend burst suddenly into view, and Sheba gasped in horror.

Its head was a massive black shell that gleamed like smooth, polished glass. Lidless obsidian eyes the size of watermelons stared at them intently, and an elongated maw that dripped with sticky yellow slime opened to reveal rows of jagged, broken teeth. The creature made a rattling hiss, pausing briefly to size up its prey before attacking. Three-foot long antennae on each side of its head writhed like serpents in the air, each one as thick as a man's forearm and covered sparsely in coarse, black hairs.

It's body was segmented, comprised of four bulbous sections that were covered in a seamless shell which was as smooth and shiny as it's awful looking head. Twelve long, jointed legs clawed at the walls and floor as the hellish nightmare prepared to lunge.

"What the hell is that!" Sheba shrieked, clutching her dagger as though it might somehow be of use.

"It is one of Skeltar's own creations," the wizard grated in reply through clenched teeth, sword held bare and gleaming in his fist. "Or more correctly, one of Skeltar's mutations." He looked back at her quickly over his shoulder. "Your fire gift would be quite handy now."

"I can't do it," Sheba replied. "It drained too much of my strength the last time, and I'm afraid that I cannot control it very well yet. Even if I could summon it……I might end up burning you as well."

"I figured as much," the wizard muttered, facing the terrible-looking monster that glared at them eagerly. He took a halting step forward, and instantly the thing leapt at him with uncanny speed.

With a mighty howl the mage struck out with his sword. It was a blur of silver steel that clove the creature's wriggling antennae in half and crashed into it's armored skull. The thing screamed hideously, and the mage deftly sidestepped another frenzied lunge, stabbing the tip of his blade into one of the creature's giant eyes. A black, foul-smelling sludge burst forth from the wound, staining the walls darkly, and the creature wailed painfully, an earsplitting shriek that was deafening in the close confines of the stone hall.

It responded by flailing at him with its long, dreadful legs, attempting to pin him to the hard stone floor. The wizard's sword moved as though it had a life of it's own, slashing, stabbing, parrying, and thrusting with preternatural speed and unbelievable power, yet his efforts only seemed to further infuriate the monstrosity, and he slowly began to yield his ground.

A sudden devastating blow caused him to lose his footing upon the slippery ooze that was spreading all over the floor, and he was driven down onto his knees. The sword was wrenched from his hand by ghastly mandibles and sent clattering down the passage.

Sheba shrieked in horror and slashed out with her dagger, hoping to at least injure the creature's other eye and buy the wizard a few precious seconds in which to regain his feet and scramble away. Her blow was blocked by one of the monster's thick, segmented legs, and a razor sharp claw nearly disemboweled her. She ducked and jumped this way and that, evading the desperate strikes of the creature and thrusting relentlessly with her dagger, but the small blade was no match against the iron-like shell that protected the evil creation. A hasty sideways glance told her that the mage was scrambling toward his sword, which had by this time been knocked further down the hall.

Sheba cried out savagely, trying her best to keep the monster distracted, but it too had seen the wizard's movements. It tried to turn itself around, but it's body was much too long and rigid to allow for such a maneuver in the confines of the hall. Seizing the moment, Sheba cocked her arm back and hurled her dagger with all of her might.

The wretched creature screeched, a long, piercing wail that froze the blood. It struck out blindly in every direction at once as its eyeball exploded in a spray of brackish filth that spilled over its demonic head and pooled on the floor. It thrashed and convulsed uncontrollably, pushing and clawing at the walls in utter agony. The creature was unbelievably powerful, and with a sickening groan, a portion of the stone ceiling suddenly gave away and came crashing down.

The hallway was instantly filled with an impenetrable cloud of dust, as stone blocks smashed into the creature and debris rained down all around them. Sheba stumbled backwards, gasping for air. Dust filled her eyes, making them water and sting, and somewhere in the haze she heard the wizard's voice. It rose in volume and power as the mage spoke strange words in a language she didn't recognize or comprehend; yet the intention was unmistakable.

A brilliant flash of bluish-white light suddenly leapt about the room like lightening, dancing back and forth between the walls of the hallway with an electrifying crackle. It was followed by a thunderous, explosive boom that slammed Sheba violently into the floor. Her head hit the cold hard stone with a heavy, solid thud.

Burning pain lanced through her skull like red-hot irons as she struggled to rise, and she collapsed, unable to move, her body limp and numb. Her head felt like it was spinning, and it seemed as though she were plunging into a sea of darkness--into an empty, bottomless abyss of endless black.

# 9

*"Tell me a story."*

Sheba looked quickly about to see who it was that had spoken. *How did I get here?* she wondered silently. A moment before she had been in a hellish nightmare from which there had seemed to be no escape. *Perhaps it was all just a dream.....*

She was home, standing in the courtyard at the top of the Temple of the Moon in Lothair. The night air was cool and moist against her skin, a slight breeze tossed her hair gently about her shoulders, and her senses seemed to be more alive and heightened than ever before.

She was acutely aware of the buzzing of insects, the chirping of crickets, the cooing of doves nesting down somewhere nearby for the night. And farther down in the valley she could hear the creatures of the jungles--creatures of the night--moving about on padded feet, some hunting, stalking their prey, others fleeing a pursuing predator or swimming in the pools and eddies that swirled along the edges of the winding river. *Where is my mother?*

She tried to concentrate, to see how much further her perception could reach, and suddenly her mind became a jumbled mass of confusing images and convoluted conversations, all of which made no sense to her whatsoever. On the contrary, they swept into her mind with all the fury of a storm--as though her mind now trembled upon the brink of insanity--and it was all that she could do not to scream at the top of her lungs.

Then suddenly there it was.... *that voice again!* But now it was louder than anything she could have ever thought imaginable, and she knew instinctively that she needed to pull her perception back into her body. Whoever it was that had spoken was now standing close by. What was they had just said?

"*I asked you to tell me a story,*" the voice answered in response to her unspoken query.

She spun instantly, but there saw no one. Then she looked down to see two young children....obviously twins.....one a boy, the other a girl. *That's odd,* she thought. *What are children doing in my house?*

"What did you...." she started, then.…... "what are you doing here?"

"The sun won't be up for two more hours," the boy said. His hair was like golden threads of silk, and his voice had a musical quality to it, like the clear sound of a silver trumpet at dawn. "Can you tell us about our father?"

"Certainly," Sheba responded, feeling completely bewildered. "I...I mean I could if…..... if I knew who he was..."

Both of them had the same color of eyes as she did, the same emerald green.

"*I'm being serious,*" the child admonished playfully.

Sheba gasped. *He had fangs! The child had fangs just like….*

She turned to stare at the little girl. She hadn't spoken yet, but there was something strange about her. She had long red hair, and she too had fangs. Her eyes were emerald green too, and.…...*wait! They had suddenly turned blue as sapphires……*

"If you won't tell me a story, then how about if I tell you one?" said the boy.

"Oh…. I'm sorry, honey," she apologized, feeling suddenly embarrassed. "I would love it if you told me a story." Her surroundings were distracting her attention just as much as the presence of the children. All of this felt so real, yet at the same time her instincts insisted that she was dreaming.

"Do you like our home?" he asked.

"Yes, I love it very much. Once I left it for a long time, and I missed it so much…."

"I'm the one telling the story, mom, remember?"

*Mom? Are these my children? But I don't have any children….*

"Sorry," she replied absently. "Go on." *Apparently these children were hers.*

"I like our Kingdom. Someday I will be its ruler," he paused. "But there is just one tiny little problem."

"Problem? What do you mean? We have lived here for thousands of years. There is no problem. When you're older you'll understand." *How old were they anyway? Ten? Twelve?*

The child's voice became indignant. "I don't need to be older! I already understand more than you do! I understand that our father was an abomination, that this country is just not big enough for both of us."

"What are you saying?" she asked. "I'm sure your father was a good man. You don't know what you're talking about."

*"No, mother, you don't!"* he retorted precociously.

The little girl moved closer to stand beside her brother. She had a very peculiar smile on her face, one that Sheba couldn't quite interpret; yet it caused her to suddenly feel alarmed. She was saying something to her telepathically, but at such a tremendous rate of speed that Sheba found it impossible to keep up, and she quickly became confused and disoriented. Her mind filled with a cacophony of unreal images, tormenting, agonizing, overwhelming. She instinctively covered her ears with her hands in a futile effort to shield herself from the malevolence of the child's mental assault.

The boy thrust his hand into the folds of his clothing and withdrew a long, slender blade. His features began to change, to transform before her very eyes, and his face took on a hellish appearance. The mere sight of his face twisted the mind into madness and caused her to instantly shrink away in revulsion.

"What is going on here?" Sheba demanded.

The children stepped toward her. Both of them now held gleaming daggers in their diminutive hands. As they moved closer they raised their blades, preparing to strike.

"I'm glad that we were able to have this talk," said the boy.

"But we're not done," Sheba countered.

*"Yes we are, mother,"* he replied icily. *"And we've decided that you have got to go!"*

# 10

"Come back!"

A hand smacked her hard across the face and fire spread instantly over her cheek.

"Sheba, come back!" the voice commanded again. "The time is not yet. Hear my voice calling you back, and obey!"

Sheba suddenly sat up with a jolt. She was sprawled out upon the stone floor of Skeltar's keep. Her whole body was covered in dust, and she could feel a trickle of blood running warm and sticky from her scalp and down the side of her face. Her head throbbed and ached badly, and the strange little wizard was bent over her, preparing to smack her once again.

"Touch me one more time and I'll...."

"Now, now!" the old man chuckled. "That is no way to treat the one who has just saved your life."

Sheba snorted derisively. "More like you nearly killed me!" she exclaimed. She tried to get to her feet but her legs wouldn't respond.

"Take it easy," the old man told her softly. "You'll be fine in a few minutes. I had no other choice but to use a blast of power against Skeltar's guardian. Unfortunately, the blast hit you as well. It was a risk that I was forced to accept."

"My body feels strange," she mumbled, still a little confused. "I was having an awful dream...."

"Dream?" the mage laughed and shook his head. "Not likely. Most other people would have been killed by such a force, yet you were not. Nonetheless, where you were, dreams no longer exist."

"And where would that be?"

"Your soul was separated briefly from your body," he said. "You were in a place that lies between the world of the living and the realm of the dead." He sat down across from her and leaned back against the wall. "Tell me what you saw."

Sheba shook her head. "I'd rather not. It wasn't pleasant."

"As you wish," said the mage, "but I can tell you this; what you experienced was not a dream, and it wasn't an illusion either."

"Then what was it?" she asked wearily. "It seemed just as real as this."

"It was a possible reality," he replied. "A likely future. You were not seeing it as one does in a dream, from a mere mental perspective. *You were actually there.* This happened because you were struck by the blast of power."

"If that is the future, then it is an evil one indeed," Sheba muttered bitterly.

The wizard leaned toward her and smiled. "Do not be fearful. The place you are now in is evil. It is Skeltar's stronghold, and everything within it has been infected with his depravity and corruption. So also was your experience, because your physical body was here whilst your soul did roam the realms beyond. It may have contained some small potion of truth, but it was also greatly distorted."

Sheba surveyed hey surroundings. The monster had been literally blown to bits. Pieces of it were strewn everywhere down the length of the corridor. The mage followed her gaze.

"Deep in the jungles beyond Ramaya and Zhenya, there exists a place very few know of," he told her quietly. "In that land there exists a curious species of ants. They grow quite large--commonly longer than a man's arm--but they are easily influenced and controlled by spells and sorcery. They are a creature that was created by the meddling of the Morashi. Fortunately, they do not form colonies as do other ants, else I fear they might easily overrun the world. Skeltar brought this creature across a very great distance, and I would imagine that he has kept this one for over fifteen years, at the very least. It appears his knowledge of the Black Arts is more extensive than I had first thought it to be."

"Did you find what you came for?" she asked, brushing her tangled hair out of her face.

"Yes," he replied. "Soon Skeltar's hold upon the King can be broken."

Sheba thought for a moment in silence, then looked up at the wizard. "Do you mean to tell me that everything that enters this place will be affected by Skeltar's evil?"

He nodded solemnly. "Yes."

"Then you had better get me out of here as quickly as possible," Sheba told him, her voice filling with a sudden urgency.

"We will be all right," the mage reassured her. "You need to gather your strength. Your battle is not finished yet."

"Some wizard you are!" she snapped impatiently and jumped to her feet. "My concern is not for myself!"

"Then for whom?" asked the mage.

Sheba glared at him angrily. "I'm pregnant, you fool! *With twins!*"

# 11

It was still early in the evening, but a thick blanket of dark clouds had swept over the heavens, extinguishing the light of the stars and smothering the pale glow of the moons. There was a feeling of foreboding and dread in the air, and even the weight of his sword, gripped tightly in his fist, did little to assuage Joktan's growing anxiety as they moved stealthily toward the city.

The dragon had kept his word. No harm had befallen any of them during the flight to Zebulon. Be that as it may, Joktan had breathed an inward sigh of relief once his feet had at last come to rest upon solid ground. They had soared to unimaginable heights, high above the clouds, and in truth, it was to prove to be an experience he would remember for the rest of his life.

Chia led them swiftly to the secret entrance of the tunnels that ran beneath the city of Zebulon and the Imperial Palace. Once inside, they moved along single file, guided only by the women's familiarity and the dim flicker of torches that cast strange, deformed shadows that slithered along the walls. It was like the descent of the dead into Hel, and no one spoke. The only sounds that could be heard were those of dripping water and softly falling footsteps. The passages quickly became a bewildering maze of tunnels that branched off and separated at every turn, and Joktan was amazed at how deftly the women moved along.

In many places there were deep, yawning pits that fell away into total darkness. Such spots could only be crossed by leaping over them, and although they appeared to be bottomless, he knew instinctively that most of them probably ended in sharpened spikes and other devices upon which the unwary would fall and be impaled. He'd half expected the women to blindfold him, but now he understood that there was no need for them to do so. It would be impossible for him to ever find his way back out alive.

As they rounded a corner and turned off into yet another branching tunnel, Chia motioned them to an abrupt halt. They stood absolutely still for several moments, then she turned to Liona.

"We are not alone!" she hissed in the shadows. "There is someone up ahead of us."

"We will sneak up and overtake them unawares," Sonya whispered.

Chia shook her head. "There is no need to. Whoever it is, they are moving towards us."

Chia extinguished the touch, and instantly they were swallowed by an impenetrable darkness, so utterly pitch black that Joktan could not even see his hand in front of his face. The sound of stealthy footsteps grew closer from up ahead, and the five of them pressed their backs to the moist earthen walls of the tunnel and waited in silence, their weapons drawn. Spiders lived in the tunnels, large, hairy arachnids half the size of a man's hand, and he found it difficult to restrain himself from swatting at one of them as it crept slowly across his cheek.

As the moments passed, his eyes began to slowly accustom themselves to the blackness, and presently a dim light could be seen coming steadily on down the passage.

It was a soft, pale silvery light that shone steadily, not the wavering flicker of a torch's flame. A dozen or more paces away it stopped, and in the silence Joktan could hear the women's breathing cease as they prepared themselves to attack. Suddenly the strange, tiny light burst into a dazzling radiance that was so brilliant it blinded them all instantly and made their eyes sting.

"Who are you!" a man's harsh voice boomed in the tunnel. It had a powerful, commanding quality that seemed unnatural.

"Tell us your name first," Chia responded loudly, attempting to shield her eyes from the painful glare.

There was the sound of quiet mirth before the man spoke again. When he did, his tone was considerably softer. "Does not my daughter know the sound of her father's voice?"

"Father!"

"Yes, it is I," the old man replied merrily.

Chia ran to Quan Chang Xu and embraced him joyously. "How did you come to be down here?" she asked, her features clouding with worry. "It is very dangerous in the tunnels."

"Don't worry, my girl," said the wizard. "My feet have trod many paths during my long years. These passageways pose no threat to my safety."

He noted the jewel that hung about her neck. "I see my old friend found you."

"Aye," Chia replied. "Though at first we were quite untrusting of him."

Her father merely smiled. "As I knew you would be. That is why I chose to give you the Heart of Tana."

She touched her fingers lightly to the jewel. "How did you acquire this?"

"That, my girl, is a long story," the wizard replied, winking at her with a devilish grin. "And one which I promise to tell once we have the time."

Chia's face grew stern. "These tunnels are one of the kingdom's most closely guarded secrets, father. You really shouldn't be here."

The wizard's eyes sparkled with amusement. "Don't you worry, my dear. I did not come down here alone."

"Oh?" Chia responded curiously.

Suddenly a female form detached itself from the shadows behind the mage and stepped into the light.

"It can't be...!" Chia started in shock.

The other women present let out a startled gasp, and Joktan's jaw nearly hit the floor. "Sheba!" he exclaimed, running to throw his arms around her. "I feared I might never see you again."

He squeezed her tightly to his chest, and she put her arms around him and hugged him back just as hard before pressing her lips to his and kissing him passionately.

"The wizard told me that you were alive, but I did not believe him," she admitted. Tears of joy began to well up within her eyes, and she quickly tried to wipe them away. "I have much to tell you!"

"And I also have much to share with you," he replied, "but it can wait for the moment." His gaze traveled over her body lustily for an instant.

"I see you have no sword," he commented.

"Just this," she replied, holding out her dagger.

Joktan hastily stripped away his broadsword and offered it to her. "I cannot give you Avatare, but this should serve you nicely."

Sheba accepted it gratefully. "I feel much better already," she smiled, strapping the weapon to her hip. Then she turned to Chia. "Where are the others?"

Chia shook her head in dismay. "They did not survive the saurgs." She was a warrior through and through, the equal of any man, but the death of her companions still pained her greatly, and her feelings of loss were evident in her gaze.

"I'm truly sorry," Sheba said. "They were brave warriors."

"They died with honor," Chia intoned respectfully.

"Yet their absence is evident, and each of them will be sorely missed," Sheba replied softly. "I offer all of you my condolences."

There was a brief moment of awkward silence, then the wizard spoke up. "Well, now that everyone that can be is reunited, we must get down to business. Skeltar is moving fast now, and he will reach Zebulon very soon. He has a small army of men with him, but when he reaches the city he will use every means at his disposal to kill the king and take the city for himself. He also intends to kill Sheba, to use her blood for a most unholy purpose."

He looked at each one of them intently. "It is up to us to see that he is defeated."

"Then we had better get to the king at once," Chia declared. "He will be most anxious to meet with Sheba and Joktan."

They started off down the tunnels once more, now guided by the wizard's strange, brilliant light, past countless yawning openings that led off into abysmal darkness. Some they entered and continued down for some distance before plunging off into yet another such passage, while others the women avoided with the utmost care and caution. They moved quickly, yet to Joktan it seemed an eternity before they halted at last before a stone entranceway over which hung a thick, heavy tapestry.

"Wait here," Chia instructed them. "I will spy out the chamber before we enter." She passed through the curtain and disappeared, and it was several minutes before she returned.

"The King is resting upon his bed in the great pool," she informed them. "Elliasha lies with him."

The wizard turned to her quickly. "There is something you must know," he said gravely. "There is treachery within the King's chamber. Elliasha has been aiding Skeltar."

Chia's eyes went wide with surprise. "Elliasha?" she hissed. "Are you certain of this?"

"Most definitely," the mage replied with a nod. "I watched with my own eyes as the saurgs descended upon Skeltar's keep with Sheba in their clutches, and it was Elliasha whom they delivered her to. She then took her within, aided by two men, and they carried her into the lower dungeons. I do not know what role she plays in this game, but rest assured, she is a traitor."

"Have you told the King of this?" Sonya asked, still in shock by the nature of this unexpected news.

"No, I have not," replied Quan Chang Xu admitted. "He is deeply attached to the woman--they have had a son together--and I fear he will not believe me." He looked at his daughter sternly. "It would be wise if you did not tell him either."

"The King has a right to know!" Liona broke in defiantly. "His life is in danger, and we have all sworn oaths to protect it. He *must* be told."

"Aye," Sonya concurred. "If he were to discover that we knew and said nothing....."

"You are right, of course," the wizard agreed, holding up a wrinkled hand. "He needs to be told, but not by any one of you. He must hear it from Elliasha's own lips if he is to believe it. And there is one more thing you should know also."

"I fear to ask what that is," Chia growled angrily.

"The King's son is dead."

"No!" Chia gasped in dismay. It took a few seconds for it to truly sink in, and when she turned back to her father, the woman's eyes were narrow, burning slits.

"Was this also the work of Elliasha? Is she so sick as to kill her own first-born child?"

"I'm afraid so," the wizard responded. "The King still mourns the loss as we speak."

"That traitorous bitch!" Fjora exclaimed murderously. "I shall lop off her head, next we meet!"

"First you will have to get past my blade," Sheba snarled, her lips curled horribly with malice. "I have a score to settle with that slut!"

"Your father is right," Joktan cut in. "Your King will have to see her treachery for himself to truly believe it. Until then, everyone will have to keep their wits about them, for she could strike against him at any moment, and if she suspects that any of you know the truth, she will no doubt seek to kill you as well."

"Agreed," Chia resolved. "No rash behavior, is that understood?" She looked at each of her companions and they nodded in turn their consent. Her gaze lingered briefly upon Sheba and she smiled slightly. "We will need to get you cleaned up before meeting the King. This passage skirts the Royal chamber to another room where both of you can be refreshed before he sees you. The King is expecting to meet the daughter of a Goddess. No offense, but you look like one who has just escaped from a dungeon!"

Sheba looked at herself and suddenly became aware of just how disheveled she truly appeared. Her clothing was tattered and torn, and her body was covered in dust and grime. "That would be most appreciated," she confessed.

"Fjora can announce our arrival while we tend to you, but we must be quick about it." Chia motioned to the other woman, and she nodded, before vanishing like a phantom through the curtained doorway. "Let's go in."

"Wait!" Joktan grated just as she was about to part the curtained entrance. He still held his sword tightly in his fist, and his features were taught with apprehension. "Your King has a price on my head, remember?"

"Not anymore," she replied. "It was lifted the moment you chose to aid us."

He stared at her skeptically for a moment. "Do I have your word on it?"

"You have my word," she confirmed. "And you have everyone here as witness to it."

He stared at her intensely, as if trying to make up his mind, then grinned, sheathing his sword with a shrug. "Then what are we waiting for?"

# 12

Dust billowed into the air from the pounding hooves of their steeds on the dry packed road as General Namindi and his twelve closest captains brought their mounts to a sudden halt. It was late afternoon, yet the sun continued to burn with unforgiving intensity in the cloudless sky, and the heat caused both man and beast to sweat profusely. Even the creatures who made their homes amid the tall grasses that hemmed in the road on either side had returned to their burrows and nests in an effort to escape the burning heat of the sweeping plains.

Slightly ahead of the soldiers, some thirty yards or so, a man dressed in tattered rags was running towards them, his arms waving desperately in the air. The riders waited, spears and swords held ready to strike, as the newcomer stumbled toward them. He collapsed exhausted, panting for breath on his hands and knees before the General and his men.

"What do you want?" one of the armed men demanded harshly. The poor wretch stared up woefully at Namindi, his sunburned lips cracked and swollen from thirst and exertion. He gasped for air in unsteady, rattled breaths, and the soldiers began to quickly grow impatient.

"Speak up, if you know what's good for you!" one of them commanded, his voice betraying neither sympathy nor concern.

"Please, I beg of you!" he sputtered feverishly. "I am but a poor slave, but I bear urgent news for the King."

The General leaned forward curiously, sudden interest glimmering in his keen pale stare. He motioned for his men to put away their weapons with a wave of his gloved hand, then dropped down from his mount and strode forward. He was a young man, scarcely twenty-five years of age, yet he was over six feet in height and built like an Adonis. The scarlet cloak which fastened at the shoulders of his shining Imperial armor swirled around him as he walked, and he moved with the ease and confidence of a lion as he drew near to the ragged man that had thrown himself prostrate upon the ground.

His dark auburn hair had been cropped squarely about his massive shoulders, his mustache neatly trimmed. He bore himself with obvious pride that bordered carelessly on arrogance, but then he was, after all, the Chief Commander of the kingdom's northern defenses. Never before had a man so young achieved such a high position in the Straltonian military, and Namindi was not one to let such facts go unnoticed, even by the filthy peasant slave that now crouched diminutively before him, shaking with fright.

The General was a descendant of old nobility, a lineage whose forefathers had been chieftains and princes back in the days when the kingdom now known as Straltonia had been nothing more than a handful of city states held together by loose alliances and oaths. Although that had been more than four hundred and fifty years ago, the ancient bloodlines had somehow managed to maintain their grasp on power and positions of importance, and Namindi was the son of such stock. He stared down at the man in the dirt before him with an air of aloofness that was unmistakable.

"How is it that a poor wretch such as yourself has come by such important news?" the General inquired imperiously. "Speak up!"

The fearful man stared up at Namindi, his eyes dilated with trepidation, and his voice wavered weakly with an obvious eastern accent as he spoke.

"I am but a peasant of Sidon. I was captured many weeks ago and brought by caravan to Straltonia to be sold as a slave."

Namindi peered at him skeptically. "Slave trading is forbidden in Straltonia," he snapped. "I have no time to listen to such lies." He started to turn away, but the man cried out in protest.

"Asherah be my witness, it is no lie!" he wailed bitterly. "I was not brought here alone. There were many more with me, some from lands of which I have never heard tell of. We were all shackled and chained inside of a wagon, over which a heavy tarp was fixed to conceal us."

Namindi studied the man's facial features carefully. He had not attained his position by being ignorant. Not only was he well educated; he was also possessed of a certain degree of discernment which exceeded that of most ordinary men. He had an impressive knowledge of foreign kingdoms, and could spoke a dozen or more languages almost fluently. He quickly addressed the man in his native tongue.

"How is it that you came to be free, if you are truly a slave?"

A look of surprise swept the frightened man's face. "By a wizard named Skeltar. How is it you know my language?"

Namindi's heart leapt within his chest at the mention of the sorcerer's name, and he ignored the man's question. Lately many rumors had reached him about Skeltar, a mage whose fame and reputation were well known in the Westermarch even by the most backward peasants. It was said that King Xalton had given the wizard command of a hundred Imperial troops, and that he had sent him off on a mysterious journey, the exact details of which no one seemed to know anything about. But it was apparent that the King was deathly ill, and that this highly unusual mission was devised with the intention of procuring something that could restore his health. Namindi bent over and stared directly into the wretched man's eyes.

"Continue," he said in a much friendlier tone. "But speak in your own tongue. Even in the company of friends, there are many spies."

The man's wrists and ankles were raw from the recent wear of shackles. Beneath an unkempt growth of facial hair his cheeks were hollowed, his eyes sunken in their sockets from starvation, his black hair a matted tangle upon a scab-encrusted scalp. He was suffering from malnutrition and scurvy, and several of his teeth were chipped and broken jaggedly, no doubt the result of harsh treatment from his captors. In spite of being cracked and dirty, his hands were not callused from a lifetime of toil and labor, and three of his fingers yet bore the circular indent that indicated rings had recently adorned them. If he was truly a mere peasant, then at least he'd made a decent living. All this Namindi's keen eyes noted in a brief instant as he encouraged the slave to continue.

"The caravan we were traveling with was attacked by an army of men, led by the wizard, and only those of us who were to be sold as slaves were spared. Skeltar gave us two choices; we could fight for him and earn our freedom, or be put to death."

The man's eyes reflected his terror as he recounted the tale, and his voice began to croak. Namindi quickly ordered one of his soldiers to bring water, which was eagerly accepted amid many grateful thanks, and once his thirst had been slaked he resumed his story at the General's bidding.

"What was I to do? I had no desire to be in a battle, for I am no soldier such as yourself, but I did not want to be crucified or have my head chopped off either. I told them I would fight, and at the first chance I stole away and made my escape."

He paused to catch his breath, and his eye grew wide. "But whilst I was among them I heard them speak of their plans."

"Then you must tell me all you know," Namindi prodded, "and see that you leave nothing unsaid, for as you can see, I am General of the King's armies. If you are truly a friend of the King's, no harm shall befall you."

"The wizard is marching to Zebulon. He has an army of six hundred men, some of which are slaves such as I was, but most of which are mercenaries and soldiers. He intends to use his knowledge of the Black Arts to capture the city, and I suspect, kill the King."

"With six hundred men?" Namindi snorted derisively. "Not even a god could take Zebulon with such a small number! Even less likely a wizard."

"I swear it!" the man defended. "He will doubtless do to Zebulon what he did to Luxantia."

"Luxantia?" the General sputtered.

"Do you not know?" the man wondered.

"No, I don't!" he replied anxiously. "What has become of her?"

"Skeltar used sorcery to lay waste to the town. I was not there....that was before he overtook our caravan....but I heard tell of it. He burned Luxantia to the ground."

"How long ago?"

"A week. Maybe more, I'm not sure," the slave replied. "None escaped alive."

Namindi stared at the slave in stunned disbelief, as if his ears had betrayed him. *Could it be true?* he wondered. Luxantia was an insignificant trade town. It was certainly of no strategic importance, but destroying any town within the kingdom was a blatant act of war and aggression. The wizard would know that if he were to do such a thing, the King would be sure to respond quickly.

Namindi was responsible to the King for the safety and protection of all the northern regions of Straltonia, which naturally included Luxantia. He had been in Zebulon only four days ago, and if news had reached the King, he would have definitely been informed, not to mention being hauled up on charges before the Grand Assembly and publicly chastised in military fashion, or worse.

This could mean only one thing; as of yet, the King had not found out about Skeltar's treachery. But the wizard was no fool, either. If he'd thought nothing of destroying a small town, then obviously the King's retribution did not worry him in the least. The last time a Straltonian town had been razed was during the wars with the savages to the north. The mage undoubtedly knew that Namindi had two thousand archers, six thousand foot soldiers and fifteen hundred mounted cavalry at his command in Albana, not including a formidable battalion of thirty heavy war elephants. If Zebulon were besieged, Albana would be the first to respond. Only a madman would attempt to attack the capital city with such a tiny, rag-tag force. Or a wizard that possessed incredible arcane power.....

Namindi hastened to help the poor wretch to his feet. "Will you swear this before my captains and the King?"

"Aye," the slave nodded. "I only wish to go back to my homeland. I have a family there...."

"What is your name?"

"I am Saldir," the man replied humbly.

The General grinned. "Saldir, I am General Namindi."

"It is an honor," replied the slave respectfully.

"Of course," the General responded. "You shall come with us to Albana." He turned to one of his men. "He will ride with you. We must ride hard."

He indicated three of the other soldiers. "You, you, and you....summon the captains to an urgent council as soon as we have entered the city." He looked at his men sternly. "This is not to be spoken of to anyone else, is that clear?"

The soldiers responded in unison. "Yes sir!"

Namindi got back on his horse and grabbed hold of the reins, his heels digging into the animal's sides. "Today is a great day!" he exclaimed boisterously to his men. "Prepare for war!"

# 13

"If only the people of my homeland could see me now!" Joktan breathed, staring in wonder at the magnificence of his surroundings.

The marble floors and walls were polished so perfectly that he could see his own reflection upon them. He stared up in amazement at the carven stone arches that soared high overhead to support the lofty domed ceiling. There a huge circular framework of gilded bronze formed the edging of a magnificently crafted stained glass skylight. Upon it was featured a scene which portrayed a basilisk engaged in mortal combat with a giant serpent. From the ornate ivory arabesques inlaid into the walls and edged in silver, to the sculptures of ancient deities conferring the crown to past kings of Straltonia in grandiose fashion, the workmanship and scale of the Imperial palace and it's furnishings was truly astonishing.

He cast Sheba a grave glance. "The last time I stood in this palace I was bound in chains."

"I'm sure something could be arranged!" she smiled back at him mischievously, and her emerald eyes sparkled with humor. "If you think this place is spectacular, you will be speechless when we get to Lothair."

Joktan was about to reply when the oak and gold doors were thrown open and Chia, along with several of her companions, entered the room.

"Follow me," she directed quickly, "we need to get you ready."

The pair followed closely behind her as they were led hurriedly into an adjoining chamber. This room had been constructed to the same mammoth scale and proportion as the last, and the ornamentation was no less extravagant. In the center, a pool of bubbling water over twenty feet wide steamed invitingly, and Chia motioned for them to strip off their clothes and bathe. Sheba did so immediately, but Joktan was a little more hesitant. Chia urged him to hurry. "Don't worry," she said teasingly, "it's nothing that we haven't seen before."

He glared at her darkly for an instant, then shrugged his shoulders and complied, leaving his garments and weapons in a heap and quickly stepping to into the water to immerse himself completely. It had been a long time since he'd had a hot bath, and the water felt immensely soothing on his muscles. He would not, however, relinquish his sword, and this he kept within easy reach for the duration of his time in the pool.

Soon several nude servant girls approached, bearing trays of strangely colored liquids in crystal vials. These, Joktan discovered, were filled with scented exotic oils and sweet perfumes. They began rubbing Sheba down from head to toe, and she lay back upon the floor at the lip of the pool, seemingly enjoying herself. Joktan, however, vehemently refused, and Sheba burst into a fit of uproarious laughter when one of the maidens persisted and he drew his sword. She jumped away frightened, and Liona moved to intervene.

"It's all right," the warrioress reassured the trembling servant, finding the situation comical. She motioned the girl away and turned on Joktan. "You scared her terribly. Shame on you!" she scolded.

"I'll not reek like a Denderian whore!" he growled.

Next another maiden approached with an armload of clean garments. She peered at Joktan timidly, then set them down before him and quickly scurried off.

"What is this?" he demanded, giving Chia a forbidding look.

She regarded him with amusement. "Those are clean clothes," she informed said. "Most civilized people are familiar with such things." She gathered them up into a ball and tossed them at him, but he made no effort to catch the bundle, and the garments scattered about him on the floor.

"You *will* wear them," she admonished.

"The hell I will!" he snarled belligerently, but when he turned to snatch up his own clothing it was gone.

"Where are my clothes?" he demanded .

Chia was still laughing, as was Sheba and Liona. Apparently they found the situation to be quite hilarious. "Do you mean those old, ratty rags and matted hides?" Chia replied. "I had them burned!"

Resentfully, Joktan picked up the garments and inspected them, muttering a curse beneath his breath and giving Chia an angry glance. He was used to wearing clothing that had been fashioned out of furs and hides...not the silk attire of a palace trollop...but nonetheless, he donned the silken loincloth, tunic and new leather boots. The breeches he tossed back at her with an undisguised glower of disdain, then strapped on his weapons. Of these, all that remained were his bow, an empty quiver, a long dagger and Avatare, the sword that Lamashtu had given him. All his other weapons had been lost during the battle with the saurgs, with the exception of the other sword that he'd given to Sheba.

"I'll need more arrows for my quiver," he grumbled, more to himself than any one else that was present.

"We'll see to that later," Chia promised, "but I don't think you will be needing them in the Royal Chamber."

Liona did her best to frown. "You cannot go before the King bearing arms anyway," she said. "You'll need to leave your weapons at the door."

"They go with me," Joktan retorted hotly through clenched teeth. "You can try to take them if you like, but this sword was given to me by Lamashtu herself." The look on his face was one of open defiance. "I'll not be taking another step without it."

"Leave him be," Chia sighed to her companion. "I'll vouch for him." She gave Joktan a playful wink, but his only response was to eye her and the others even more suspiciously.

Since entering the king's palace, his mood had changed significantly. Perhaps it was his vengeful nature....or the inborn, wary uneasiness that all savages feel when confronted by the hideous glare of civilization....but one thing you never did to a savage was attempt to relieve him of his weapons. Joktan had spent several years in more cultured environs, but his instincts were just as primeval as those of his forefathers. Chia had become well aware of this by now. She had no desire to make even the slightest attempt of disarming him, but nonetheless, she did enjoy teasing him every now and then.

Sheba had been ushered briefly into an adjacent room, and now she reemerged, and the sight of her caused Joktan to suck in his breath. She was dressed in a loincloth, a long, thin, scarlet strip of silk that had been embroidered heavily with gold. It was held in place by a thin belt of gold cloth and a golden chain that fastened with ornate buckles on each hip. Ornate breast cups barely constrained her abundant cleavage, and her feet were shod with new boots of soft red leather that laced up to her knees.

Even in such scant and simple attire, she looked like a goddess personified, and he eyed her with undisguised lust. She caught his gaze instantly, but her look was one of silent approval and satisfaction. A hint of a smile tugged gently at her full, red lips.

Chia led them out of the room and down a winding marble corridor, past countless guardsmen in suits of shinning armor that stood in rapt attention at regular intervals, then up a spiral flight of stairs and down another seemingly endless hall. On they strode, passing scores of King Xalton's watchful Imperial guards, until at last the hall ended abruptly before a great set of cedar doors that were heavily carved and inlaid with ivory. Each massive door was encrusted with dazzling jewels, any one of which, Joktan surmised, would make a man considerably wealthy.

Through these they entered into a vast, lofty chamber, where elegant tapestries from far away Zhenya hung from golden rods, covering the walls and reaching down within a few inches of the floor. Their feet sank into thick, plush carpets that had been crafted in Peran and imported by ship across the Senja Sea, and Joktan began to wonder just what vast amounts of treasure this King truly possessed, for never before had he witnessed such a wanton display of opulent riches. Perhaps he would have time to search the palace treasury....

Chia guided them across the broad expanse to pause before one of the many brilliantly hued hangings. She swiftly pulled it aside to reveal a hidden cleft in the marbled wall. Placing her slender fingers purposefully upon the stone, she pushed forward softly, and suddenly a doorway that had been all but invisible to the naked eye slid open before them without a sound.

One by one they passed through, with Joktan and Sheba in the middle, and Fjora, Liona and Sonya following closely behind. Now they were moving down a narrow stone passage that curved off slightly to their left, and presently they arrived at a low, arched entrance over which a thick curtain hung on each side. Quan Chang Xu was awaiting them impatiently.

"What took you so long?" he scowled at his daughter in fatherly fashion.

"We had to make them presentable," Chia explained quickly. "It's only proper!"

The wizard rolled his eyes, which she seemed not to notice as she turned and addressed them in a low voice.

"Are you ready to meet the King?"

# 14

Namindi sat at the head of the heavy wooded table in his conference chamber. He waited quietly while his captains entered the room and took their appointed seats one by one, but the calm and collected exterior he presented to those present was merely just a mask that in reality hid tremendous feelings of inner turmoil and anxiety.

Casually he held a silver chalice to his lips and sipped wine. When everyone he was seated comfortably, he motioned to his guards to leave the room, closing the door behind them. He studied their faces intently, and in their eyes a he could see the nervous expectation they sought inwardly to repress. These were men he'd known most of his life, all of whom he had carefully selected three years earlier, when the King had conferred upon him the rank of Chief Commander.

Namindi had no doubts about their loyalty to him. He knew he could trust them to the last man, and their allegiance was unquestionable. These were men from lineages such as his own, descendants of the ancient nobility that secretly harbored resentment towards the King.

Each man at the table was powerful in his own right. All were young, ambitious captains, sons of dukes and barons, the would-be inheritors and beneficiaries of wealthy estates and prestigious titles. They represented important connections to some of the most influential men in Straltonia, and many were the clandestine leaders of dissenting factions.

There would be found no sympathy for the present ruler within these walls.

Xalton had built numerous libraries and institutions for learning. He had renewed friendships and trade relations with foreign nations that his father had thoughtlessly destroyed, and under his reign the kingdom had been free from war and turmoil. Perhaps it was because of these things that many were inclined to forgive his indulgent lifestyle, but his flagrant squandering of wealth on whimsical eccentricities left no room for the nobility to enrich themselves.

Under previous monarchs, the fathers of these captains had grown rich and powerful. Even though the royal coffers had become bankrupt on occasion in the past, their families had steadily grown wealthier, for the spoils of war had been filtered through their greedy hands long before it ever reached the palace treasury.

Conquest often brought ruin and desolation, but there were many who were deceitful enough to use the guise of war as a means to gain huge tracts of valuable land and the coveted estates of their rivals. Kings were, of course, not ignorant to such activity, but every ruler needs men of power to further his desires, and more often than not, they were inclined to turn a blind eye to such atrocities, so long as they their own ends were achieved and their gluttony for power sated.

Not so, however, since King Xalton seized the crown with his sword. He'd used the influence of the old nobles to support his bid for the throne, but after his position had been secured he'd all but forgotten about the ones who had backed him. The bribes had dwindled, the favors had ceased, and the new laws he'd introduced seemed to be aimed more at protecting the peasants than empowering the rich. He had repaid the money lenders of Dendera and Amurdon. And all the while he basked in lavish abundance and built new treasuries in which to store his ever-increasing wealth.

The old nobles had seen enough. No longer would they sit idly by and watch the King grow fat without receiving their rightful share. Civil war was brewing in Straltonia, and every man present in this room was waiting like a crouching tiger for the slaughter to begin.

Now they looked to Namindi to lead them. He was young and ambitious, as were they, but he had that certain quality of leadership which every great man throughout the ages has possessed. He exuded charisma they could only dream of, and when he spoke, everyone listened intently. It was not just his brilliance and charm that held their attention and made them want to follow his command; it was the fact that all of the old nobles seemed to like him. They knew that he would not forget about the ones responsible for handing him the crown if the opportunity ever arose. They also knew that the commoners were tired of old men running the kingdom.

A new, young, energetic king would seem like a breath of fresh air. He would be a hero, the man that had brought an end to all the unrest and bloodshed that the coming civil war would unleash.

Namindi pushed back his chair and stood to his full height before his men.

"Firstly," he started, "I want to thank all of you for coming so quickly on such short notice," he said. They nodded their reply, and he continued swiftly.

"For three years we have met in secret in this very room. Many long nights have we held council, till the pale hours of the red dawn. We have sworn oaths to each other, and we have pledged solemn bonds of brotherhood, and once more this night we meet, united in one common interest, against the tyranny that has turned our once great nation into a land of spineless cowards."

His words resounded loud and powerfully within the room, and when he paused for a moment to sip his wine, the sudden silence was ominous.

"I have just come from Zebulon, and I bring welcome news. The King's son is dead, and Xalton's illness yet lingers on. I have looked upon the face of the King myself, and I can assure you, the rumors we have heard are all true." He placed his huge hands upon the table and leaned forward, a triumphant gleam sparkling brightly in his pale eyes. *"It will not be long before he joins his spawn in the grave!"*

At this one of the captains stood and raised his goblet. "Here, here!" he cried joyously. Namindi snatched up his drink and joined his comrades in a toast to King Xalton's impending demise, then motioned for silence.

"All this while we have been planning on taking the kingdom by force of arms," he said, "but it seems the gods have granted us a rare stroke of luck, and by this strange twist of fate, in a few days the kingdom will be handed to us willingly. There will be no need for bloodshed."

At this his captains started in surprise, but Namindi merely smiled. "I know that you have all heard the rumors, claiming that the King sent a wizard off on a secret mission to find a cure for his ailment. I stand before you now to confirm those rumors. The wizard's name is Skeltar, and into his command the King entrusted a hundred of his men. But it would seem that this mage had ulterior motives, as all wizards surely do, and he intends to attack Zebulon, the purpose of which can only be to take the throne for himself."

This unexpected news caused an instant murmur to arise, but Namindi silenced them with an upheld hand. He was preparing to continue when one of his men, a young captain by the name of Valentius, spoke up.

"How many men does this wizard have?"

"Six hundred," the General replied. "Mostly dissidents and mercenaries, with about a hundred soldiers."

Valentius burst into laughter. "Six hundred!" he exclaimed incredulously. "Is this sorcerer insane? We have border patrols with more numbers!"

"Aye," Namindi agreed, "but this wizard has burned Luxantia to the ground."

All laughter within the chamber ceased abruptly and they stared at him in disbelief. "He is crazy then," Valentius murmured lowly. "Does the King know of it?"

Namindi shook his head. "Not yet," he replied, "and I intend to keep it that way for as long as possible. If he were to find out, all of us would be called before the Court. But that is of little importance now. Skeltar has no doubt reached Zebulon by now. Six hundred men might not be enough to take the city, but it will be a large enough to cause the guards to seal the gates. The wizard didn't destroy Luxantia by force of arms. According to my sources, he used his foul arts to accomplish it, and that is what he intends to do to Zebulon."

"We could join forces with him then," one of the other captains reasoned.

"Yes, we could," Namindi nodded. "That was my first thought as well. But if we were to do so, we would be seen to be in open defiance of the King, and every one would know our intentions. If the assault were to be a success, we would no longer be bound by the will of a tyrant. Instead, we would be under the control of a wizard's mummery. The commoners would hate him, and us in turn, for aiding him in his cause, and I doubt that this wizard much cares about our interests."

"Then what shall we do?" Valentius asked. "Surely you don't believe he will be able to take Zebulon with a tiny band of rebels?" It was more of a statement than a question.

"Who can say?" Namindi responded with a shrug of his broad shoulders. "What if his witchcraft prevails? I know the thought of it seems preposterous, but what if........*what if it were to happen?*"

He paused thoughtfully. "This mage is no fool," he said lowly. "There may be a chance he knows something we do not."

Namindi slammed his fist down hard upon the table, his pale eyes gleaming with an eager fire as cold as the ice fields on the great Northern Sea. "I say we ride out to Zebulon," he declared, "but hold back just far enough to watch and see what happens. If Skeltar's magick fails him, we will swoop down and wipe out his army before they can flee. The king will die regardless....we all know that it is but a matter of time. The throne will be ours for the taking, and the nobles will support us, while the commoners will think us to be their saviors."

"Then we could tell the king that we followed him from Luxantia," Valentius offered.

"Aye!" Namindi agreed. "My thoughts exactly."

"And what if the wizard's magick works?" one of the other captains asked.

"Then so be it!" the General replied. "We have but to ride into the city behind him. Who will know in the chaos of battle that it was not the mage that killed the king?"

"In which case we will still be looked upon as heroes by the people, and the kingdom will be ours," a seated captain surmised quickly. Namindi thrust his wine into the air, spilling nearly half the contents of his goblet onto the table, and his captains leapt to their feet to join him in a resounding cheer as he made a toast.

"I drink to you, my brothers!" the General proclaimed, "and to our dying king! May he die like the pig that spawned him, and may his soul rot in the bowels of Hell!"

# 15

The throne of Straltonia was a masterpiece of rare craftsmanship, a perfect blend of function, decadence and beauty, to which few, if any, in the known world could compare. Certainly there was no equal to its splendor and value throughout the kingdoms of the Westermarch.

It was comprised of a massive eagle, the Imperial symbol of the nations might. The body had been cast in solid gold, with sweeping wings curving outwards slightly to form the seat, then rising nearly six feet high and crossing at the tips, constituting the arms and backrest in an impressive display of artistry and design. Each filament on every feather was vividly portrayed and intricately etched, the tips encrusted with glittering diamonds whose value was incalculable.

The massive head was carved of solid ivory, and it had been crafted with the same unerring attention to detail as had been the rest of this spectacular seat of power. It jutted forward imperiously between the King's thighs, the powerful beak of rhinoceros horn partially open, as if voicing it's eternal dominance. The piercing eyes were two exquisitely faceted sapphires, the size of a grown man's palm, and they dazzled menacingly ahead in a stare that was equally intimidating as it was breathtaking.

The seat and backrest were padded with plush, silk cushions, and the feet of the mammoth bird of prey's feet, complete with vicious-looking ivory talons, formed the base that supported the entire throne. It seemed the malachite crystal dais upon which this rested had been thoughtfully chosen to represent the vibrant hues of the endless, swaying grasses of the expansive plains over which the king presided.

The King himself was clothed in his most regal finery, his long robes of white silk and satin, a scarlet cape of soft velvet and cloth of gold, hemmed along the edges with ermine and mink. The royal crown, two golden eagles with outstretched wings that wrapped around his head, sat firmly upon his brow. Countless rubies and diamonds struck fire about his forehead beneath the shimmering glow of the brightly lighted chamber.

It was rare indeed that King Xalton went out of his way to impress a visitor. He much preferred the comfort of the thick cushions on his floating bed, but now his body was weak, and sitting upright for extended periods was more than he could bear. At least the marvelously sculpted throne provided solid support for his aching back, and it afforded him the opportunity to be in closer contact with his guests.

Through bloodshot eyes he peered intently at Joktan and Sheba, and deathly silence pervaded the sprawling interior. Sheba bowed her head slightly, then regarded the King with an even, steady gaze. Hers was not the bow of someone who is in the company of a superior, but rather the polite acknowledgment of an equal. This seemed to startle the King somewhat, but not nearly so much as did Joktan's insolent posture.

He stood fully erect, feet spread slightly apart. The savage's bearing portrayed no sign of meekness nor a shred of humility, and his hand rested lightly upon the jeweled hilt of his mighty broadsword. Something in his eyes told Xalton that should Joktan be reprimanded or punished for his flagrant display of impudence, he would never be remorseful, regardless of the severity. They burned with the unquenchable fire of all savages, a wildness that remained untamed, a spirit that was indomitable, in spite of countless battles and bloody wars. The man had not yet been born to which this adventurer would bend his knee, nor likely ever would there be. He stood before the king of the mightiest nation in the Westermarch, with no intention of groveling nor paying homage at his sandaled, scented feet.

He stared about the chamber curiously, noting each of the numerous naked beauties with a natural, masculine interest. Joktan made no attempt to understand the habits and pastimes of civilized men--the sports of athletes, the daring acts of circus performers, the drama of theater and prose of poets--such things were of little interest to a primitive tribesman, not to mention bewildering.

But here, at least, was something he could comprehend. Each was a woman possessed of rare, exquisite beauty, some from countries so far away that most western nations considered their existence to be nothing more than a fanciful myth. Joktan recognized only a handful of nationalities in their comely features; the rest he could only guess at.

Nonetheless, his wariness and caution were obvious. The last time he'd stood before this Ruler, he had been bound in heavy iron chains. It had not been in this private inner sanctum of opulent splendor, but in the palace court over which King Xalton presided, and now the savage eyed the cultured suspiciously.

Joktan studied the King's countenance. His skin was ashen and gray, his cheeks hollow and emaciated. Folds of wrinkled flesh sagged in bags beneath his sunken eyes and under his chin. There was no brightness in his dim, gaunt stare. The skin on his fingers was shriveled and creased, the thin bones in his hands twisted as if with old age and arthritic disease. Had he not seen this man himself before the strange illness had taken hold, he certainly would not have believed him to be the same person. The king had obviously lost a great deal of weight, and to the tribesman he seemed a corpse without a cask.

Under other circumstances king Xalton would have taken great offense to Joktan's indifference, but he was too consumed by pain and sickness to concern himself with flamboyant protocols and etiquette for the moment. The ivory image of Sheba's scantily clad figure immediately distracted his attention and aroused him with fascination. Her stunning beauty was both regal and sensual, and for an instant the king was utterly speechless.

Elliasha had suddenly tensed and nearly burst out in a startled exclamation when Sheba had first entered the room, but she caught herself quickly and chose to bite her tongue. Now, as they stood only a few feet away from each other, her face began to pale, her dark eyes seething with malevolence and hate.

Sheba found it difficult to ignore the woman's vengeful glare, and although the king himself could not see it....as she stood off to his side....Liona and Fjora noticed it immediately. They glanced at their companions without a word, but it was a knowing look that passed between them. Perhaps the king was unaware of the hussy's treason, but it had been solidly confirmed for the others by her murderous glare.

For a brief second, Sheba's eyes met Elliasha's, and there was no forgiveness in her molten stare. An unmistakable malice caused the concubine to quickly avert her gaze and turn away.

This silent exchange lasted only a split second, but some inner faculty of intuition....the source of which even she did not fully comprehend....alerted Sheba to a sudden startling realization. If her rage were to remain unchecked, another uncontrollable burst of angry fire would quickly ensue. It was all she could do to repress her feelings of revenge and focus her attention once more upon the king.

Chia stepped forward, bowing with a flourish and breaking the ominous silence that prevailed.

"My Lord!" she addressed the king. "May I present to you Sheba of Lothair, the daughter of the Blood Goddess, and her consort Joktan, of the Sabertooth Tribes."

"Welcome!" the king said. "I know you have both come very far at my request, and have endured many troubles and hardships. For this, you have my gratitude." His voice was trembled as he spoke, and Xalton directed his gaze at Joktan. "What man can fathom the mind of fate?" he wondered aloud. "The thief whom I condemned to die….."

He turned to the warriors who had accompanied the pair and smiled warmly. "Not once did I question whether you would be successful," he said.

If the women doubted his word they did not show it, for Xalton's praise had an instant effect. The pride in their eyes was unmistakable. He looked once more at Sheba and Joktan.

"Never before have any of my women lost their lives during the fulfillment of their duties in my service," he informed them sadly. "They were like daughters to me." Joktan considered the incestuous overtones of this statement, but made no comment.

"They were true warriors," Sheba offered. "You have our most sincere condolences."

Xalton nodded his acceptance and thanked her, then pointed a frail finger towards Quan Chang Xu. "Without question you have played an important role."

"Perhaps," replied the wizard graciously, "but there is much that yet needs to be done. We must tend to your illness. The king must be strong," he advised. "You cannot let your enemies see your weakness."

"Have you spoken to them of my…….ailment?" he asked the mage, spitting out the last word as though it were a poisoned fig.

"Yes," she answered for him. "He has told me."

"Then what do we do next?" he asked.

"I have secured the blood that Skeltar took from you," the wizard informed him hastily, holding up the king's cherished goblet for all to see.

"Where did you find it?" Xalton shuddered. He almost didn't want to know.

"In his keep," Quan Chang Xu replied. "There it was fiercely guarded by such things that should only dwell in nightmares, but with the aid of Sheba, I was able to retrieve it intact." He grimaced his disapproval. "Skeltar placed an evil spell upon it, but that is broken now."

"Then what must I do to be healed?" the king sighed anxiously. "Will my strength return at once, or will it take several hours?"

"Please!" the wizard exclaimed good-naturedly, "one thing at a time! I cannot say with certainty how long it will take your strength to return. But you can be assured that it will come back to you quickly."

The mage turned to Sheba. "Are you ready?"

"Aye," she replied, thrusting a pale wrist toward him. She looked at Xalton. "I do this willingly, but know one thing; my blood is sacred, and you may see many things."

He nodded his agreement. "What will I see?"

"Things in your mind....images....things both ancient and very recent...." she hesitated, her voice husky and low. "Even I cannot say for sure, but what you see may be most unpleasant, albeit true." She shot Elliasha a deadly glance. "You may also witness some of my own experiences. See that you treat them with respect, and never speak of them to another living soul."

The wizard reached into his robes and withdrew a small, sharp object. With this he pierced her slender wrist while she held it out over the king's goblet, and instantly her blood began to flow. It was hardly more than a small prick, and within the space of a breath the bleeding slowed to a mere trickle, then quickly ceased, yet to the mage it seemed enough for the purpose at hand. She held up her wrist so that all those present could see the incision, and to their startled amazement, the wound closed and disappeared before their very eyes.

The King gasped, and even Elliasha stared in disbelief while many of the other women in the chamber who had been born in southern nations threw themselves upon the floor in silent dread and awe. No one need explain to these maidens from distant lands such as Mahalla, Rodinath, Khasdim and Arvad who the Blood Goddess was, nor relate the stories of her terrible might and fearsome powers. Well they knew the myths that Sheba's mother had inspired--had even sung songs that told of her amazing feats of prowess around the evening fires in their homelands--and in that brief moment, every doubt they might have had regarding the validity of the legends of the Blood Goddess had been unequivocally dispelled.

Only Joktan seemed unconcerned, but his knowledge and experiences with this warrioress from Lothair far surpassed that of any other. Their intimacy had shown him first hand the origins of her abilities, with a clarity that no one else could possibly begin to comprehend or even try to understand. Although he yet harbored many lingering questions, by now come to accept them. His savage intellect was not inclined to dwell on the abstract for very long, and not withstanding her unique abilities, to him Sheba was a woman much like any other. The only difference was, she possessed a part of him that few would ever truly see.

"Like I said," Sheba intoned, "my blood is sacred. From the moment you sip of this cup, until the day that you die, there will be a connection between us. It is unavoidable....a side effect you might say....but nonetheless it will exist."

The King assured her that he understood, and as the mage whispered a barely audible incantation and passed his right hand over the cup, she continued in a stern voice.

"You must therefore swear to me, that peace will prevail between us from this day forward."

"Of that you have my solemn oath," Xalton replied.

The wizard passed Sheba the jeweled goblet, and she in turn handed it to the King. He lofted it between his trembling palms, eyed it apprehensively, and to the bewilderment of all that looked on, she withdrew her dagger. Holding it by the blade, she gingerly reached forward and placed it upon the sovereign's lap. He looked at her uncertainly, but Sheba's smile seemed to reassure him.

"Go on," she urged softly. "You'll know what to do when the moment comes."

With a sigh of finality he closed his eyes and raised the cup to his lips, paused, then drained the contents in one long draught. No one said a word nor made a sound, and indeed, one could have heard a pin drop upon the polished stone of the chamber floor in that moment. They watched tensely, and the anxious hush prevailed. Presently the King slowly lowered his hands and sank back into the cushions on his throne, the goblet slipping from his grasp and crashing to the floor with a dull metallic ring, yet all remained standing, watching and holding their breath.

Slowly his face began to change color as his deathly pallor was replaced with a ruddy, healthy glow. Where his skin had loosely sagged, vitality appeared, filling out his hollow features as his strength magically returned and coursed through his veins. Before their very eyes his sickness faded and disappeared, and in its place youth and vigor rushed in to take their place in a miraculous transformation that defied the senses.

Even Joktan looked on in disbelief as the creases and wrinkles on his gnarled hands and twisted fingers vanished, and suddenly a different man sat before them. He was in his prime, without any trace of disease to be seen, and a fire which had long been absent now burned in his eyes as he opened them slowly and stared at Sheba.

Chia let out a squeal of joy, and instantly the room was filled with the tumult of laughter and exaltation. Elliasha stared at the king as if in shock, then joined in halfheartedly. Sheba turned to Joktan and smiled, letting out a deeply held breath. Even she had not known what to expect, it seemed. No one noticed the King's hand move toward the hilt of the dagger upon his lap, nor the whiteness of his knuckles as he clenched it in a vise-like grip, nor the narrow, sidelong glance brimming with seething indignation .

With such explosive speed as none could have ever imagined him capable of possessing, the king sprang from his throne like a leopard and spun on his feet. With his left hand he grabbed Elliasha by the hair and wrenched downwards. She shrieked in fright and craned her head back to stare in terror at her lover, but he forced the treacherous maiden to her knees with an indifference born of overwhelming animosity. His fist was a blur, and there was a brief flash of steel. Then his dagger slammed into her naked chest, the foot-long blade buried to the hilt between her rounded ebony breasts and protruding between her shoulder blades from behind.

Blood gurgled from the woman's lips amid frantic, high-pitched pleas, erupting in a crimson torrent from the fatal wound in her chest. It streamed down the shapely contours of her stomach, hips, and thighs as she screamed in agony.

Suddenly Elliasha's features underwent a horrible change. Her flawless complexion wrinkled and withered, transforming before their very eyes into a hideous and decrepit form. Her perfectly sculpted figure became grotesquely misshapen, like a corpse recently unearthed from a musty, earthen tomb.

King Xalton gaped in horror, at once recognizing the familiar, decaying face, yet staring dumbfounded, immobilized by shock. All the moments he had ever shared with the maiden he'd known as Elliasha came rushing in upon his mind at once, making the grisly truth he now witnessed all the more difficult to accept and comprehend. Well he knew the once delicate lines and symmetry of that face, an image he'd not seen for more than twenty years, for it belonged to his long-dead mother!

All who watched fell back in terror, unsure of the reality their eyes beheld. King Xalton's rage had broken a sorcerous spell, exposing not only a traitor, but a spirit conjured to life in the reanimated body of the woman who had given birth to him. Now the glamoury was shattered, and the soul inhabiting her corpse shrieked like a demon loosed from the seething bowels of hell.

He was jolted to his senses, and again the dagger rose and fell with bitter hate. Her blood sprayed over his golden throne, staining the ivory eagle's head a sickly red. Still he drove the blade through her chest again and again with violent fury, until his rage had abated, and her blood ran out over the malachite dais of his throne like thick red spoiled wine. It spread wetly over the floor in a steaming, slippery pool, then slowly it changed from a crimson fluid to an oily, brackish sludge.

King Xalton stood there, his chest heaving from exertion, fingers still tangled in the black, wavy locks of Elliasha's lolling head, his royal robes soaked in gore. Slowly his fingers uncurled themselves from the dagger, and it clattered dully to the floor. He released his grip on the dead woman's hair, and her lifeless body slumped limply forward upon the dais. Everyone stared at him in stricken silence, and even Joktan had been taken aback by Elliasha's awful transformation and the sheer brutality of Xalton's wrath.

So too, it seemed, had the King himself. He stared down at the cadaver beside his feet, then staggered backwards wearily and fell upon his throne. A blank expression glazed his eyes. This was the second time blood had been spilt upon this dais by his own hand. The dying image of his father flashed before him, and he sought to force it from his mind, but one realization struck him profoundly.

He had slain both of his parents upon this very spot.

After a few moments he turned to Sheba, and when he spoke his voice sounded distant and detached.

*"I saw her!"* he breathed, as if relating a nightmare's scene. "I saw her throw you into the dungeon, saw her pay the men who helped her....*I even heard her say their names!"*

The dazed expression faded as his mind began to clear, and his voice was a whisper filled with revulsion. "I saw her kill my only son," he said with finality. "That's why I had to take her life."

His expression began to sicken as the import of what had just occurred finally registered completely in his mind. The ruined body at his feet was not that of the youthful, exotic beauty he had intimately caressed just hours before.

"I don't understand..." he blanched and wretched violently in revulsion.

*Small wonder her touch felt so familiar!* He thought grimly. "Long have I cherished my mother's memory," the king confessed. "Now it has been forever tainted....the price I now pay for the throne....and my life."

The eastern mage stepped forward. "Skeltar used necromancy to give life to your mother's body. He placed a spell upon her, and a powerful one at that, for even I have been beguiled."

"But I had a son with….with that…*that thing!*"

"No!" the wizard assured him. "Do not allow such thoughts into you head! The baby couldn't have been your child. Skeltar must have stolen it, and I dread to think of what evil he used upon the baby's actual mother."

The king shook his head in dismay, then turned to Sheba. "Now I know what haunts you. You must live with a terrible burden." He paused and closed his eyes in grief.

"We both do," she replied.

"Aye," he wept. "Bitter memories are an inextricable thorn in the hearts of men."

Sheba nodded in understanding. He regarded her much differently now than he had before. No longer did the king see her as a beautiful, exotic warrioress, another foreign maiden who stirred his loins and ignited the flames of his masculine lust.

Now he truly understood the rare gift of which she was possessed, with all of its power and greatness. And he also felt the bloodlust with which she lived every day of her life.

Chia stepped to the king's side and shoved the limp body away from the dais of the throne. It made a sickening sound, rolling unceremoniously onto the floor.

"I couldn't have done it better myself!" she conceded. "Welcome back to the world of the living, my Lord!" She said, joyously embracing him.

"Indeed," he replied solemnly, looking blankly away. "I knew that I was being played for a fool, but never in a million years would I have expected something this foul and hellish!"

She withdrew her arms and grew serious once more. "That," she said, gesturing at Elliasha's bluing body, "was the easy part. What we have just witnessed was as evil a thing as any could ever be, but you cannot dwell on it any longer. There's a storm of trouble coming, and we have little time in which to prepare. The city gates must be closed, and the palace guards tripled at once."

"Obviously there is much that I am unaware of," he surmised. "No doubt that bitch saw to it…."

"Aye," she conceded, "I do not doubt that she did. My father tells me that Skeltar is returning to Zebulon. In addition to the soldiers you gave him, he has picked up more men, mercenaries I would imagine."

"Let him come!" the King roared. "No army has ever breached our gates nor scaled our walls. And it will take a lot more than what he's got to do it."

"It's not his army of men that you need fear," the wizard spoke up. "He will conjure up another army....if he hasn't already....the likes of which I can guarantee this city has never seen before. Gather every soldier you that you can and put them on the walls. If I am wrong, then at least your life will not be in danger."

The King rested his chin on his knee and frowned. The only man that could understand the intentions of a sorcerer was another mage. "Damn his black arts!" he cursed bitterly. "At least the politicians that oppose me do so for reasons that are simple to ascertain!" He sighed heavily, then suddenly exclaimed, "my own mother! I still cannot believe my eyes!"

"In any case, we will guard you as always," Chia told Xalton flatly. "No one will get into this room unless it is over our dead bodies, but we need someone we can trust to guard the palace itself."

"Who do you suggest?" he asked. "Brutus was my best man for the job."

"Then put Joktan here in charge of it," she suggested. "You know what he did in your dungeons! I have seen him in battle, and he is better than any twenty of your men!"

"You are too kind," Joktan replied dryly, "but I cannot watch over your palace." They looked at him in surprise.

"You can't refuse!" Chia cried. "At least not if the King orders it."

"He's not my King!" Joktan retorted, then added, "no offense. But I didn't come to Zebulon to save his life. That was Sheba's task. I'm here because I swore an oath to slay a wizard and a devil, and by Dagon's scaly member, that is what I intend to do!"

# 16

Dawn swept across the plains in brilliant hues of bloody, crimson fire. As the burning orb of the sun arched upwards along it's eternal lofty trail, the morning mist dispersed unnoticed and stifling heat prevailed. The tall grasses of the vast expanse outside the city's intimidating wall swayed and tousled like an endless sea of beryl and jade beneath azure, cloudless skies. Noon passed with no less comfort than the heat of a blacksmith's forge, yet still no sign of Skeltar nor his band of renegades could be seen.

The soldiers upon the wall cursed the blistering temperature profanely while perspiring beneath heavy helms and breastplates of steel and thick coats of chained mail. Straltonian armor was some of the finest in the world, but being forced to stand in it all day long high upon these walls and parapets of solid stone could quickly suffocate the hardiest of men, and soon the heat began to take it's toll.

To counter this, the captains gave orders to rotate positions regularly, and abundant supplies of water were made readily available. Even so, with no enemy in sight, a high spirit of morale would be difficult at best to maintain.

In spite of Chia's continual insistence that the gates remain closed, as the day wore on without any noticeable signs of attack, the King relented, with the provision that a thorough search be made of all persons and belongings entering or leaving the city. Anything that seemed suspicious was immediately investigated, with those who were belligerent being roughly detained and questioned.

It would be impossible to maintain a heavy guard without arousing the fears and suspicions of the inhabitants. Although the King desired to prevent this from occurring at all costs, there was little choice in the matter. Without proper vigilance, any city could be easily taken, and it was not inconceivable that a small band of well-trained men could overpower the palace guards. It would not be difficult to enter the city in disguise, and Skeltar had a hundred soldiers at his disposal who were all well aquatinted with the precincts of the palace.

While trusted generals and captains were placed in charge of preventing just such a thing from taking place, Chia and the rest of the elite female guards made preparations to secretly escort the king to a hidden inner chamber should the need to do so arise.

It wasn't that they lacked complete confidence in the abilities of the military. They knew with total certainty that any assault could easily be repelled, for only the best of the Imperial Troops were stationed here in Zebulon. As well, Skeltar had such a tiny force to contend with that it was laughable, but it wasn't his rebels that gave the warriors cause for concern. Indeed, it was the wizard himself, and the terrible arcane forces he was said to be able to wield with ease.

The withering temperatures of the day eventually faded into the shadowy ashes of evening dusk. Night fell like a thick black curtain strewn with millions of shimmering diamonds, and the coming dawn routed the gray tinged specters of the night with golden promises of incinerating heat. Like the one before it, this day passed without any noticeable signs of the wizard or his men, and the next four days that followed proved to be equally monotonous.

There was no apparent threat of attack, and the numbers of soldiers upon the city walls quickly dwindled.

If Skeltar had planned some sort of assault, it seemed unlikely that it would now be forthcoming. Perhaps the mage had suddenly realized the futility of such a foolish attempt and had wisely decided to abandon his efforts. The King's health had fully returned, and he was in excellent spirits. Skeltar's sorcerous hold upon the King had been broken, and the atmosphere of doom that had hung over the palace for so long was now forgotten.

However, it was obvious that the wizard was still out there somewhere, and until he was caught and dealt with, the King's life would be in jeopardy. No crime against the King could be allowed to go unpunished. Someone would have go out and track the mage down to render justice upon him.

Joktan and Sheba continued to be guests of the palace during this time, and by the King's orders, they were free to come and go as they pleased. There were very few rooms in the palace from which they were prohibited, and Joktan suspected that these liberal arrangements had been made more in courtesy to Sheba than himself.

In truth, he felt that he had done little, if anything, that had so far been of any benefit to the King. His only commitment had been to accompany Sheba, and it was her and Quan Chang Xu who had been responsible for ridding Xalton of his mysterious disease.

Nonetheless, he was quick to take full advantage of such unusual freedoms. When her and Joktan were not busy lovemaking, Sheba spent her time conversing with Chia and the others, leaving him with plenty of time to explore the palace from one end to the other. His curiosity was limitless, although he tried to keep it concealed for the most part, but soon he was wandering the endless halls and passages with as much ease and familiarity as did the myriad courtesans and nobles.

Most of the men that Joktan encountered wore white linen robes, with richly decorated belts that secured about the waist, and a long broad sash slug diagonally over the shoulder.

The women wore simple white silk robes that fell nearly to their feet, many of which were so shear and flimsy they left very little to the imagination. Nearly all wore light leather sandals, and gold and silver jewelry, consisting of jeweled armbands, bracelets, anklets, chains and rings.

A number of the younger women stared a him with obvious interest and did their best to pose alluringly as he passed by. Straltonian women were known for their sexual escapades, and it wasn't every day that one saw a real savage in this part of the kingdom, not to mention in the palace itself. The older, wealthier women picked up their pace however, as if in fear of being robbed. Needless to say, he definitely stood out in his simple loincloth, leather boots, and broadsword. Few men dared nor deigned to speak with him.

This amused Joktan more than anything else, and he began making a special point of giving those he saw a wide smile....one that best displayed his fearsome looking canines, often accompanied by a menacing growl. If the sword didn't send them scurrying away, the fangs worked every time.

It wasn't long before his roaming brought him into the armory, where he spent a great deal of time examining the vast display of diverse weapons and assorted armor. He helped himself to a fine chained mail corselet and a broad leather belt from which hung a short mace, an ax, and a short, double-edged sword. After filling his quiver with arrows, and thrusting a couple of daggers under his belt, he returned to the chamber he and Sheba had been given. There he stowed away his newly acquired weapons before setting off once more, this time in search of the palace kitchen.

The servants, who wore simple, linen robes secured by a length of braided hemp or leather, were fairly startled by his sudden appearance, but within a few moments he found himself engaged in a lively discourse. They were not as aloof as the other folk he'd encountered, and Joktan immediately felt right at home in their midst.

Slavery was against the law in Straltonia, and commonly people from the lower classes earned a modest living employed as servants by their wealthy countrymen. Many of them wore copper and silver jewelry, cowry shell necklaces, and simple sandals, the predominant style of footwear throughout the kingdom. Shortly Joktan went to exploring once more, having filled his gullet with a joint of mutton and quenched his thirst with a liberal quantity of expensive cherry wine.

As the days progressed he grew more and more restless. There was little for a man to do in the winding halls of the palace, and he spent a great deal of time exploring the city. It had been little more than a year since last he had walked these streets, and a grim smile was his as he strode past the Temple of Dhampir.

He was instantly reminded of his oath to Lamashtu in the ancient grove out on the plains, and for a moment he considered the prospect of sneaking into the temple in search of their evil god. He knew that he would not find the demon there no matter how long he searched, but the prospect of slitting a few throats tempted him greatly. He turned back toward the palace once more, knowing that he would have to find Skeltar before he could fulfill his oath to the Goddess.

During such forays out into the city, Joktan was quick to notice the diminishing numbers of sentries posted at the gates and fewer guards along the walls. However there was nothing that he could do to prevent it....other than reiterate his misgivings to Chia and the King....and while the warrioress was inclined to sympathize with his fears, the King felt otherwise and merely brushed his comments aside. To Xalton Joktan was just a primitive savage, and what could a wild tribesman possibly know about defending a palace, much less a city? Even so, those same primeval instincts that these civilized people disregarded as ignorance and savagery had been the deciding factor between life and death for him on countless occasions. He was not about to ignore them now.

The tribesman could only surmise how Quan Chang Xu felt. The strange little mage from Zhenya had been right in every other regard, but he had told them very explicitly that Skeltar was coming. That had been several days ago, and so far his prediction had not come to pass. Joktan hadn't really spoken to him, other than a few quick words in passing.

It had been six days now, and Joktan's sense of unease and apprehension had not diminished. Instead, it had grown increasingly stronger, and as he meandered aimlessly through the opulent precincts of the palace, he suddenly found himself in the royal gardens. Looking around, he noticed the wizard seated with his back turned toward him a short distance away. Joktan, having little else to do, strode over immediately and spoke to him. The mage peered up at him as though he'd been awaiting his arrival.

"It's about time you got here!" the wizard chuckled jovially. "I've been waiting for nearly an hour."

Joktan frowned. "What are you talking about, old man?" he asked. "I don't recall saying I would meet you anywhere, and my memory is pretty good."

"Of course you don't remember," the wizard replied. "I never actually spoke to you. Nonetheless, I did call you not more than an hour ago."

"Then what do you want?" he demanded. He knew that no one had called him, but decided that he would humor the old man. Perhaps he was becoming senile.

"It's not what I want," the wizard responded knowingly. "It's what you want. You are here to honor your oaths, but so far, nothing has happened. Now you are becoming bored, wondering what you should do."

"True," Joktan admitted, "but that is all plain enough to see, wizard or no."

"I told the king that Skeltar was coming, yet so far he has not. Do you think I was wrong?"

"Of course!" Joktan replied, "but what difference does it make, other than you probably feel a little foolish, but who wouldn't? Even wizards make mistakes. Every one knows that."

"Except for the fact that I made no mistake," Quan replied flatly. "There is a reason why Skeltar has waited, and it has to do with you a little."

"Me?" he snorted. "I highly doubt it. I've never met him, and it's doubtful that he has any idea of where I am. It is the King and Sheba that concern him."

The wizard laughed. "Don't be so naïve, Joktan! Your destiny has been linked with his ever since you were born. If I can see that, he certainly can. He knows that you have been put in his path for a reason, but he hasn't figured out what that purpose is yet. I know he has been trying to determine how you fit into the puzzle....perhaps he has by now....but I don't think he realizes who your father was."

Joktan frowned. How could this mage from the Eastermarch know anything about his father?

"You are surprised that I know of your father?" the mage asked. "I know many things."

"How?" the tribesman queried curiously. "You come from Zhenya, a place so far from my homeland that my people consider it to be a myth."

"Yes," Quan Chang Xu laughed softly, "but I am a wizard! I hear ancient voices upon the wind. They speak in tongues that have not been heard by men in over a thousand years, or even ten thousand years. In the mornings the sparrows sit on my shoulders and whisper, which is why I come to this very spot each day at dawn, but now we are getting sidetracked. I am not here to tell you about winds and birds."

A huge bumblebee suddenly flew past them, and the mage held extended a frail hand. Instantly the black and yellow insect alighted, and the old man spoke to it in a strange language that Joktan couldn't understand. A few seconds passed, then the wizard smiled and the bumblebee darted away.

"I know exactly where Skeltar is," the wizard continued, as if nothing had happened. "But no one will listen to me now. Chia sent out a scout to look for him, one of her trusted warriors in fact, but the woman failed to discover anything, and now even my own daughter is secretly doubtful of me."

He peered up at Joktan knowingly. "Nonetheless, I am correct. He is using magick to hide his location, which is why Chia's scout found nothing, but he is quite near. He waits to attack because an army from Albana is camped not far to the north."

"Albana?" Joktan scowled. "That could only be General Namindi."

"You know of him?"

"Aye!" he replied darkly. "I had dealings with him a year ago, after escaping from Xalton's dungeon."

"Well, Namindi has heard of Skeltar's intentions. By what means I do not know, but he has brought his army down, and they are waiting for Skeltar to make his move."

"From what little I know of Namindi, I can assure you that he doesn't have the King's best interests at heart," Joktan informed him. "Not unless he's changed his mind within the last year, and I highly doubt it."

"No, he has not changed," the mage sighed sourly. "Namindi desires to be King. I have tried to warn Xalton of this, but he will not listen, especially now. He refuses to speak of it, preferring to occupy himself with his women instead of political intrigues. He thinks that no one would dare to openly oppose him, but in this he is mistaken. If Namindi can find a way to capture the crown without causing the citizens to see him as a villain, he'll do it. So now he waits for Skeltar to make his move. If Skeltar fails, Namindi will attack, and the people will see him as a hero, in which case he will have to put off his bid for the throne a little longer."

"And if Skeltar wins?"

"If he does, or at least gets into the city, Namindi will sweep in and destroy his forces, but he will see to it that King Xalton is killed during all the confusion that ensues."

"The King no longer has an heir," Joktan considered. "From what I understand of Straltonian law....which is not much, mind you....Namindi could be crowned if he had the support of the people, as could anyone for that matter."

"Exactly," agreed the wizard. "And he'll have it if he comes in behind Skeltar."

"And I will only aid him by killing that foul wretch and his pet demon!" Joktan surmised with a sudden curse.

Quan Chang Xu nodded. "That could very well be the case."

Joktan ground his fist into his palm as he paced anxiously. "Well I care not what becomes of this lousy kingdom once I leave," he growled. "King Xalton can rot in Hell for all I care! My business is with Skeltar."

"Fair enough," the mage allowed, "but I care about my daughter. If Namindi succeeds, he will have Chia executed, along with all the others at her side. They are strong warriors, but Namindi has vast numbers on his side and they won't stand a chance. The women will surround the King to protect him, and the general's men will mow them down to get to him. They won't stand a chance."

He stood and looked Joktan straight in the eyes. "I don't want my daughter to die!" he lamented, his voice a whisper of passion and sorrow.

"But you're a wizard!" the tribesman responded. "Can't you save her?"

Quan Chang Xu shook his head, then sat down heavily on a nearby bench. "Not in this case," he said woefully. "There is a limit to what even wizards can do."

"Then what do you want from me?" Joktan demanded harshly. "My hands are full as it is! I have Skeltar to worry about, and that in itself is a tall order, not to mention some demon that he's managed to conjure up from the underworld or wherever. And supposing that I live through all that, I still have Sheba to think about....and chances are, she'll be with your daughter and I'll have to hack my way to only Dagon-knows-where to find them. By that time Namindi's men will be swarming the place, and it's going to take an awful lot of killing to get through them."

Suddenly the wizard leapt to his feet with the speed of a tiger. "Listen!" he exclaimed, his voice roaring like thunder sweeping across the open plains. Joktan started and jumped back, staring at the mage incredulously, his hand instinctively gripping the hilt of his great broadsword.

"There are realms of existence few ever see but magi." The volume of his voice returned to normal as he spoke, but while he continued, his eyes burned with a fire which was frightening to behold. "They are separated from this world by an invisible curtain, which we wizards call a veil. There are many such veils, each one of which is but the entrance to another realm. While they are impossible to see with mortal eyes, they are easily opened and entered by those who delve deeply enough into the arts of magick."

"I myself have passed through seven of these veils at one time or another, and it is within such a place that Skeltar has concealed himself and his men. That is why Chia's scout failed to see them, and it is why Namindi cannot see them either. But he is there nonetheless, waiting for the general to pack up his army and go back home."

He paused to catch his breath and be certain Joktan was paying attention.

"I'm listening," the savage growled irritably. "Go on."

"You must flush Skeltar out of hiding," the wizard declared. "To do this, you will need to leave the city and ride to the east before sunrise. You need not travel far, only a mile or so, then wait quietly. At dawn you will see Skeltar's encampment. It will be nearly invisible to your eyes, and it will last but a few moments....therefore you must be vigilant.....but you will see it."

"And then what?"

"You cannot enter it. It must be opened for you, and he will certainly not do that, so you must light the grass on fire. His camp is merely concealed. They are behind the veil, not in it. Although I doubt this makes any sense to you at all, it is of little difference. Light the grass on fire, and Skeltar will be forced to come out into the open, where any mortal will be able to see him plainly. Then come back to the city at once."

"If I do as you say, Namindi will see him too, right?" Joktan questioned.

"Yes," the mage nodded. "That is why you must come back here at once. The soldiers upon the wall will see him, and then Chia will believe."

"That still leaves Namindi's men to worry about," Joktan reminded him.

"Correct," the mage responded quickly. "And I'm betting that Skeltar will keep them occupied with something if you flush him out of hiding ahead of time."

"Like what?" Joktan wondered. "Namindi has thousands of men."

"I don't know exactly, but trust me, it won't be pretty. He is most likely planning to use something of the sort against the city too. He doesn't have enough men to storm his way through, but he's not stupid either. I'm thinking that he'll show up at the gate and make a big fuss....that way the guards will seal it up tight....then he'll use some kind of spell against the King's soldiers. After that it will be easy. A few men can climb the wall and open the gates, and then Skeltar will head for the palace."

"And you're sure about all this?" Joktan asked dubiously.
"Well, maybe not one hundred percent," the mage admitted, "but at least it's more of an idea than anyone else has around here. Once you light the grass on fire, Skeltar will have no choice but to come out. Then we'll find out what his plans are in a hurry."

"And where does Dhampir fit in to all of this?"

The wizard looked thoughtful. "I think he'll conjure him up right here in the palace. That way he can go about his business without fear of interruption. That's why you will have to make it here as fast as you possibly can."

"I don't think that will be much of a problem," Joktan growled. "At least not if everything goes like you say."

"Well, I could be wrong here or there...." Quan Chang Xu confessed. "So once you get back here, have Chia take the King and all her warriors....including Sheba....to Skeltar's keep. It is west of here, and no one will look for the King within his enemies lair. Namindi will be hard pressed to get his men to enter that accursed place, for there are still many demons lurking about the outer grounds."

"Great," Joktan muttered. "More demons."

"Don't worry yourself about that," the wizard snapped. "There's an underground passage that can be used to enter his keep. Elliasha had it constructed not long ago, and she used it to meet with Skeltar in secret. It leads from the tunnels you passed through when you entered the city several nights ago. Chia and Sheba both know where it is."

"Very well," Joktan agreed. "And where will you be?"

"In many places," Quan Chang Xu replied. "In the mean time, you will have Skeltar and Dhampir all to yourself. The women can hold Skeltar's keep easily enough....there will only be one way in."

Joktan mulled everything over in his mind. He didn't like the idea of trusting a wizard, but this one had saved Sheba's life, which was definitely a point in his favor. The whole scenario sounded a little confusing to him, but at least it was *something*. And it sure beat hanging around in the palace doing nothing. The idea of forcing Skeltar's hand prematurely appealed to him considerably, and presently he turned toward the wizard with a shrug.

"Sounds good to me," he decided at last. "I'm willing to give it a shot. Just be sure those women are safe."

"I will," the mage assured him.

"You better," Joktan warned, turning to leave. "Because after I've finished with Skeltar, I'll be looking for Sheba, and if anything has happened to her....." He gave Quan Chang Xu a menacing grimace. "I'll be looking to gut another mage."

# 17

General Namindi squinted his eyes and tried to shade them with his hand as he gazed out over the undulating grasses that thickly carpeted the rolling plains. Far in the distance, the white outer walls of Zebulon reflected the sunlight, causing the city to look like a gleaming diamond set adrift in an endless sea of green. From this vantage point, the nation's capitol looked like a tiny speck on the horizon. It seemed difficult to believe that this minuscule dot of dazzling light was one of the biggest cities in all the kingdoms of the Westermarch.

The bulk of his army was camped far behind him in one of the few gullies to be found between Albana and Zebulon. Generally referred to as the Valley of Dead Kings....the reasons for which had already been lost in antiquity a thousand years ago....it would take over two hours of hard riding to reach. Zebulon was almost the same distance from here though, and that made his position most advantageous indeed. It was imperative that he keep his soldiers out of sight from the city as well as passing caravans, no easy feat with several thousand men in polished steel armor on the open plains.

Behind him he had over three dozen men spaced out between himself and his army. Each had been given a torch made of equal parts of sulfur, charcoal and saltpeter, a mixture that burned extremely fast and produced a billowing cloud of thick smoke. The stench was enough to make a man gag, but such torches were remarkably effective as a means of passing along signals at a distance.

Upon his order, the first man to his rear would spark his torch, and the next man would see it and light his in turn and so on down the line. In this manner, it would take a matter of minutes to reach his army with a signal. It was a brilliant tactic that he himself had developed only a few years earlier, one of the many secrets that had kept him one step ahead of his enemies and rivals alike.

Namindi frowned, then pulled out a silk cloth and wiped the sweat from his furrowed brow. The heat was unbearable, even for a man that had been born and raised upon these very plains. There was no sign of Skeltar and his men. If the slave had spoken the truth, and the general had no reason to believe otherwise, the wizard should have been here several days ago.

"Send out another scout," he barked at the captain lying nearest him in the grass. "Tell him I want to know what's going on in the city. And send another one to circle around to the other side. Something's up."

"Yes sir!" the captain complied immediately, rising quickly to carry out the general's order.

"Get down, you fool!" Namindi exclaimed with an accompanying stream of profanity.

The captain dropped instantly, and the general glared at him angrily. "They can't see us from the city, but it's possible that the wizard might be able to. I don't want him knowing we're here, so you keep your belly on the ground at all times or I'll gut you myself, is that clear?" The man nodded that he understood, then slid away to carry out his superior's bidding, and Namindi turned to the others that were concealed about him.

"That goes for the rest of you too!" he snapped, giving them all a sour look.

His soldiers flattened themselves into the long grass, disappearing from sight entirely. Namindi was usually even tempered, but for the last few days his fuse had grown steadily shorter. He'd been in a foul mood since morning, and it certainly hadn't improved within the last few hours.

A startled cry shattered the silence and brought the soldiers instantly to their feet, as Valentius sprang to into the air, screaming in agony. A huge cobra, over twelve feet in length, had sank its long white fangs into his right hand. Its teeth had gone through his palm completely, and he danced about wildly, insane with fear while the poisonous serpent writhed and held on tenaciously and it's venom dribbled down the young captain's arm.

Namindi leapt towards him, his sword already in motion, and his blade clove the deadly reptile asunder a foot below it's broad neck. The cobra's body fell thrashing into the grass, but it's head still attached to the captain's hand, and Namindi's weapon struck once more. This time, however, it was not brown and tawny scales through which razor steel sheered, but human flesh and bone. The general's sword split the man's skull from scalp to teeth in a crunch of splintered bone, and Valentius crumpled into the grass, his face a mangled obscenity of brains and spouting blood.

The other captains about him looked on in horror. Namindi slung the gore from his blade and sheathed it, then resumed his previous position in the grass.

"He was a dead man already," he told them flatly. "Better to end his life quickly than prolong it in senseless torment."

"Never have I seen such a huge cobra!" one man breathed in amazement. "The body of this thing is bigger than the width of my arm!"

"Aye," Namindi concurred. "'Tis no ordinary serpent to be sure."

"Valentius was a good man," another intoned wistfully.

"That he was," the general agreed. "I'll not relish the task of informing his father that he is dead. Notwithstanding, we must be even more wary than before. One of us should have noticed a snake that size among us....but none did." He turned his gaze back across the plain, but all was as it had been before the commotion began.

"Perhaps this Skeltar is closer than it seems," one of his captains muttered, voicing the thought that each man now silently considered.

"Don't make more of it than what it is," Namindi snarled. "It was merely a snake. I have seen many such creatures, some of which were even larger than this one," he lied. Inwardly he shared in their suspicions, but the last thing he needed was his captains loosing their nerves.

Perhaps it was simply an inbred superstition, something that yet lingered within the subconscious regions of men's minds....an enduring memory of the unholy abominations that had been unleashed upon the sons of men by ancient necromancers such as Therion and Kethros....but no army felt at ease when it was a wizard who opposed them. Straltonians believed in a vast number of gods and goddesses. Every city and town in the kingdom contained a special section in which only temples and sacred groves were built, each one dedicated to a different deity.

The lower classes were a superstitious lot, but the wealthier and more educated populace were generally more inclined to view such things as religious rituals and sacred rites to be nothing more than the old trappings and traditions of their forefathers. And while most indulged in the ceremonies and festivities of various religions, they did so more for entertainment and social revelry than righteous zeal.

It was rumored the very elite participated in secret rituals that reeked of foul arts, but such ideas were laughed at by most sane men.

Nonetheless, soldiers and fighting men existed day after day in a world were death stalked grim and grinning. More often than not, his harvest was a bloody bounty of grisly corpses, many of whom were once friends and comrades of those fortunate enough to survive.

Thus soldiers usually proved to be even more suspicious than most commoners, and nearly every man bore some sort of pagan talisman or charm about his neck or wrist, in the belief that it might somehow protect him if he should be ordered off to war.

Namindi wore no such objects.

His faith rested firmly in his sword, his confidence in the superiority of numbers and carefully planned and executed strategies. There had been very few times that he'd been wont to believing in anything that smacked of the supernatural. Yet even as the bravest of men are sometimes stricken with fear in the lonely watches of the night, and so it was that Namindi now found himself wrestling with his own secret fears. He'd thought himself to be above such foolish imaginings, yet they sprang into his mind unbidden, a shadow that grew steadily in the darkest corners of his brain.

He wondered if perhaps Skeltar was waiting just as he. Could it be that the mage was watching him through some arcane means? It was said that wizards could easily control beasts and reptiles, that such creatures lacking intellect could be compelled to perform their bidding. The unusual size of the cobra that had bitten Valentius led him to wonder; what would happen, should Skeltar summon a horde of such serpents, setting thousands of them loose upon him and his men all at once?

He shuddered at the thought, then peered out over the plains again. *Where are those scouts?* He wondered suddenly. *They should have been back by now…..*

# 18

Later that afternoon a tiny puff of cloud appeared on the western horizon. At first it was hardly visible, and to the soldiers who stood watch upon the city walls it might as well have been a bird soaring high off in the distance. A slight breeze whispered softly over the plains and imperceptibly picked up speed, and its touch was almost soothing to the men who sweltered beneath heavy helms of polished steel.

No one seemed to notice as the insignificant speck of gray became a small black line of smoky clouds. Within the city, where the towering walls obscured all view of the land beyond, the residents went about their normal daily routines, oblivious of the approaching storm.

Steadily the winds continued to grown, and soon they battered the armored watchmen with all the fury and violence of a hurricane. Many of the silken banners on the battlements were ripped loose from their rigging. The air was choked with dust and sand, driven furiously by the howling wind. It stung painfully, biting into the skin and blinding the eyes.

An hour before dusk the sun was blotted from the heavens. The seething skies were blacker than a witch's hate.

Brilliant streaks of bluish-white lightening lashed out from above. It was as though some celestial deity had been unwittingly provoked, and now he was aiming his bolts of electric rage directly at the city itself. These flashes were closely followed by deafening bursts of rolling thunder, and such was their fervor that even the palace walls shook and trembled from the roar.

Joktan stood with Sheba, gazing fiercely into the havoc upon the lip of the eastern wall. Here the wind was at their backs, nearly pushing them over the edge, but they planted their feet wide and firmly braced themselves against the maelstrom of the night. At regular intervals along the parapets, soldiers could be seen crouching, clutching desperately at their long scarlet cloaks, but their numbers were few as far as Joktan was concerned, and he uttered a long stream of vulgarities that were quickly swallowed up and lost in the swirling chaos of the night.

"If the wizard was right, Skeltar is out there somewhere," he intoned. "I don't doubt that this storm is his doing."

Her gaze held his for a long moment, and the woman's concern was hard to miss. "Do be careful," she implored, punctuating her request with a passionate kiss.

He nodded, but made no reply. Many hours before he'd conferred with Sheba and Chia, informing them of his plans for the night and coming dawn. Although the latter had expressed her misgivings in no uncertain terms, Sheba had been insistent about accompanying him.

Joktan, however, would hear none of it. He was sick of speaking his mind, only to have his words fall upon deaf ears, and he needed her to stay with Chia and the other warriors. He knew that they would listen to Sheba and do as she directed, and he had to have someone he could trust at the gate to let him back into the city, just in case everything turned out the way Quan Chang Xu had predicted.

After a few more words with Sheba, he descended the wall and mounted a great black stead, procured earlier from the king's stables. Then, after casting one last glance over his shoulder in Sheba's direction, he slipped through the heavy iron gates and disappeared into havoc of the storm.

Joktan guided the horse to his left, keeping his head low and crouching down in the saddle as he skirted the city, and the beast regretfully complied. Digging in his heals, he drove the stead onward at a gallop through the bitter winds, until presently the gale was at his back. His mount moved faster now, carried along by the force of the storm at their heels, and it took little time for him to reach the eastern wall.

Here the wall protected both man and beast from the severity of the terrible onslaught that swept in from the west. As of yet there had been no rain, but he had little doubt that it would be forthcoming. Such violent storms always brought equally furious downpours, and he angrily cursed his luck in terms so profane as to shock the most barbarous of men. Even though the wall offered considerable shelter, his cloak flapped wildly about him, and Joktan stripped it away, securing it to his mount. The last thing he needed was a garment obstructing his ability to grasp for weapons quickly.

He knew that somewhere up above him, Sheba was probably peering about for him, but the dust in the air was so thick that he could barely see ten feet over his head. Lightening lanced the darkness with blinding brilliance, and the resulting crashes of thunder shook the ground beneath his feet. The thought suddenly struck him that, if the sunlight of dawn could reveal Skeltar's position, surely the intense illumination of the bolts that were slashing across the sky could do likewise. He made no pretense of understanding the metaphysical nature of the veils that Quan Chang Xu had spoken of earlier. It was merely a hunch, but to his uncivilized mind, it seemed that perhaps it was not the time of day that mattered most, but rather the brightness of the light involved.

Joktan knew that were he to step but a few paces from the wall, the full power of the storm would instantly assail him. Savages, however, were not easily intimidated by such mundane discomforts as foul weather. With a grim look of determination defiantly etched upon his sunburned features, he tightened his sword belt up a notch and stepped confidently out into the raging winds.

He'd taken but a few steps when the small hairs on the back of his neck began to rise. The air seemed to come alive, as if charged by an invisible, mysterious energy which he had never before experienced. Reacting purely by primitive instinct, he suddenly leaped headlong into the grass, rolled to his feet, then jumped once more.

Maybe it was just sheer fluke, but the moment his feet left the ground, an effulgence of unimaginable intensity exploded as if out of nowhere, and a bolt of lightening struck the exact spot where he had been standing only moments before.

Blinded momentarily by the brilliant flash, he slammed into the dirt face first, nearly splitting his skull open on an exposed rock that jutted up through the grass. His vision was a blur of multicolored dots as he lay there for several minutes, his eyes burning as if struck by red-hot irons. He felt something warm and wet upon his face, and even before he wiped at it and looked at his hand, he knew that it was blood. There was a nasty gash above his ear, but other than that he had miraculously managed to avoid certain death.

He knew not if it had been some kindness of the gods or simply fate itself that had saved him, and not being inclined to conversing with any one deity in particular, he decided to thank himself for reacting so quickly. The only goddess he'd thus far spoken to in his life had been Lamashtu, and he still was not entirely trusting of her, being prone to suspicion as he was.

Presently his sight returned and the pain subsided. Breathing a sigh of relief, he pulled himself upright once more and stepped lightly forward. The thought occurred to him that perhaps the lightening bolt had been the work of Skeltar. It was entirely possible that the wizard was nearby, and that he'd already seen him approaching. If so, then who was to say that the mage hadn't used his knowledge of the Black Arts to hurl the lightening at him?

The thought caused Joktan to growl angrily and he quickly drew his sword. The cold touch of steel immediately seemed to allay his fears, and he carefully continued out into the plains, casting many furtive glances over his shoulder as he went.

The elements continued to vent their indignation, and several more bolts of lightening struck nearby, some of which came dangerously close to hitting him, yet Joktan pressed on. The wind at his back lent speed to his feet, and the blackness that surged about him was darker than the reeking slime in the pits of Hell.

It felt as though he had been walking for hours on end when he suddenly stiffened and froze in his tracks. Within the impenetrable haze of dust he'd caught a fleeting glimpse of something else. It seemed to be moving slowly in the darkness….

He gripped his sword in both hands and peered intently into the gloom, attempting to determine if what he'd saw had been real or simply an illusion. Icy pangs of indescribable fear tore at his mail-clad chest as he realized that indeed, something *was* moving about, and it was coming in his direction!

Tendrils of smoky, purple mist worked their way steadily towards him. They glowed ethereally, like the fingers of a massive spectral hand. They wended through the tall grass like ghastly serpents, becoming increasingly larger, and he stood with his feet rooted firmly to the ground, unsure of what to do. It had nearly reached him when Joktan was galvanized into action. With all the strength he could command, he swung his sword in a sweeping arc, but his blade might as well have been slicing through empty air.

The phantasmal visage was clearly unaffected, and now each vaporous tentacle began to merge, coalescing into one giant, shapeless, mass. Joktan jumped back, his blade held ready for a vicious thrust, and he stared in horror as the specter slowly took form and solidified. What he beheld was not a man, nor a beast or devil, but an unearthly obscenity of the three, an abomination that could only be spawned by the foulest necromantic blasphemies.

Another man might have cringed or dropped his sword and fled screaming in terror through the darkness, but Joktan was a savage, bred by a culture that most civilized men called heathen. In the pantheons of his world, all manner of creatures existed at which the peoples of educated kingdoms openly scoffed. Goblins, ghosts, trolls, and ghouls....and they were no myth nor fairy-tale. He accepted their existence, believed it to be nothing less than a matter of fact, and he was not afraid to meet any of them, with nothing more than the trust he had in his own ability to fight and the keen edge of a steel sword gripped fiercely in his knotted fist.

The thing that stood before him now was a mockery of nature and humanity. Long pointy ears swept back from a broad, bulbous brow. Two huge red eyes glared wickedly upon him, and horrible jaws the size of a crocodile's in length and twice as wide slowly opened, displaying over two dozen fearsome teeth, elongated and jagged. They were not arranged close together, but spread unevenly apart, and when the demon closed its mouth these teeth jutted out and protruded over it's upper and bottom lips like ivory daggers.

From this gruesome maw dripped sticky filth that he knew existed only in the deepest pits of hell. It slathered down the demon's neck in gelatinous globules, dripping over its hairless body onto the ground. The grass began to smolder and burn from the acidity of this slobber, and the stench was so revolting and noxious that it was a struggle in itself just trying to resist the overwhelming urge to gag.

Two long, slimy arms, bulging with gargantuan, rippling muscles, hung down from slightly stooped shoulders nearly four and a half feet wide. It had four fingers on each misshapen hand, but each one ended in a long, deadly talon as black as the forbidden knowledge which had given birth to this monstrous nightmare.

The beast had feet like those of a bear, with claws just as menacing as the talons on it's fingers, and a long tapering tail trailed out nearly six feet behind. It twitched and writhed in serpentine undulations, as though it had a life of it's own, and ended in a point shaped very similarly to a spearhead. At least nine feet tall, the grisly demon towered over Joktan to stare at him from orbs that seethed with horrific intent. It had definite intelligence, but that of a mind possessed completely by the most unimaginable depravity spawned in the sulfurous regions of the damned.

Joktan's knew that this foe could only be the work of Skeltar, and that meant that the wizard had to be close by. His expression was truly frightening to see, but it was momentarily replaced by one of shocked amazement as the demon suddenly addressed him in an almost human voice.

"I know your face, boy!" the demon roared mockingly. "I saw it when you first crawled out of the bloody gash of your mother's womb, soaked in her fluids, gasping for breath! How I longed to lay my hands upon you then, to rend your tender flesh into juicy strips and savor the rare flavor of your lineage!" The abhorrent creature made a sickening, drooling noise that made small bumps begin to rise on Joktan's skin. "And I saw you more recently as well."

"Well here I am!" the tribesman challenged, no longer startled. "Come and get a piece of me if you dare!"

"Oh!" exclaimed the visage, it's voice oozing contemptuous mirth and it's eyes burning with malevolent amusement. "You are a feisty morsel indeed! How fortunate am I to have bode my time!"

It studied him lustfully, like a glutton eyeing his next meal, and licked its black, flabby lips with a forked, crimson tongue. "And now there is so much more of you for me to enjoy!"

"Well, I see you know my name," Joktan growled. "Tell me yours."

"Why should I?" the demon scorned. "Do you think that knowing my name will give you some sort of power over me?" It snorted in contempt, and gruesome strings of putrid slime spurted from its flaring nostrils as it continued to rant.

"Well it won't!" the thing declared. "You would need to be a magician, and clearly you are not." It eyed him with ravenous greed. *"But you do look tasty...."*

Joktan gripped his sword with both hands and moved into a solid fighting stance, his feet spread wide and planted firm. He needed time to figure out what to do, and since the beast seemed to be in a mood for conversation, he quickly determined to use its disposition to his best advantage.

"I just want to know the name of the fiend I'm sending back to Hell!" he snarled at the demon, his eyes azure coals of glowing fury.

The abomination laughed diabolically as it prepared to spring. "Very well!" it agreed derisively. "It will be of no use to you this night. My name is Nischoaz, and the sacred eye that bears my name was set upon the seal which you bore to Luxantia."

"Bah!" Joktan exclaimed tersely. "Small wonder that bauble brought me such ill luck."

"You ignorant gnat!" the demon retorted. "Did you think to be rid of me so easily? The seal upon which my jewel was affixed belongs to one named Kawisu. He is my superior, and it is his name that is engraved upon the golden disk. Therefore men call it the Seal of Kawisu, and the jewel is called the Eye of Nischoaz. They are but a portion of the Black Scroll."

"I only asked you for your name," Joktan growled. "Save the lengthy explanations for your friends in Hell. Come meet my blade!"

"Fool! You are but a fish recently crawled up from the sea!" Nischoaz's terrible laughter roared even louder than the thunder crashing overhead. "I, however, am immortal!" he cried vehemently.

"To me it was but yesterday that your kin were simple monkeys swinging mindless through the trees, and now you think you can destroy me? It was I that brought you to ruin at every turn whilst you carried my emblem! It was Dhampir who destroyed Luxantia at Skeltar's bidding, and it shall be he who does the same to Zebulon this very night. Kawisu shall also play his hand in the slaughter, for he and I are dukes under Dhampir. It's too bad you shall not live to meet him also. Alas! the pleasure is mine alone to savor. And enjoy it I shall, with every mouthful of your juicy flesh."

"That remains to seen," Joktan replied dryly. While the demon had been talking, the rain had finally began to fall, and now rivulets of water trickled down the grotesque features of his foe. He was quick to notice this, for in truth, he wasn't sure if his sword could kill this demon. It had been nothing more than mist and smoke only a few minutes before. Now a sudden surge of hope coursed through his veins, for he realized that if this demon had become solid enough that the rain could wet it's flesh, then it must be real enough to slay with steel.

"Know this!" Nischoaz proclaimed. "While the legions we command are feasting upon the flesh of soldiers, I will be amusing myself with your precious Sheba. All of us want her, you know! It's her blood that makes the woman such a valuable commodity, but I will get to her first!"

"Not if I can help it," Joktan spat, tossing his dripping hair back out of his face.

The horror threw it's head back and let loose a cry that shook the very ground beneath the savage's feet, then he fastened his evil glare upon him. "Now I'm going to kill you!"

"How?" the tribesman retorted. "By boring me to death with your senseless chatter?"

Nischoaz snapped his teeth together anxiously. "First, I'm going to strip the flesh from your bones," he boasted. "Then I'm going to rip your eternal soul to pieces!"

"By Mithra and Dagon!" Joktan swore in exasperation, knowing full well that the demon was only talking in an effort to distract him. "If you're not going to fight me then I'll bring the fight to you!"

He leapt at the fiend, his sword cutting a silvery arc through the air. Nischoaz jumped back with astonishing speed, and the savage's blade made but a tiny scratch across the demon's belly. It might have been a mere flesh wound, but it was yet enough to confirm Joktan's suspicions. The demon stared down at his stomach in disbelief, not seeming to realize until that very instant that it could actually be in serious danger from a mortal weapon.

"You don't seem so immortal after all!" Joktan taunted the thing.

The horror vented its wrath and charged in, arms out wide, seeking to crush him up into its powerful grasp. Joktan ducked low and tried to roll out of his path, but his enemy moved with uncanny speed and agility. It failed to sweep him off the ground, but nonetheless he was knocked nearly senseless by the sheer force of its attack. He was sent sprawling over the ground, gasping for air, but still gripping his sword. He was back on his feet in an instant, uninjured by the blow, his anger molten as a volcano's blistering fervor.

The demon spun around, its eyes burning with hatred such as even the savage had never seen before, and it stepped forward, albeit this time more cautiously than before.

"By Mithra's left tit!" Joktan cursed venomously. "I'm going to send you back to the Hell bitch that spawned you....in pieces!"

The demon roared and came at him again, but this time the human wasn't caught off guard by it's unnatural speed. Joktan knew what to expect, and ran straight at the nightmare, sword held high above his head, without even trying to dodge it's massive arms and raking talons. Just as the monster's arms began to close like the steel jaws of a giant trap, he brought his blade smashing down upon it's hideous skull in a splintering stroke that almost split it's head in half and sheered away the left ear completely.

The demon howled in agony, jumping backward in surprise, and Joktan rushed in for another vicious blow. The blade of Avatare slammed into the demon's shoulder. It ripped through Nischoaz's preternatural flesh and crunched right through his bones, and the demon toppled to the ground. As it fell it struck out at him, hurtling the savage through the air like a stone from a siege engine, and this time when he struck the ground it was with such tremendous force that he was momentarily rendered unconscious.

He rose slowly, shaking his head and checking for broken bones, then he realized that his sword was gone. It would have been impossible to locate his foe in the darkness of the storm, were it not for the demon's unearthly shrieks that pierced the din of the chaos about him. Gripping his ax in his left hand and the mace in his right, he staggered uneasily toward the tormented cries and of his foe, his vision a blur of dirt and blood.

His skull throbbed like a beating drum, and he was vaguely aware of a nasty gash along his ribs where the demon's wicked claws had torn through the steel mesh of his mail, but as he sought out his foe his senses began to return, his sight cleared, and suddenly the thing loomed before him in the blackness. The demon bellowed insanely, and flames of fire spouted from its hellish eyes, yet the sword was still firmly embedded in its shoulder. It wrenched upon the blade mightily, and Joktan watched as the steel bent from side to side, but it did not break, and the demon was unable to remove it.

As it struggled futilely and screamed it's ire, Joktan felt his strength well up within his body just as powerfully as the storm that crashed around him, and he fell upon the devil with a barbaric battle-cry, his mace and ax a whirlwind of brutality and death. Vainly the fiend struck at him time and again, it's talons seeking to rend his flesh to ribbons, to smash his bones like brittle clay, but he avoided each attempt expertly, swinging his mace and ax with the frenzied fury of an enraged panther. The foe was yielding ground, and every time it fell back Joktan swarmed in with a lethal flurry of blows.

He ducked a sweep that should have torn his head from his neck, then hurled the ax with desperate, adrenaline-driven might. It spun through the air and slammed into the demon's forehead at an angle, burying itself deeply with a solid thud. The jarring momentum caused Nischoaz to reel and stagger backward, and the savage moved in with his mace to hammer mercilessly at the thick bones of its knees.

The demon staggered drunkenly, and Joktan palmed a long, narrow dagger and thrust upwards, slicing the horror's belly open wide. It collapsed upon the ground in a spreading mound of slippery entrails, and Joktan leaped upon it's misshapen chest and cried out triumphantly.

"Eat my flesh, will you!" he shouted like one possessed of madness. "The only thing you're going to eat is my mace......as I pound you back down into Hell!"

With both hands, he gripped his mace and wielded it with all his strength. Every drop of savage rage he felt was poured into his strokes, an anger so primitive and animalistic that no other man would have believed his eyes if he were to have witnessed it.

This was not the anger of a man, but rather the outright livid fury of a beast gone utterly mad. The heavy bronze bludgeon turned the demon's flesh into a gory pulp, smashing its distorted features into slivers of teeth and shards of bone. Its body shuddered, its pointed tail thrashed, and its unnatural blood pooled like rotted, reeking bile upon the sopping, muddy ground. Over and over he swung that mace, until long after the nightmare's body had finally quivered and lay limply dead. Even then, he continued to bash at its corpse until his anger began to subside.

His heart thundered in his chest, his blood roared in his ears, and his mind swam with vengeance and bloodlust, until at last he dropped his mace and tore his sword out of the demon's carcass. Perhaps the demon's enormous strength had not been able to withdraw the blade because it had stuck just so, severing vital muscles and tendons. Or maybe it had been due to some spell placed upon it by Lamashtu, which prevented a demon from ever wielding it.

Joktan neither wondered nor cared.

He raised the blade of Avatare high into the air, then brought it down with brutal finality, and the demon's head fell away into the grass. Then he plunged his sword into its chest and tore out its wretched heart. He didn't stoop down to pick up his mace, nor the ax that he'd buried in the demon's thick skull. His dagger also he left behind, protruding from the belly of the mangled corpse, as he wiped the blood from his blade and strode away from his defeated foe, tossing it's vital organ out into the impenetrable darkness.

He had no thoughts of turning back toward the city. He'd come out here on this plain to flush Skeltar out of his hiding place in the other realm, and now he knew that the wizard was close....very close.

There were spots here and there upon his legs, arms and chest where the demon's spittle had burned him, even through his mail armor, but the rain, which had by this time ceased, had washed the foul slime and slobber from his skin, neutralizing the acid. Slowly the burning subsided, becoming little more than a slight irritation that was soon enough forgotten. He was tired from physical exertion, and the cuts and bruises he'd sustained made his muscles stiff and sore.

How far he walked, he didn't know, but it was clear that he would not be able to set the grass on fire if it were soaked by rain, so he kept on going, and presently he noticed that the grass was dry and the mud had ended, so he sat down to wait for dawn.

Battling the saurgs had left the vile taste of defeat upon his lips. He wasn't used to losing, and the memory was a bitter one indeed, but the past week of boredom and inactivity within the palace had been every bit as unbearable.

His struggle with Nischoaz had been taxing, but it had served to reawakened his senses and made him feel truly alive. Now his primitive survival instincts came rushing to the forefront in a flood of vitality and vigor, washing away the stench that a week in civilized environs had left clinging to his flesh like a festering disease.

As he waited the skies cleared, and he sucked the cool morning air deeply into his lungs in giant breaths. It felt truly refreshing, and as it was still a good while before sunrise, he kept himself occupied by chewing up bits of chickweed and rubbing it as a poultice on his wounds. Shortly the first tinges of light began to spill over the horizon, painting the heavens in saffron, crimson and gold, and he stood to gaze about.

Now he could see the walls of Zebulon far behind him, and he guessed that he'd walked nearly five miles in the darkness. Ahead of him he saw nothing, save for open plains and an endless expanse of green. He waited a little longer, then turned back toward the city with a heavy sigh, and suddenly something caught his attention.

It was barely visible. Indeed, an ordinary man might have missed it entirely, for even Joktan's keen eyes had scarcely saw it, but before him he noticed a vague, transparent outline, the edges of which shimmered in the glow of the rising sun. It was the shape of a tent, and instantly his heart skipped a beat as he began to discern other images as well.

He saw what appeared to be the shapes of men and horses, but the sight of them was truly perplexing. While he could make out their contours and see that they were moving about, at the same time he could look right through them, as though they had been cut out of crystal-clear glass. Then instantly the vision faded, and he was left shaking his head, wondering if it had been merely a mirage.

He strode over to the spot where they should have been, but there was nothing. Only grass and dirt and the usual insects of the plains, yet he was sure he'd seen something for those few, fleeting seconds. The wizard had said that he would only be able to see them for a few moments, so perhaps he really did know what he was talking about after all.

Even so, he was supposed to be between Skeltar's camp and the city. Now he was on the other side of where he reasoned the mage should be, and the thought of walking further through the area made him shudder.

What if Skeltar's men could see him as plain as day? The idea that he could be surrounded by invisible foes....against which his blade would be of no use....did not appeal to him in the least. He decided to light the fire where he was and see what happened. If an armed host suddenly sprang up about him, he'd just have to hack his way through them as best he could and hope for the best.

Setting down his torches, he made a small mound of tinder on the ground between his knees, then struck flint to steel, keeping a wary lookout for ant signs of attack. A thin wisp of smoke appeared, and raising the fluffy bundle in his cupped palms, he blew gently until the smoldering ember flared to life. When the flames sprang up, and he dropped the tinder quickly, snatched up a torch, and held it into the small fire.

With two blazing torches in hand, he quickly went about setting fire to the grassy plain, making a line of flame that swung out in a wide semi-circle behind the area where he judged Skeltar's camp to be located. The grass burned slowly at first, as some of it was still damp from the rain that had fallen only a few hours before, but the blistering heat that had scorched the land over the last six days had turned the plains into a veritable tinderbox, and before long the flames licked up into a roaring inferno that burned wildly out of control.

The fire spread out in every direction. It burned all within its path and left behind only smoldering ashes and blackened ruin, and a huge column of dark smoke billowed high into the sky. Several small rodents scurried past him in a frenzied panic as their habitat went up in the blaze. As if out of thin air, men began to spring up everywhere, and suddenly Skeltar's encampment burst into open view.

Joktan ripped his sword from the sheath with a guttural oath and took off at a dead run as men and soldiers clambered about him in confusion. He knew there was no hope of reaching the city if he tried to skirt the flames. The fire was now enormous, sweeping over the grass with frightening speed. He raced toward a tethered stead as fast as his legs would carry him, slashing out with his sword at everyone he passed along the way.

A desperate man rushed at him, a short sword gleaming in his hand, but the savage parried the thrust and disemboweled him, then hacked off another man's arm without breaking his stride.

The reins on the horse's bridle were tied securely to a post that had been driven deeply into the ground. Joktan cut the leather straps and bounded up onto the animal's back in a single leap, and the frightened stead reared up, it's dark eyes wide with fear, hooves flailing the in the air, but he held on tenaciously and dug in his heels. From a nearby tent a soldier appeared, only half dressed, with an arrow notched and drawn, but the savage's instant reflexes sent the assailant gasping into the dust, clawing at a hurled dirk that protruded from his throat. An instant later both man and beast were dashing toward Zebulon in a cloud of dust and feathered shafts, as a dozen or more soldiers armed themselves and vainly plied their bows.

As he sped toward the city, he cast a furtive glance over his shoulder to see several riders giving chase, and he crouched down lower upon the charger's back, urging it to greater haste. He was circling the walls and nearing the main gate when a shaft struck his mount in the rump. The poor beast cried out in pain, going down beneath him as a flurry of spears and arrows tore into its sides and rear. The next few seconds were a cloud of kicking legs and blinding dust, then a spear shot past Joktan's head as he tried to jump away from the horrified, thrashing stead.

His sword leapt into his fist, and he slashed the beast's throat, then grasped the spear and turned to face his foes. The first he impaled head on, burying the hardened steel point deep in the attackers chest with a powerful, well aimed thrust.

Then his sword was singing a song of death as half a dozen men dropped from their mounts and swarmed around him like flies on a rotting corpse.

A soldier wearing a steel helm and breastplate confronted him, his short sword clashing against the stout blade of the savage in a spray of brilliant sparks. But Joktan had the longer reach with his mighty broadsword; he smashed his enemy into the dirt with a single brutal blow, his helm riven, and a gory cleft along his skull that spurted blood.

He turned as two more rushed in, thrusting for his throat and chest. Joktan dropped to one knee with a hideous roar, and his blade sheered through kneecaps and bone like a hot knife through butter. As he rose he sidestepped another attacker's spear, jumped away, and chopped the haft in two with a knife-edge blow of his bare hand, all the while parrying thrusts at his chest and midriff.

The man with the spear was momentarily startled, and Joktan wrenched the shaft from his hands and stabbed it through his throat. His foe staggered backwards, blood pumping from the wound, as the tribesman's next stroke clove away another man's right shoulder and arm in a single sweep, and he fell away, screaming in agony as his life gushed onto the ground.

One man remained, and he came on warily indeed, as he stepped over the mangled carnage of what had been his comrades only a few minutes before. Joktan could see the fear in his eyes; this was no soldier, nor was he a mercenary. He was just a commoner with a blade.

"Go back!" Joktan growled harshly. "You are no fighting man. If you come a step closer, it will only be death that you find here this day."

The man didn't seem to hear him. His eyes were like those of a cornered dog, and his hands began to tremble violently.

"By Dagon's scales, man!" Joktan warned. "Killing you is like slaying a child. Drop your blade!"

With a sudden cry the wretch came on, his sword held high over his head.

"Fool!" the savage exploded. His sword flickered with blinding speed, and the man's cry ended abruptly as he crumpled into the dust. Joktan had struck him with the blunt edge of his blade, and the wretch lay there unconscious upon the butchered remains of his fellow companions.

The thump of an arrow striking into the dirt beside him made Joktan's head jerk around, and with a muttered curse he saw several more riders galloping toward him at a furious pace. Behind them at a distance trailed the rest of Skeltar's horde, and the raging fire followed closely at their heels. More shafts streaked through the air about him as he turned on his heels and made a frantic dash for the city gates. He knew that if he didn't get there in time the guards would lock him out, and he could now hear the thunder of hooves beating the earth somewhere close behind him. He was greatly relieved to see Sheba waiting anxiously just outside the massive iron doors.

"Hurry!" she yelled, as if he needed further encouragement.

She was armed with a crossbow, and as he sprinted past he caught a glimpse of her raising it to fire a bolt in the direction from which he had just come, and from high up on the wall a cloud of arrows sailed out to meet his pursuers. He didn't stop running until he was safely inside, where Sheba quickly joined him.

"What took you so long?" she demanded angrily. "I was beginning to think you weren't coming back."

"I had a little trouble to deal with," he panted.

"So I see," she frowned at his shredded mail. Between the demon's claws and the swords and spears of Skeltar's men, his armor had taken quite a beating.

"I'll explain soon enough," he promised, "but we need to get to the palace."

"Hold on," she said. "You've got an arrow in your leg."

"What....?" Joktan was startled to see the broken shaft sticking out just below his left buttock. In his flight toward the gate he hadn't felt it pierce him, but now as Sheba grabbed hold of the wooden barb and tore it from his flesh, he winced and had to bite his tongue to keep from crying out. Blood seeped liberally from the wound, and he cursed angrily.

"This is the last thing I need right now," he grated. "It'll be stiffening up before too long."

She regarded him with a teasing smile. "Don't worry," she laughed. "I'll tend to it when we reach the palace," and she gave him an unexpected slap that smarted painfully on the wound.

"Wench!" he growled beneath his breath. "Some nurse you'd make!"

"You're not the only one that's had it rough. We've had a long night too," she informed him as they headed off down the street at a jog.

"A foul darkness came over the walls like a fog. It killed nearly two-thirds of the soldiers on guard, and those that did not fall down dead on the spot are now dying from a strange disease. They've piled the bodies in a warehouse, while those that yet live are laid out on stretchers in another."

Sheba swept a lock of hair out of her eyes. "The king is in a safe place....for now, at least.... but I think my job here has been completed. If we had not given our word, I would leave this city in an instant. I have my own country to worry about."

"That cursed wizard set some demon upon me last night," Joktan grunted. "Put up one hell of a fight, too!"

"Well, it looks like the real battle is just beginning," she replied. "I'm sure that Skeltar is in a rage right now, what with you lighting that fire and all. He'll retaliate quickly, and what happened last night is most likely just a small taste of what we can expect from him now."

"Whatever it is," he frowned, "it won't be human."

"There's no way to tell," she considered. "Though I would tend to agree."

"Trust me," he replied. "The demon I fought last night was boasting that some devil summoned by Skeltar destroyed Luxantia. It claimed that he intends to do the same thing here." He grinned at her proudly. "Then I bashed its brains out! I think Skeltar planned to attack last night, though. By killing his minion, I stalled him a little. No doubt that fire will buy us some time as well."

"You conversed with a demon?" Sheba asked incredulously.

"Aye," he confirmed exuberantly. "Right before I cut its ugly head off and ripped out its heart!"

By now they had reached the palace, and once inside, Sheba hurried him along, pulling him into an alcove once they were in their chamber. She drew the silken curtain tight. Joktan wondered what was up, but she pressed a slender finger to his lips and had him sit down on a cushioned, marble bench while she stood in front of him.

"I missed you terribly!" she admitted, her voice a subdued whisper. "The truth is, I was worried about you last night. After you left, I stood upon the wall for hours. I peered into the darkness of the storm with my mind." She looked at his tattered chained mail knowingly as he stripped it off and let it drop to the floor with a metallic clink.

"I saw the thing you fought, even before it saw you."

"I figured as much," Joktan conceded. "Is that why you wanted to go with me so bad?"

She nodded. "I didn't want you going out there alone," she confided. "And Xalton made a pass at me, that fat pig!"

Joktan couldn't help but laugh. "I suspected he would," he said honestly. "The man loves beautiful women, and I certainly can't fault him there. I'm sure you would be the jewel in his crown of conquests."

"I'll be dead before that happens," she snapped.

"You never know," Joktan mused. "It wouldn't be the first time he bedded a corpse!"

Sheba scowled at him angrily. "You're humor is sick," she snorted. "And to think I saved that bastard's life!" Her expression changed and she looked at him seriously.

"But truly, I did worry over you a lot last night. I am not accustomed to such feelings."

She leaned over and put her arms around him tightly, holding his face against the pale, softness of her shoulder. The pair had spent nearly every day together for weeks now, and together they had survived some harrowing situations. The true depth of their feelings for one another became startling clear now that they'd been separated only a short time. They shared an intimacy between them of which very few could ever dream of even possibly understanding. Although neither of them sought to try expressing this bond in words, it was nonetheless undeniable, and each could read in the others mind the things which words could never truly say.

Joktan kissed her tenderly and ran his hands along the outside of her shapely legs. Presently their lips met, and as their tongues touched he grabbed her roughly and pulled her onto his lap. Sheba sat straddling him as he tore away her brazen breast cups and fondled her firm, ivory breasts, caressing them with passionate kisses.

Her head fell back in pleasure as she pressed her turgid nipples into the warm wetness of his mouth, and her fiery locks spilled down her back and buttocks to brush lightly over his naked legs. Joktan's arousal was immense, and she moved her body sensuously against the iron bulge that swelled under his loincloth, rocking gently back and forth.

His hands slid down to the buckles that fastened Sheba's silken shift about her curvaceous hips. He stripped it away, tossing it carelessly to the floor with one hand while the other explored the moistness of her velvet femininity. She arched her back and wrapped her arms around him even tighter, breathing erratically in his ear.

"Remember the first time we did this?" she asked, her voice a whispered moan of pleasure.

"Yes!" he replied hoarsely, pulling aside his own loincloth and rubbing his erection against the swollen lips of her womanly mound.

"Bite me again!" she urged, sliding her moistness along the length of his raging hard-on. "My blood will heal you," she continued, turning her head to the side to expose the sleek contour of her neck.

He placed a firm hand on each of her rounded buttocks and positioned her appropriately upon his lap while kissing and nipping gently at her neck. She sighed expectantly as the engorged head of his throbbing manhood slid between her tender pink folds, slipping up and down along the length of her slit, the natural lubrication of his pre-cum making his contact with her even more wet and slippery.

Joktan's mouth opened wide as he sealed his lips over her jugular, and she sucked in her breath with a deep, startled gasp as his stiff shaft sank into her burning hole and his sharp canine fangs mercilessly tore into the soft flesh of her neck. She could feel herself stretching to accommodate his rigid thickness as his jaws clamped down hard upon her neck like an iron vise and her red blood spurted thick into his waiting mouth.

Her sucked down harder while impaling her with the full length of his massive cock, and she cried out intensely, her essence gushing hotly between his thirsty lips, her long nails clawing frantically at the rippling muscles on his back.

Now came a torrent of visions and images, the sum of his lifetime and the eternity of hers, coalesced into tormented moments of indescribable bliss. She pressed her swollen clitoris against his pubic ridge and rubbed herself rhythmically back and forth against him, stimulating herself as he drove his manhood into her soaking pussy relentlessly, penetrating her as fully and completely as her body could possibly allow.

His thrusts became more violent, her motions more frenzied, as her orgasm grew like a hungry fire raging deep inside of her, and all the while her blood continued spilling freely through his lips. He gulped it like a parched and dying soul in need of drink, and then suddenly she screamed in erotic fervor as her orgasm exploded with the thunderous roar of fireworks, in brilliant, exhilarating hues that only she could possibly sense and witness. Her lithesome body trembled and shuddered from the overwhelming intensity, and all the time his manhood surged and plunged between the steaming velvet of her quivering lips.

She felt him stiffen further....found it hard to believe it possible....and he ripped his fangs out of her punctured flesh, throwing his head back against the stone wall and groaning painfully, his features contorted in ecstatic euphoria.

His orgasm filled her with a molten rush. He bucked powerfully against her thighs, gripping her buttocks and slamming her ruthlessly with his granite phallus. His fingers gripped like talons of steel as he pumped inside her, his semen erupting like a fountain of fire, filling her with his thick, milky seed.

Their bodies glistened with silvery perspiration in the dim interior of the alcove, and her firm nipples pushed against him, her chest heaving in labored breaths. For a long while they sat there, doing nothing more than simply staring deeply into each other's eyes, his manhood still twitching firmly inside the silken interior of her dripping femininity.

"I believe your wounds are healed," she said at last, her eyebrows arching as she considered him playfully. "How do you like my nursing abilities now?"

"I think my leg still hurts," he feigned a frown. "Perhaps you should tend to my wounds just a little longer."

"Perhaps….." she smiled. "However, you no longer have any wounds, so I guess there isn't any further need."

"I can fix that," Joktan laughed. "I still have a bit of slaying to do." He shot her an impish grin. "I'm sure I'll have a few injuries before I'm done!"

"A woman can always hope!" she teased demurely.

He smirked good-naturedly, but as she rose from his lap to get dressed, his expression became suddenly serious. "Why didn't you tell me?"

"Tell you what?" she asked, unsure of what he was referring to.

"Why didn't you tell me that you're pregnant?"

"I didn't know until just recently when I was in Skeltar's dungeon," she explained. "I fully intended to tell you, but so much has happened lately…..I just wanted to wait until we had some time alone…..until we were gone from here…." she paused. "But how did you know?"

"How do you think?" he snorted. "I drank your blood. You are pregnant with twins. I even saw their faces."

"Twins?" she gasped in amazement. "You saw them?"

"Aye."

"What did they look like!" she asked excitedly. "I mean, I suspected, but…."

"They're beautiful," he whispered. A distant look had filled his eyes, as though he were looking into a dream. "They look just like you."

Sheba's face instantly lighted with a glowing, ethereal radiance, and Joktan suddenly seemed to almost become embarrassed. "They look exactly like you," he smiled sheepishly. "Except that one's a boy, of course…."

"A boy!" Sheba exclaimed. "Are you sure?"

"Absolutely," he confirmed. "Just as sure as I'm sitting here right now."

"That can't be…..!" she cried, her eyes wide with bewilderment and sudden fear.

He sat there quietly for a few moments, not knowing what to say in light of Sheba's reaction, and thoroughly confused. He'd expected her to be enthused, but the look on her face told him that something must be wrong, and it was clearly something which he definitely did not understand at all. Presently she fixed her on gaze on him with a thoughtful frown.

"So how do you feel about all of this?"

"Why don't you tell me," he replied quietly. "You know my thoughts better than anyone else." His eyes searched her face intently. "Look into my heart and tell me what you see."

She sat back down on Joktan's knees and rested her forehead against his temple. Her breathing slowed, she fell silent, and her eyes lightly closed.

"You feel very happy!" she said after a moment, "yet unsure. The wanderlust is strong within you, and because of it you know that it would be impossible to settle down and be a father."

"Aye," he confirmed. "In which case I would be a poor parent indeed."

"That's O.K.," she continued. "It's not a father that these children are going to need. They will be very different and unique.......the first of their kind."

"How do you know?".

Sheba was silent for a moment before she spoke. "Because the women in my lineage....the ones who have become queens....have never given birth to more than one child, and always a female. It has always been forbidden, in an effort to prevent the possibility of a struggle for dominance, to have more than one."

"How have they done this?" Joktan wanted to know. "Surely someone must have decided to break the tradition. A queen can do as she pleases."

"Not us," Sheba replied. "We have no control over when we become pregnant. Our bodies seem to decide that for us....as well as the sex of the child....which is why I am confused about my current situation. But once we give birth, we are immediately made queen, and after that, we are incapable of having children ever again."

Joktan stared at her incredulously. "Why? Is it on account of some cruel rite? What manner of people is it that dwell in your land?"

"No!" she laughed softly. "There are no barbarous rituals involved. Everything is done as it must be. You'll have to trust me, that is all I can say."

"Why do I get the impression that I'll never be permitted to see them?" he demanded. "That is what you were going to say, isn't it, before you thought better of it?" He glared at her. "I saw it in your eyes."

"Well....yes," she admitted slowly. "We have learned, through many trials and grievous errors, that men are more prone to violence than women. It is part of human nature, and inevitable. Women are nurturing, while men are dominating and aggressive. Such an influence would be disastrous after becoming queen, and because of this, our children have always been raised by women. And so must it be with mine, even more so than any others."

"We'll see about that," he growled. "Your country sounds like a very strange land indeed, and I think you know that if I decide to see my own children, no tradition, demon, or Hell itself will ever stop me."

She kissed him tenderly on the lips, then looked him in the eyes. "I know, but you must trust me about this," she assured. "Once we are there everything will make sense to you........ I promise."

# 19

General Namindi's forbidding mood had not been improved by the dreadful storm. The fact that his scouts had failed to return did not help matters either, and as all subsequent attempts at locating them had proven fruitless, his disposition was such that his men now gave him a wide berth.

All night he and a handful of captains had kept watch. The ferocity of the storm had been no less than spectacular, and Namindi had moved closer to the city under the cover of darkness, taking three of his most trusted men along with him. The blackness of the strange storm had been so utterly impenetrable that he had walked right up to the very gates of Zebulon without being detected by the guards. The massive iron doors had been all but invisible even to his keen eyes, and he'd nearly stumbled into them headfirst in the pitch-blackness of the foul night.

Mingled with the din of thunder had been other sounds as well, noises they knew should not have been there. Once, in particular, it had seemed as if a strange voice ranted in the dark, but the words were difficult to hear and impossible to decipher. Convoluted as such intonations might have been, they had nonetheless raised gooseflesh upon even the General's skin, and he was not a man that spooked easily by any means.

A lone horse had been discovered along the eastern wall. There was no sign of its rider, but the stead clearly belonged to King Xalton's stable. The General wondered if perhaps the king had sent out a few scouts of his own. If so, at least one of them had not yet returned, for it seemed that the mount had been standing there for quite some time.

After returning to their former position, Namindi had decided to remain where they were for one more day. Although there had so far been no evidence of the wizard and his army of renegades, a nagging feeling in the pit of the General's stomach told him that something wasn't right. The king could have stationed scouts of his own outside the city. They could have hidden in the grass unnoticed, just as he and his captains were now, which could easily explain why the scouts they had sent out earlier had not returned. The king's men could very well have captured them, in which case Xalton might suspect that Namindi was close at hand. There was only one place between Zebulon and Albana where an army the size of Namindi's could be concealed, and their encampment would no longer be a secret.

However, Namindi's scouts were tough and hardy men. They knew the risks associated with their duties, and in the event of capture, their silence could be virtually guaranteed. Most of them carried some sort of deadly poison which they could quickly swallow if captured, preferring to die with honor than in cowardly disgrace, or worse yet, in agonizing torment upon the torturer's cruel rack.

However, if the king had discovered his scouts, he would have certainly made some sort of move by now, and since that was not the case, Namindi felt confident that they had met with some other demise. What that might be, he could only venture a guess, but his military instincts told him that their disappearance had something to do with Skeltar.

At dawn his suspicions had been confirmed. A lone man had been spotted to the east of Zebulon by one of Namindi's captains. He definitely wasn't a soldier, which meant he had to be a scout, sent out by the king, no doubt. The General watched in puzzlement as the scout set fire to the plains, but his reasons for doing it had become immediately evident. As the flames grew in size and swept toward the city with increasing speed, Skeltar's army had suddenly appeared, as if materializing out of nothing by some dreadful form of magic.

Now the wizard's small force had positioned themselves in front of the city gates, just far enough away to be out of the reach of the king's archers. Namindi knew that the king would seal up the gates; Zebulon could withstand a siege indefinitely. There was no possible way a few hundred men could breach the city's formidable stone walls, and any attempt to break down the gates with battering rams would be utterly futile. Those mighty iron doors were nearly two feet thick.

The king would wait until the attackers realized the hopelessness of their assault, and once they turned to leave, his army would rush out upon them like a tidal wave of gleaming steel death. The renegades would be outnumbered a dozen to one, and the slaughter would be over in a matter of minutes.

Namindi watched with no small amount of curiosity as Skeltar's men took their places in a semi-circular line, and the spectacle was such that he and his captains couldn't help but laugh. Unless the mage had arranged for another army to join him very soon....one that was significantly larger....he was setting himself up for disaster. Skeltar had not become the most feared wizard in the Westermarch through stupidity. Clearly, something was amiss, and only time would tell what the wizard had in mind. There was nothing to do but sit back and watch for the moment.

"That wizard is a fool!" one of his captains cleared his throat and spat into the grass beside him. "I say we cast bets to see how long he lasts. If we can't take the city, at least we can make a bit of coin out of this excursion."

Namindi actually smiled. "Cast all the bets you like," he laughed darkly. "I say the mage breaches the gates tonight."

His captain raised his eyebrows doubtfully. "With six hundred men?"

"Aye," the General answered with a nod. "That mage has been here all along, and we failed to see him until this morning. Obviously the scout who set that fire this morning knew what he was doing. How he figured it out I'll never know......perhaps he just got lucky." He gave the captain a knowing stare.

"If Skeltar was able to hide his army in plain sight like that, then obviously he is no idiot, and right now you should be wondering what else he is capable of. Even the most ignorant peasant knows that a city such as Zebulon cannot be taken with so few numbers. There is purpose in what he is doing, though I'll be damned if I can figure it."

"Does that mean we will be staying here another day?" the captain asked hesitantly.

"Yes."

The captain grunted disapprovingly, and his superior's temper flared. "You dare to doubt me?" he snarled, anger flushing his cheeks a dark crimson. "By tomorrow morning you will all see why I am the youngest General in Straltonia's history, and why you are all only captains!"

The man apologized instantly, but the General continued. "Make bets, you say? I'll make you a wager, dog! If the wizard hasn't entered the city by night's end, I'll give you ten pounds of gold."

The captain's brow furrowed dubiously. He had not intended to rouse the General's ire, but ten pounds of gold was a small fortune, and he knew full well that Namindi could pay it with ease. "And if by some chance the mage actually does makes it in?"

Namindi grinned horribly. "Then I will name my price. What do you care? You're going to be a rich man, right?"

The man considered a moment longer, then smiled thinly. "Deal!" he agreed at last.

"Good then!" the other proclaimed, his eyes sparkling with satisfaction. "The rest of you dogs take heed!" he commanded, knowing that they had all heard the details of the wager. "And in the mean time, send word back along the line. I want the foot soldiers and archers to start moving forward. When they are within sight of the city, they are to separate into groups of ten and spread out on their bellies. It is of utmost importance that they keep out of sight. The first man I see moving up behind us I will gut myself! Once they accomplish this, I will have further instructions. Go now, and be hasty!"

He turned to the captain with whom he'd struck the bargain. "And you'd better pray to Mithra that I'm wrong," he warned. "Ten pounds of gold is a pittance to me, but loyalty and trust........those are qualities which I consider to be priceless."

# 20

"Skeltar has sent us his terms," Chia informed the king. "They are but two things; he demands your complete surrender….."

"Over my dead body!" Xalton ejected, fiercely interrupting her.

"That is the second option," she replied wryly.

The king's laughter was sardonic as he turned to Quan Chang Xu. "And what is your advice?"

The little mage shrugged his frail shoulders lightly. "It is no laughing matter, My Lord. He fully intends to storm the city, that much is obvious. How he has devised to do it remains to be seen, but it would be most wise to prepare for the worst."

"Some help you are!" the king snapped anxiously. "I've made enough preparations to withstand the assault of an army a hundred times the size of his pathetic band of renegades."

"He will undoubtedly wait for nightfall," the mage advised. "Of that you can be assured. Midnight is the hour of greatest power for any sorcerer. To those who delve into the arts of magick, it is known as the Witching Hour."

"It grows dark already," Chia commented, "although the sun is yet visible in the sky."

"Yes," Quan Chang Xu confirmed. "Skeltar gathers the forces of darkness to him, even as we speak. Did you send more torches to the wall as I asked?"

The warrioress motioned affirmatively. "Of course, father. And I left instructions for all of them to be lighted at dusk."

"Good," the wizard replied. "Fire may prove to be more useful than steel."

Suddenly the oaken chamber doors were thrown open and Joktan burst into the room with Sheba close at his heels. He strode quickly to where the king and his confidants were seated, a grim expression creasing his deeply tanned features. He addressed Chia briskly, gesturing at the king.

"What is he still doing here?" Joktan demanded. "He should be in the keep by now!"

"I know," she bristled, "but he refuses to go."

"That's right!" Xalton confirmed defiantly. "I'll not have some foul mage drive me out of my own palace!"

Joktan turned on him angrily. "You foolish wretch!" he growled. "Your life is in our hands. You'll do as we tell you if you want to live."

The king stared at him incredulously. "How dare you talk to me like this!" he exclaimed indignantly. "I am the King!"

"Maybe so," the savage retorted, "but if you do not heed our advise you won't be for long. You clearly know little about defending your own city."

"What has gotten into you?" Chia demanded. "You had best bite your tongue!"

Joktan spun, his eyes filled with menace, and his hand moved instinctively to the hilt of his sword. "Are you going to silence me, wench?" he snarled.

Sheba stepped between them, and he stood glaring about the room like an angry, wild beast.

"Both of you settle down!" Sheba shouted in such a commanding voice that the warrioress and tribesman obeyed her instantly. Her words were like an unseen force that compelled them to obey, and silence filled the chamber instantly. She turned to Joktan.

"Tell them," she intoned. "And mind your temper."

"I have just come back from the plains," he said.

"That was this morning," Chia replied sourly. "You have already told us about it."

"No, I went out again," his said tersely. "I've just returned."

She glared at him doubtfully. "Impossible. The gates are locked, and you could never find your way back through the tunnels."

"No," he agreed, "but while your soldiers crowd the western wall like circus spectators, they leave the rest of the city virtually undefended. I slipped over with a grappling hook and some rope, then circled out into the plains."

"For what reason?" Chia asked. "We can see Skeltar easily enough."

"And that is what worried me," he replied. "I thought perhaps he might have another army, one which we have not yet seen."

"Go on," she urged.

"The smoke from the fire I started this morning and the tall grass gave me plenty of cover," he continued. "As you probably suspect, I saw exactly the same thing which you have seen from the wall, but as I was preparing to come back, I caught the brief glint of steel farther out and toward the north, so I decided to investigate, and what do you think I found?"

"Enlighten us," the king responded sarcastically. "What was it?"

"A massive army," Joktan replied. "Countless numbers of soldiers, divided up into groups and scattered widely over the plains to the north. They are lying in the grass as we speak, which is why they cannot be seen from the wall. They are your Imperial Troops."

Everyone stared at him in disbelief, but he ignored their looks and went on.

"It is General Namindi. I know that Quan Chang Xu warned you of his presence earlier, but you refused to listen, just like you did when he told you that Skeltar was close by days ago."

"If it truly is Namindi," the king reasoned, "he would have already attacked Skeltar's camp."

"No he wouldn't," Joktan disagreed.

"And how would you know?" Xalton snorted. "You're a northern savage."

"That I am," he retorted, "but you are a foolish king."

Xalton stiffened, and Joktan continued without the slightest concern. "A year ago you locked me in your dungeon. After escaping, I fled to the north, where General Namindi caught me. But instead of bringing me back here, he gave me a choice; I could carry out a ridiculous mission for him, or have my head lopped off in the city square. Naturally, I chose the quest."

"I've heard nothing of this," the king admitted.

"Of course not," the savage responded. "And what a surprise! All that you care for is your concubines. Meanwhile, unrest has been fomenting like a plague throughout the kingdom, especially among the nobility. General Namindi told me this himself last year. He wanted your crown then, and he wants it now."

"If what you say is true, then why have you waited to tell us?" Chia demanded.

"You wouldn't believe your own father," he answered lowly. "Why should you listen to me? I'm a savage, remember?"

Xalton rested his chin on a plump fist thoughtfully. He'd known that there were factions throughout kingdom that resented his rule, but never had it been more clear to him just how serious the situation was until this moment.

"What was the purpose of the mission Namindi sent you on?"

"It makes little difference," the savage replied. "It was a fools quest."

"Then humor me," the king urged.

Joktan shrugged nonchalantly. "Very well. He sought an ancient sword. It was supposed to render its bearer invincible in battle. According to an old map he'd obtained, it was hidden in the Dead Land of Muspell."

Quan Chang Xu started. "What did he call this sword?"

"Trfing."

The wizard's face suddenly blanched. *"The ancient blade of Therion!"* he breathed. *"Did you find it?"*

"Aye," Joktan replied bitterly. "But I did not give it to Namindi. I lost it in one of the bottomless chasms of Muspell, and as it was beyond my abilities to retrieve, I left it there and journeyed west. Like I said, it was a fool's quest."

The wizard seemed to breath a sigh of relief, and the tribesman turned to face the king.

"I came here to kill Skeltar and one other," he stated. "After that, I'm gone. I care little about you or your kingdom, but fulfilling my personal obligations will be much more difficult if you are killed."

He looked at the king knowingly. "If Skeltar breaches the walls, Namindi will follow at his heals like a vulture. There is no hope of holding off his troops here in the palace, and the fighting will ravage the city. I know that you dislike the idea, but you must go to the keep. Your women can defend you there with ease, and chances are, no one will even think of looking for you there……..not even Skeltar. He will be busy trying to take the city, as will Namindi, I suspect. No one will consider that the king might take refuge in his enemies stronghold."

Xalton stared at Joktan intently. "Very well," he said at last. "If Chia agrees, then I will too." He looked at the warrioress for approval, and she nodded affirmatively.

"He is right," she allowed.

"And what about you, wizard?" asked the king.

"My thoughts have been made well known," said the mage. "However, I will be where I am most needed. Where exactly that will be, even I do not know for certain as of yet."

"Then I will have some of my guards accompany you," Xalton offered.

"Don't waste them on me," the wizard objected. "I will be just fine, and they will be put to better use elsewhere."

Chia objected instantly, but her father merely laughed. "I am a powerful sorcerer," he reminded the young woman gently. "I need no protection."

Joktan moved to Sheba's side and spoke to her discretely. "Go with Chia," he whispered. "See that she is safe....for her father's sake."

She started to say something, but he quickly cut her off. "It will be more beneficial to have someone inside the keep as well as outside of it." Sheba looked unsure, and he added. "Don't worry. I'll be O.K."

"But my duty to the king is done," she countered. "I should be with you." She wanted to tell him about how the evil within Skeltar's keep could possibly harm her unborn children, but if she had tried everyone else would have heard.

"I would like for us to be together also," he explained. "However, I promised the wizard that I would keep an eye out for Chia. I cannot be in two places at once."

"It would have been nice to have known sooner," she retorted, clearly displeased with the tardiness of his disclosure.

"I've had little time," he replied dryly.

"I know," she said, her features softening instantly. "And we're stuck here now until the battle is over."

"Aye," he muttered, touching her arm gently. "Be careful."

He nodded and crushed his lips against hers briefly. Then he turned and left the chamber. Outside the doors he paused for a few seconds, wondering silently if he would ever see Sheba's beautiful face again. The thought of losing her seemed to pierce his very soul. He forced it away with an angry growl, then started toward the palace armory.

# 21

Skeltar sat upon a heavily cushioned divan within his broad canvas tent. His withered fingers grasped an oval mirror of polished silver, at which he gazed intently while uttering an arcane spell. The surface of the looking glass slowly took on a purple metallic sheen, and he continued to chant the ancient incantation in a barely audible tone. Presently a vague image began to appear within the mirror, at first nothing more than a faint mirage, but as he continued to voice the magickal syllables the vision became crystal clear.

Seeming satisfied with the results of his endeavor, the sorcerer traced an invisible symbol over the image with the twisted forefinger of his right hand, then placed the gleaming mirror on a small wooden table that had been placed nearby. The sound of approaching footsteps drew his attention toward the door. They were confident, yet hasty, accompanied by the clank of heavy armor, the telltale signature of Brutus' imperious stride.

"Come," the mage intoned as the sandaled footsteps neared the door. The canvas curtains of the entrance were cautiously swept aside, then the soldier stepped quickly into the room.

"I heard your voice," he said flatly in a tone as devoid of emotion as his dark eyes. "How my I assist you, My Lord?"

Skeltar gloated with an arrogant sneer. Lately he'd been using a form of telepathy to call Brutus to him whenever the need arose. Often he'd used the same method of communication with his former servant Cral, but there was something about that insolent miscreant which had always seemed to annoy his master. Perhaps that was why the mage had derived such satisfaction from demeaning him audibly.....

"My plans for this evening will make the destruction of Luxantia look like child's play," Skeltar boasted. "Within a few short hours the sun will rise, and I will be the ruler of Straltonia."

"Yes, My Lord."

"I realize, of course, that King Xalton was once your master, and Zebulon your home," the wizard hissed. "Not withstanding, you have served me well thus far. Do you have any misgivings that I should know about?"

"No, My Lord," the soldier responded hollowly.

"Are you sure?" Skeltar insisted. "You may speak freely. I will do you no harm."

"A few weeks ago I served an overindulgent king," Brutus replied. "I was not aware of what an ungrateful man he truly was, but you have since opened my eyes. You have paid me well, and although there have been times when I've considered your methods to be somewhat......extreme, you have always kept your word."

"My actions are justified by their results," the wizard's voice rattled dryly.

"Aye," he responded. "And I've sworn my loyalty to you, by oath and by blood. I will not break either one."

"Excellent!" Skeltar sneered. "Tomorrow you shall be the second most powerful man in all the Westermarch!"

"I already consider myself as such," the soldier proclaimed meekly. "No one can stand against your power."

"You are an eloquent man," the wizard rasped. "And very astute. Now listen closely to me. Send some men and a stout battering ram to the needle's eye, with instructions to break it down. Send another group to the northern wall with four catapults and plenty of stones. They are to begin their assault immediately. Another detachment will be likewise sent to the south wall, with catapults and stones. The rest will be spread out along this western wall and in front of the gates. They will attack with arrows and the remaining catapults. Is that clear so far?"

"Yes."

"Good," the wizard intoned. "That will cause the king's men to spread out, even though the threat we pose to them is a joke by all appearances."

Brutus frowned thoughtfully, but said nothing, and Skeltar continued. "I am going to give you a very important mission." He picked up the silver mirror from the table and handed it to the soldier. The image on it was still as clear and bright as before, and Brutus, who had expected to see his own reflection, stared at it in slack-jawed amazement.

"The man you see there is a formidable foe," Skeltar said. "He is a very good swordsman, and not to be underestimated. I warned you of him at Luxantia. Once we are inside Zebulon, he will no doubt make a nuisance of himself."

"I can handle him," Brutus promised. "Where will I find him?"

"You won't have to," the mage replied. "He'll find us both soon enough, and when he does, I want you to bring me his head."

"Consider it done," he said. "Anything else?"

"No, that is all, but after you leave, see that I am not disturbed until I call for you."

"As you wish." The soldier turned and disappeared through the door flap, checking to be sure that it was securely closed so as to prevent those who might be curious from peering in. Skeltar went to the far corner of the room and flung back the lid of a large, oaken chest. He withdrew several items, all of which had been designed and crafted with a specific unholy purpose in mind. Having collected these, he closed the lid and positioned himself at the center of the earthen floor. He set down his arcane implement and produced a small dagger from his robes. It was an athame, a double-edged knife created for the sole purpose of commanding magickal powers, and as he raised it into the air a hideous grimace writhed over the parchment features of his awful face.

*"This moment marks the end of an era!"* he whispered in a serpentine hiss. "No longer shall I be bound by the curses of long dead magicians. My youth shall be restored! I shall be invincible, and the whole world will henceforth cower at my feet!"

He gazed upwards with the expression of a madman gone insane. "Nay, not only the world, but even the Legions of Hell itself!"

For a few seconds it seemed as if he had truly lost his senses, but then he lowered his athame and picked up a tiny object from the floor. It was one of the items he'd retrieved only moments before, and he held it almost reverently as a molten light began to glow within the orbs that should have been his eyes.

*"But for my first act of power, I must take care of Namindi......!"*

# 22

A strange, pale mist sprang up as if from nowhere. It spread out over the grassy plains and drifted lightly through the breezeless night air like the ghost of a murdered man. It crept toward the soldiers that lay motionless in the tall expanse of green, three thousand armed and armored men that waited anxiously in anticipation of Namindi's signal.

The vaporous effluvium was seemed to carry with it an almost preternatural chill, yet the General welcomed it gratefully nonetheless. Fires still burned hungrily in the distance, and although they seemed to be inexplicably dying out, they cast a bloody glare along the far horizon. In their wake the plains had been transformed into a smoking ruin of lingering embers and gray-white ash, leaving behind nothing that would offer concealment.

Namindi had been forced to order his troops further back into the grass, out of the path of the raging inferno. While his men were perfectly concealed, they were now farther away from Zebulon than he had planned on. The dense fog would provide the cover needed they to move closer to the city walls without detection.

Darkness had begun to fall even before the sun had sank out of sight, and he didn't seem to notice that the vaporous mist hovered only over the portion of the plains wherein his soldiers were now positioned.

He watched with curiosity as Skeltar's men moved into place around the city walls, laughing silently as they wheeled their catapults and cumbersome ox carts laden heavily with chunks of jagged stone.

*What is this mage doing?* he wondered. It would take thousands of such cartloads before Zebulon's massive walls would ever yield. The wizard's ammunition would only last a couple hours, after which his war machines would be useful only as firewood.

A sudden shrill cry brought Namindi to his feet. The sound was quickly joined by a dozen more, and within seconds the plain came alive with soldiers. They jumped up in a panic from the grass like a plague of screaming locust, swords drawn, slashing about their feet in utter terror. The scene was one of total chaos, and within the few brief moments that it took for the General to rise and look about, at least two dozen armored soldiers plummeted to the ground, thrashing and howling in torment. He started forward, and suddenly a cold shiver clawed at his spine as he realized the source of their terror.

There was no wind this night, yet the tall grass swayed upon the breast of the plain like a sea whipped by a cyclone. Everywhere soldiers sprang into view, only to plunge back to the earth, arms and legs flailing wildly before their frenzied cries slowly died. Even as the dead men's screams ended, they were replaced by countless others, and Namindi stared aghast as the ground began to churn about his feet.

"Snakes!" he yelled, as if his men didn't already know, but they were well aware of what it was that caused the earth to crawl like maggots on the dead flesh of a festering corpse.

Even amid the blackness of the night, the identity of this evil could be recognized with ease. Death adders, vipers, cobras and dreaded tiger snakes were but a few members of the reptilian wave that swept thickly over the ground. So vast were their numbers that they swelled over each other like a darkly broiling flood, foaming with certain death. Every manner of poisonous snake writhed and twisted sickeningly, striking out at anything and everything that moved, including each other.

The peril this nightmare presented was immense. While soldiers in neighboring kingdoms such as Perga wore high-topped leather boots, Straltonia's infantry wore only sandals. The serpents boiled over their feet and wrapped around their legs. Again and again, countless pairs of terrible fangs dripping with deadly venom sank deep into exposed, Straltonian flesh.

Some managed to escape, running blindly into the impenetrable blackness of the night, but those who did were very few indeed.

Namindi was one of them. Suddenly a horse appeared in front of him, and he recognized it instantly as the one which he'd found yesterday along the eastern wall. The beast charged toward him wildly, the whites of it's eyes virtually glowing amid the gloom, and as it passed the General grasped onto the reins. He swiftly swung into the saddle. His heels hammered the beast's ribs like iron sledges and he drove the terrified mount through the desperate, screaming mob.

It was impossible to believe that only minutes before these men had been an organized army of highly trained and seasoned soldiers. They reached out desperately....as if he alone could miraculously spirit them all away to safety upon a solitary stead....and Namindi's short sword flashed in his fist, a tongue of glistening death that flicked out merciless and cruel.

He struck insanely at the very men who had loyally followed him all these years, his sword smashing polished helms and cleaving waving arms in two like brittle twigs. It seemed like a nightmare from which he could not be free, a blur of unearthly horror, and he roared unintelligibly like a possessed fiend as his blade ripped through the pleading face of a onetime childhood friend.

Then suddenly he broke away from the hideous tumult, charging furiously over the plains as fast as the horse's legs could carry him into the night.

# 23

Joktan stood upon the wall as the first barrage of flaming shafts arced up towards the battlements. He grinned savagely at a nearby soldier and ducked behind the crenellated stone, just as a half dozen arrows splintered on impact mere inches from his unprotected head.

"Seth and Tana!" he swore. "Are they aiming only at me?"

"Of course they are," the soldier beside him commented dryly. "You're the only fool dumb enough to stand in open view!"

"Bah!" Joktan scoffed. "I'm also the only man on this wall that has killed fourteen of Skeltar's dogs tonight!"

His words were true. The soldiers on the wall were all hardy men, but the memory of the previous night's arcane assault was still fresh in their minds. Few desired to present themselves as a target. They were justifiably afraid that the wizard would unleash another sorcerous attack against them, and not a one was inclined to be his first victim of the night. Joktan, however, had faced many evil adversaries, the likes of which none of these men could have possibly imagined. He knew that if someone didn't raise their courage soon, Skeltar's victory would be all but assured.

The savage notched a shaft to his bowstring, then quickly stood. In a single, smooth motion, he took aim and fired, then drew two more arrows and loosed them in a blur of movement before turning to the man beside him.

"Make that seventeen!" he informed the cringing soldier. "Isn't there a single dog amongst you that's man enough to try and best me?" he roared brazenly.

He knew that none of these soldiers would take kindly to being called dogs, especially by a Sabertooth Tribesman. His ruse worked excellently. Further down the line of crouching men behind him, a boisterous voice rose to the challenge.

"Aye, tribesman!"

Joktan turned to see one of the captains now standing, brandishing a cocked and loaded crossbow in each meaty fist. The man was middle-aged, taller than him by a hands breadth, deep chested, and possessed of a bear-like build. He grinned wolfishly beneath his crimson plume and polished helm.

"Who are you?" Joktan bellowed, seemingly unconcerned as a flurry of feathered shafts tore through the air about him.

"I am Cassius, Captain of the Fifth Imperial Battalion!" the soldier declared. "I'll teach you to boast under my watch! Seventeen you say?" He glance around at his men. "Why, I've slain more with naught but my bare hands and manhood!"

The other soldiers let out a noisome cheer in support of their captain, a man whom they obviously regarded with a great deal of admiration. A wicked smile split the burnished features of the tribesman's face. "That's the spirit!" he laughed as he strode quickly to the captain's side. "But by Dagon's member, you've some catching up to do, captain!"

The look in the man's eyes told Joktan that he recognized the ploy for what it was. Cassius slapped his shoulder firmly with a powerful hand, still grinning broadly. He gave the savage a knowing wink and a slight nod, then turned to his men.

"Come on, dogs!" he roared. "Are you going to let this simple savage show you up? Stand on your feet, and send those son's of Seth back to Hel!"

Another wild shout broke lose, and suddenly the archers were standing. Joktan took up a position near the captain, drawing his bow and taking aim.

"Fire at will, boys!" Cassius shouted.

The archers had already notched arrows to bowstrings, and amid of chorus of sharp twangs, a cloud of arrows streaked out and downwards from the wall. Their fletched shafts sprang into the air like a swarm of angry bees and furiously pelted the attackers in a sheet of steel tipped death. Suddenly the darkness below the walls became black as pitch, save for tiny wreaths of flame that flickered on the arrows and torches of Skeltar's men. Nonetheless, cries of anguish and pain drifted up from the void as the soldiers plied their bows in earnest, launching successive volleys against their foes.

Joktan paced along the battlements, shouting battle cries and encouragement, and presently he felt a strong hand grip his shoulder. He turned to meet Cassius' wide grin.

"Well done, friend," the burly soldier beamed approvingly. "That was just the spark to get them going." He motioned the savage off to the side and lowered his voice. "I've heard rumors, that some of those men down there were once Straltonian soldiers. Hell, we've all heard them." He stared intently at him.

"You're the only man that has had the chance to see them up close yet, so tell me. Is it true?"

"Aye," he confirmed darkly. "About a hundred of them at least. The rest are mercenaries and renegades, best I could tell."

"Few men relish the though of fighting those who were once their comrades," said the captain. "My men are no cowards, but what happened here last night was enough to strike fear in the heart of even the bravest soldier."

"'Tis no pleasant affair, fighting a wizard," Joktan replied.

"No," the captain agreed, "yet I was on the wall when you were out there on the plain. You're a good fighter, with a stout heart. Men respect that."

Joktan wasn't used to receiving compliments, but he nodded gratefully. Relations between Straltonia and the Savage Tribesland were stained by a long history of blood and war, and he knew that the captain truly meant what he said.

"After this is over, come and see me," Cassius told him. "I could use a man like you."

"That would be a first!" Joktan chuckled heartily. "A savage in the army of Straltonia?" He smiled at the captain. "Thanks for the offer, but I have other commitments to keep. This little battle has been a damned distraction. I shall be on my way as soon as possible."

Cassius smiled warmly. "Nevertheless, my offer yet stands."

A sudden clamor interrupted their conversation and brought both men instantly about. They set off along the rampart at a dead run, and as he sprinted past the defending soldiers along the lip of the crenellated wall, Joktan shouldered his bow and drew his sword. He carefully dodged stray arrows that hissed through the open spaces between the battlements, then dove and rolled to safety as a stone launched from a catapult sailed dangerously past him. It struck with a heavy crash in a spray of shattered debris, mere inches from where he'd been a second before, and he sprang to his feet, continuing on without a pause.

Cassius bounded alongside of him, matching the savage's stride easily, even beneath the considerable weight of his steel armor.

Along the southern wall they could see soldiers pointing out into the darkness, their faces painted masks of fear and trepidation. Joktan skidded to a halt and peered over the wall at the ground below. Icy fingers stroked his spine, and the short hairs at the nape of his neck pickled and stood on end. The soldiers about him fell back in horror, and he stared grimly out at a visage that defied all natural laws of evolution. He heard Cassius suck in his breath sharply as he came to an abrupt stop beside the tribesman and instantly froze, gaping unbelievably at the nightmare before them.

Out on the plain, a ring of torches cast their lurid, flickering glow upon a vile and hideous creature that could have only been spawned in the nightmares of the sulfurous pits of Hell. The thing stood in the center of the circle. It's thick muscles stood out starkly along massive lengthy thews as it held its arms out to each side in a terrible stretching motion. Rippling and bulging impossibly, the creature flexed its gargantuan might and clenched its talons into dreadful fists the size of watermelons.

From a disproportionately small head, two tiny yellow eyes burned like smoldering brimstone in bony sockets. A slavering maw lined with a score of pointed fangs gaped open, forming a demonic grin that caused Cassius' legs to turn to jelly. The monstrosity stood erect, over twelve feet tall, and a thick, skinless tail trailed out behind it an equal distance.

Its body was a grotesque blasphemy of natural laws and evolution; a human form mingled with demonic contours. Instead of skin, a translucent slimy film covered its horrific body, and every fiber of the demon's muscles was plainly visible. Joktan could see its tendons, thick as knotted ropes the diameter of his forearms. They were a pale, yellowish color and contrasted vividly within red ochre musculature. It's bones looked like rusted iron, and the demon's legs seemed somehow too short for the mammoth body they supported.

Joktan was utterly repulsed by what he saw, but to him it was as though he were experiencing a flashback from the previous night's unholy encounter on the plains. He did not stare in frigid terror, trembling uncontrollably like those who stood beside him on the wall. His uncivilized intellect had not been trained since childhood to fear such creatures, be they born on Earth or in the fathomless rotting sewers in the dungeons of Hell. He did not question its sudden appearance, for in truth he'd placed himself upon the wall in expectation of just such a foe.

His only concern was whether or not it could be slain by mortal weapons.

The demon roared, it's voice a thunderous abomination to all human comprehension, and in that instant Joktan sheathed his blade and stripped the strung bow from his shoulder. To those about him it seemed as if an arrow appeared from nowhere in his bow; the next instant it sprouted between the corded muscles of the monster's chest.

The demon howled in a mixture of fury and surprise, then fixed it's gaze squarely upon the savage. It was a look that brimmed with untold malice, and it sent a shudder down his back. With one of it's huge, unsightly hands it clutched at the wooden shaft and tore it free, leaving a hole in its breast from which an oily substance that was its blood oozed forth.

"Go back to Hell, Dhampir!" the savage muttered, notching another arrow to his bow and taking aim. His words were answered by an appalling torrent of wretched mirth that spilled from the demon's rubbery lips.

"I am not Dhampir!" it cried. "I am Kawisu!"

Joktan lowered his bow a little and cocked his head to one side, scrutinizing his unholy foe. Then, with a careless shrug of his shoulders, he raised the weapon and took aim.

"I care not which devil you are!" he snarled, loosing the shaft and drawing another from his quiver with blinding speed. The demon Kawisu dodged the first with unimaginable agility, but the second caught him in the side. It ripped into the demon's torso, and the malignant creature screamed a ghastly roar. It stood upright in the center of the circle of torches and spoke in a language no human ear would ever understand.

*"Maliscannae uphan dario!"* Kawisu bellowed. His outstretched palms turned upwards, and from them flames of purple fire flared to life.

*"Maliscannae dinnath darsario!"* He continued, the volume of his voice now shaking the very ground on which he stood. *"Come forth into the night!"*

Joktan guessed what the demon was doing, and turned quickly to those around him. They still stood in abject terror, but his tone was such that they were instantly galvanized into action.

"Are you men or children?" he yelled, as though he were now their leader. "Arm yourselves! Bend your bows and slay that spawn of Hell! Do it now!"

As the men notched arrows to bowstrings and loosed a storm of feathered shafts, he grabbed hold of their captain and roughly shook him.

"Cassius!" Joktan shouted in his face. "Get your wits about you man!"

Reason suddenly rushed back into the captain's slack-jawed face, and his blankly staring eyes met the savage's burning gaze.

"I'm sorry…" he started, but Joktan cut him off abruptly.

"I don't have time to for this!" he growled. "That thing is calling up more of its kind. *You have to kill it now!*"

Cassius nodded, then turned to his men, but their momentary bravery had already faded. They stood staring in disbelief down at the plains. Joktan spun and peered out over the wall, and for a brief moment he too looked on in horror.

To the left and right of the demon Kawisu, as far as the eye could see, a horde of other demonic creatures began to appear. They were not nearly the size of their hellish master, being scarcely half as tall as the average man, but they were all identical to him in every other respect.

They sprang up from the earth and stood at attention, awaiting their leader's command, a grisly army of misshapen and skinless monsters. Joktan glanced in each direction, and saw that the demonic mob was spread out facing the city walls in a sweeping semi-circle. He couldn't even begin to guess their numbers; their lines spread out into the darkness seemingly without end.

Realizing that the soldiers would need another demonstration to bolster their courage, he grasped his bow and fired a dozen or more shafts in rapid succession. His skill with a bow was astounding, and every arrow found its mark. The victims sank to the ground, screaming horribly, clawing futility at the feathered cloth-yard shafts. With triumphant indignation, Joktan turned and shouted at the soldiers.

"They might be ugly!" he declared. "Hell, some of them might even be able to speak. *But they are not immortal!* Look down there at your foes; they are stricken down with a single arrow! Now stand like men and slay these sons of whores!"

The soldiers answered him halfheartedly, glancing timidly over the wall, and he continued with brash and determined vigor.

"These demons do not come to rob your gold and rape your wives! They've been conjured up by Skeltar, and they feast on human flesh and blood! If you do not stand and fight with every ounce of strength you've got, rest assured they will glut themselves on your families, and take your souls with them back to the foul pits of Hell!"

Their eyes grew wide as dinner plates as he confirmed their deepest fears, and Cassius looked genuinely distraught. But Joktan didn't care. On the contrary, he'd hoped for just such an effect. He knew that eventually these civilized men would turn and flee. He also knew that, no matter how educated one may be, every man was yet possessed of an animal's instincts, and a cornered beast with no hope of escape was a dreadful foe indeed.

"They may scale the walls, but if they do the advantage is still ours!" he cried. "Ply your bows now, while they stand there like idiots. Once they start scaling the walls, every other man drop his bow and flay them with your swords. This is your one chance, so choose now! Will you die like sheep, or fight like men?"

His words roused the soldiers immensely, and they let out a clamorous shout before turning to face their unnatural foes. Within moments the night air swelled with arcing shafts, a hail of death and slaughter that struck down demons in countless droves. Kawisu screamed unintelligibly at his minions, and suddenly they swarmed toward the mighty soaring walls of Zebulon. They closed the gap between their leader and the city within a matter of seconds, rushing forward wildly, an inexorable angry mob. They slammed against the stone wall, a surging tidal wave of filth, and with fearsome talons clawing desperately; they swept upwards, scaling the stone walls with impossible ease.

While half of the defenders pelted their demonic assailants with arrows, bolts and spears, many drew their swords and slashed as their foes attempted to clamber over the lip of the battlements. Others still lit torches under Cassius' command, using them to ignite the buckets of oil and naphtha that were poured out over the edge and set ablaze. This proved to be most effective against the ghastly horde, and they fell away shrieking insanely, flailing at the air. Still the demons came on ferociously like an endless sea of hate.

Joktan grimly reaped their preternatural lives in butchered scores. The shining blade of Avatare swirled about him like a windmill of dismemberment and slaughter within his iron grip, shearing hellish skulls and undead flesh with merciless abandon.

Around him soldiers met their death with panic stricken eyes, and many wailed like tortured souls as they crumbled, pitching headlong off the wall. Joktan's wake was a gory swath of broken, mangled ruin, but he knew that no amount of soldiers could stave off such innumerable odds for very long.

He glared over the wall as his blade ripped a particularly nasty demon into two separate halves, and spied Kawisu yet standing in his circle of torches. His arms were outstretched, and he continued to summon his horrible servants up from the pits of Hell in countless droves. Joktan cursed bitterly and snatched up a fallen crossbow, taking deliberate aim. He willed his chest to cease it's heaving, and eased his finger against slowly the trigger.

The bolt flew like a streak of lightening, and the tribesman's aim was true. Kawisu's attention was focused solely on his task. He didn't see the quarrel until it smote him deeply between the eyes. The demon's rage was instant. He toppled backwards like an oak tree hewn by a woodsman's ax. His visage was a twisted display of insidious, slavering wrath, as he tore at the earth and knocked over the torches that formed the circle as it thrashed about.

Pain was something foreign to a demon fresh from Hell, and as red-hot pangs of excruciating agony lanced through his skull, Kawisu lashed out violently at anything that was near.

Casting the crossbow aside, Joktan got the attention of all the archers in his vicinity. Kawisu was still writhing upon the ground, and the savage pointed with his sword, yelling to be heard above the din of battle.

"Shoot him!" he commanded. "Fill his carcass with arrows! I don't care if he looks like a pin cushion, don't stop until he's dead!"

The archers acknowledged his order, and swiftly directed a relentless stream of arrows at the wounded demon while Joktan scooped up a bucket of naphtha and swung it in a circle about his head. He released his grip and the pail fell away, landing within several feet of where Kawisu lay. He must have done this half a dozen times or more before actually hitting the demon, who screamed even louder as the flammable liquid spilled onto the ground and soaked into his open wounds.

Two archers had already guessed Joktan's intent, and brandishing flaming arrows, they took aim and loosed upon the suffering fiend. Seconds later the demon burst into flame with an incredible shriek, becoming a fallen statue of living fire. Joktan was astounded by the rate at which the demon's body burned. The flames incinerated his unearthly flesh in scarcely more than a couple of minutes, leaving behind a smoldering pile of pale, white ash.

A triumphant shout was raised and carried on down the embroiled line of weary defenders, yet the demon's horde continued to pour over the walls. Kawisu had managed to summon thousands of the creatures before Joktan could slay him. A quick look around told him that the soldiers were slowly losing the fight, but the fact that they rallied to meet their foes with brave determination gave him at least a little hope. He jumped back into the fray with a savage battle cry from his homeland, startling both men and demons alike.

His blade wove a pattern of death and destruction. It cut through the demons with such tremendous ease, that often times it struck the stone of he wall behind them, hewing great chunks of rock from the battlements as if they were butter. Few living men had ever heard of Avatare, and fewer still knew the shining blades true design and purpose. None on the wall that day knew except for Joktan, and the brutal savagery he unleashed with the mythical weapon grasped tightly between in hands inspired those about him to even greater ferocity.

Suddenly a distant flash from Skeltar's camp caught his eye. A searing silver radiance dispelled the darkness as completely as the brilliance of the sun, and a dazzling globe of light some nine feet in diameter rose up silently into the air.

The soldiers upon the walls stood agape in wonder, and even Kawisu's legions halted their assault abruptly. The orb floated upward slowly, then sat motionless as if suspended by on an invisible thread.

Then suddenly it shot toward the city with uncanny speed. It passed through the thick iron gates as if they had not been there at all and darted into the city like a streak of lightening.

Joktan watched the strange ball of light settle in an empty street.....which he judged to be somewhere near the warehouse district....where the silvery effulgence inexplicably winked out. It was much too far away for him to discern the exact location, but an inexplicable feeling of apprehension gripped him, and he began to work his way toward a flight of stone steps which led down steeply from the walls.

As he moved nearer to the stairs the demons resumed their attack with renewed vigor, and Joktan glanced down from the battlements as he hacked a path through the screaming horde. In that moment he was witness to a truly grisly sight. The horde of demon creatures did not only rush the city. Here and there large groups of the bloodthirsty devils were embroiled in a bitter battle with each other, and their gory prize was plain to see.

While Skeltar's men had been busily attacking the city with their catapults and battering rams, the demons had sprung up behind them. Now all that remained of the wizard's fledgling force were desecrated carcasses and corpses torn limb from limb. The demons were feasting not only on the bodies of Skeltar's men, but also on the broken wreckage of the soldiers who had fallen from the top of the city wall.

With a sudden shudder, Joktan quickly descended the steps, then turned into the street below and raced down it in the direction of the mysterious light. The streets were nearly deserted. All of the citizens had fled to their homes and no doubt bolted the doors, while the bulk of Zebulon's soldiers had been ordered to defend the walls.

It was a strange feeling that gripped the savage as he hastened down the empty thoroughfares. The oppressive darkness was illuminated brightly by the flickering glow of countless torches. Placed at regular intervals along the streets, they were maintained nightly by the city guard, yet furtive shadows lingered as he went along. They crept eerily over the paving and cobblestones, and a chilling atmosphere of unseen menace caused the hairs along his neck to stand on end.

With bared steel gleaming reassuringly in his fist, the savage ran as fast as he could go. He made every attempt to be stealthy in his approach, but speed and silence do not make for a very compatible mixture. To Joktan's ears his footsteps sounded like the charge of an elephant, although in reality no other man in the city could have moved at such a speed and made so little noise.

Rounding a corner, he found himself in the area where he judged the light to have been before it had vanished. He saw nothing, and he paused a moment to catch his breath while gazing about into the gloom. He couldn't help but notice the pale, dense mist that seemed to roll along the streets. Joktan turned to better see behind him into the dimly lighted darkness, and icy fingers running down his back raised gooseflesh along his spine.

He was standing before the temple of Dhampir.

The savage growled throatily, and his grasp tensed upon the grip of sword. *Was this merely coincidence?* He wondered, then unconsciously shook his head. No, chance had nothing to do with it, he mussed. Obviously Skeltar had come this way for a specific reason. *He must be preparing to summon Dhampir inside the temple........!*

Joktan glanced about quickly, his keen eyes probing the shifting shadows, but seeing no one, he stepped forward, his feet treading lightly without a sound. *It was time to fulfill his oath!*

The temple was a massive bulk hewn of marble and limestone blocks. Of circular design, the building was a forbidding example of the malevolence that Dhampir represented. Six tiers of steps ran in a semi-circular arc before him, rising toward the temple entrance.

At the top of the stairs, thirteen pillars supported set at equal distances from each other supported a narrow overhang high above. Each had been carved of solid stone, into the likeness of hundreds of human skulls piled one on top the other.

A single pair of heavy mahogany and bronze doors led inside, guarded to the left and right by massive demonic gargoyles. The huge clawed feet of these forty foot high sentinels of stone rested firmly upon still more human skulls, while their jaws gaped wide in a terrible snarl of deadly looking fangs.

A spire atop the lofty roof pierced the heavens, a massive copper-plated spear point thrust up angrily in defiance of the gods of men.

Joktan was halfway up the steps when the light rustle of fabric, accompanied by the muted metallic clink of steel armor caused him to wheel about. He stood ready for action, the muscles in his legs tensed to spring, his sword held ready to block some unseen blow. Across the street a cloaked figure detached itself from the shadows and moved hastily toward him. The savage stood motionless, watching the mysterious person move closer, while keeping a wary eye for further signs of danger.

"Halt!" Joktan shouted, his voice echoing loudly off the stone buildings that lined the street on every side. The stranger did not stop, but continued toward him intently as before. There was a sureness in his step, a confidence in his gait, and a bared short-sword in his right fist.

"Hold, dog!" the savage commanded. "Any closer and your blood will wet my blade!"

The figure was that of a soldier, and he threw off his cloak without breaking stride. "I do not take orders," he replied, without the slightest hint of emotion. "I give them. Prepare to die!"

"Who are you?" Joktan demanded as the soldier started up the steps. He couldn't see the man's face clearly, and his voice was unrecognizable.

"My name is Brutus," the soldier replied, moving more warily now. "I was once a servant of the king. Now I am the right hand of power, you might say. Skeltar will soon rule the world, and I will lead his armies against every nation!"

"I care not about you," Joktan growled. "My business is with your master."

"Then it is also with me."

"Dagon and Mithra!" the savage cursed. He wanted to get to the wizard before he had a chance to summon his demon. It would be difficult at best for him to fight either one of them on their own, but together they would be nearly impossible to defeat. The longer he toyed with this brute, the harder it would be to kill Skeltar.

Brutus was circling him now, like a timber wolf sizing up its prey. He was a foot taller than Joktan, and from the looks of his bulging muscles, very strong indeed. His chest was broad, his head protected by a gleaming helm. His hands were like meat hooks. In the left Brutus held a small, circular shield known as a buckler. *Definitely not standard issue in the Straltonian military,* Joktan thought. It was about fifteen inches in diameter, and a long, pointed spike protruded from both top and bottom.

"I don't have time for this!" the tribesman grated angrily.

Suddenly another voice spoke from the shadows. "I do!"

From the shadows near the doorway of the temple, another figure stepped forward. Brutus, who had been moving in on Joktan, quickly put some distance between himself and his foe. He had no idea who had spoken, but the savage knew instantly.

Torches set in sconces upon the temple walls splashed lurid blood-hued images over the steps as Sheba stepped into the flickering glow and shrugged away her cloak. In one ivory fist she held a battle-ax, and a bared sword blade shone like molten silver in the other.

"What are you doing here?" Joktan demanded in surprise. "You are supposed to be…"

"Just go fulfill your oath," she interjected, a wicked smile playing upon her luscious crimson lips. "I'll take care of this dog!"

He glanced back at the soldier, then at her. "Let's take him together."

At that moment Brutus recognized this new opponent, and his heart skipped a beat excitedly as he backed away a little further. *This was the woman his master sought so badly! What a fortunate turn of events!* He frowned unknowingly as another thought suddenly crossed his mind.

Skeltar wanted this wench alive, and unharmed. The wizard had been clear about that.

He studied the warrioress closely, careful to maintain a wary distance from both her and the savage. She was beautiful, that much was obvious. Perhaps more attractive than any woman he'd ever seen. The soldier was sure that she would be easy to overpower. She was, after all, a woman. He could get in close and knock her senseless with the blunt side of his blade. But with the tribesman at her side, things would be much more difficult. His master would be exceedingly pleased with him for capturing the woman he so greatly desired. Hopefully Skeltar wouldn't mind if she sustained a few minor wounds in the process....

"You have other obligations," she objected, "and very little time."

Joktan glared at Brutus. His eyes noted every detail about the soldier in a single, measured glance. He cast another look at Sheba.

"Very well," he grunted. "Just be quick about it!"

*Be quick about it?* Brutus thought. *What an insult! He would kill this savage once he'd captured the woman...*

"I'll see you shortly," Sheba promised. "Get going."

Joktan looked at her one last time, then turned and bounded up the stairs as she stepped forward to meet her foe. The clash of steel resounded sharply as his hand tugged at the doors, and he wondered if he'd made the right decision. He knew instinctively that the soldier didn't stand a chance against her, but even so, he hated leaving her there to face him alone. *What if something happens to her.....?*

He banished the though from his mind as quickly as it had arose. He must have all his senses focused on the task at hand. The wizard would doubtless try to use some fell magick against him.

The interior of the temple was just how he remembered it. He padded silent as a phantom past a circular water fountain in the center of the foyer. The object looked ancient, carved with blasphemous imagery that made it impossible to focus the eyes upon clearly. How any artisan could embellish on piece of stone in such a manner, Joktan didn't care to guess. Perhaps the hands that had worked upon that stone had not been human.....

Through the foyer, a curtained arched doorway opened into the outer courts. This was as far as most ordinary people ever went. There was a row of altars crossing the center of the chamber from left to right. Six in all, they were made of black, highly polished onyx, and each one stood three feet high. The rectangular surface of each altar was about four feet long and three feet wide, and it was upon these massive blocks that the priests sacrificed bloody offerings to their grim god at the request of his worshipers. Such rites were designed to grant the supplicant certain favors from Dhampir, and were performed by the priests for anyone who could come up with enough gold. Arching upward, the walls disappeared into the lofty blackness.

Past these Joktan stole, slipping like a shadow over the cool stone of the floor toward the next doorway that loomed before him in the darkness. This door led into the inner court. Only priests were allowed to enter this area. The thought caused a horrible smile to form upon his lips; this was the second time he'd stood in this forbidden place.

Joktan strode quickly over to a grotesque, brazen idol. The thing stood nearly nine feet high, grimacing down upon all those who stood before it. Unsightly hands clawed eternally at the air, and the savage paused for a brief moment, searching his memory. The ghastly visage was disconcerting in the gray gloom, and the statue's jeweled eyes seemed to glow with a faint, unnatural light. *Which hand was it?* Something Brutus had said suddenly jogged his memory. *The right hand of power…*

He climbed up on the brazen beast's lower feet and reached high over his head. The burnished surface was cool to the touch as his fingers closed around it; he pulled down, straining with all of his strength and weight combined.

The hand moved slightly, and a metallic click sounded loudly in the silence of the chamber as a hidden latch inside the idol was released. A panel concealed upon its belly slide open, and Joktan dropped to a crouch and slipped inside.

Here he knew a flight of stairs spiraled down into a winding maze of subterranean caverns. Along the walls, human skulls had been crafted into oil burning lamps, and their wavering flames lighted the passage. The savage moved cautiously, casting a wary glance at the macabre lamps that grinned hideously from their sconces.

From here the treasure vault was just a short distance. Perhaps he would return after he'd slain the wizard and his pet.. ….

A furtive sound behind him brought Joktan suddenly about.

"Dagon's bloody balls!" he swore, as a priest lunged at him through the air, a long slim dagger shinning in an outstretched hand.

Joktan sought to raise his sword and skewer the wretch, but the robed priest had caught him unawares, and it was too late. The savage barely had time to grasp at the hand that clutched the blade before the full weight of the priest slammed into him.

Both men struck the floor hard, struggling for ownership of the menacing blade, but the acolyte was no warrior. He was not accustomed to mortal combat, and in an instant Joktan's hand clamped down over his with a powerful twist. The priest stared in horror, seeing the glittering steel point now aimed directly at his throat, but he made no sound.

He fought frantically for a few seconds longer, and as he did, Joktan slowly pushed downwards on the blade. The tip of it touched the priest's throat, and his eyes grew even wider as a trickle of blood ensued. He was struggling now in earnest, but it was much too late. The savage grinned with pleasure as the blade sank into the center of his enemies throat ever so slowly.

He pushed it gently until the point struck the floor, allowing the robed assailant to feel every inch of the steel as it sliced through his esophagus. Then he wrenched the blade harshly from side to side, nearly decapitating the priest. His blood spilled over the floor and his head lolled to one side as Joktan withdrew the dagger and plunged it to the hilt into his chest. He waited for a second, until the man's nerves had stopped twitching and he lay still and limp; then the tribesman rose with a satisfied grunt of approval and continued on his way.

As he moved forward he passed by the corpses of numerous other priests. Some bore no visible clues as to the cause of death, while others were charred and grotesquely dismembered, as if their bodies had been ripped asunder by a mighty beast. The shear number of ruined carcasses spoke volumes to the savage. Skeltar was an unwelcome guest. He was cleaning house as he passed through these forbidden halls.

There were ancient runes and symbols carved in bold relief along the upper portion of the walls, and he noted them suspiciously. There was something about the way they swirled and twisted that seemed unearthly. Had he known that this mysterious script had been inscribed upon these very walls over a thousand years before, and that even then it had been all but long forgotten, he would have cared no more nor less. He stalked onwards, staring intently ahead as the grisly lanterns cast phantasmal shadows down the musty halls, descending ever deeper into the bowls of the earth.

Presently a faint voice reached his ears, and he moved towards the sound with grim determination. As he grew closer, the voice became more distinct. It rose considerably in volume, a series of resounding cries that reverberated hollowly through the subterranean corridors of decrepit stone.

Joktan pressed his back to the wall and crept nearer, listening curiously to the arcane intonations of an unholy language few mortals had ever heard even in the primordial eons of past centuries and ages. It was a tongue that had been birthed by an evil race which had once possessed vast knowledge and power. That civilization had crumbled to dust over three thousand years before Joktan had been born.

He peered around a corner to gaze into a vaulted, sprawling chamber, in the center of which stood a darkly robed figure before an altar of crumbling stone. The mage was caught up in his vile rite, his back turned, and Joktan stole towards him, his sword held firmly in both fists.

As he drew closer he raised his weapon and tensed for the attack. He positioned himself for a devastating blow, and as his blade began to move, so too did the wizard. Skeltar spun on his heels with uncanny speed and agility, and Joktan's blade narrowly missed its mark, cutting a long line down the sorcerer's robe.

The mage cried out in surprise, for the savage had caught him off guard, a feat which few men had ever been able to accomplish. With a terrible roar Joktan reversed his stroke and swung back sharply, and

Skeltar jumped backwards as the point ripped into his robe again. *Where did this savage come from?* He thought desperately. *Brutus should have killed him already!* His shock lasted only an instant.

The wizard gripped his staff with gnarled fingers and pointed it at the tribesman, uttering a hasty incantation just as Joktan's sword made a silver arc through the air that was meant for Skeltar's neck. A brilliant explosion suddenly burst before the tribesman's eyes, and the resultant crash shook the chamber violently.

Rotted stone rubble to plummeted down from the soaring ceiling that lost itself in the blackness above somewhere far above, and Joktan was lifted into the air and hurled backwards powerfully by an unseen force.

He smashed into the wall and crumpled to the floor, the breath nearly blasted from his heaving lungs. He had not, however, relinquished his grasp on his sword, and he staggered painfully to his feet as the wizard prepared another spell. He saw Skeltar's lips moving, and knew without a doubt that the mage was going to hit him with another devastating blow. He had to distract him long enough to get his breath back....to get close enough for another thrust....

"I know your reason for coming here, but you're too late!" Skeltar declared. "I have already spoken the conjuration. Dhampir is coming."

"Don't you know who I am?" Joktan gasped, swaying on his feet.

"It makes no difference who you are," the wizard replied dryly. "I've seen you many times in my scrying glass. I suppose you must have killed Brutus to have gotten past him, but he's unimportant now. And you are just another savage whose time has ended."

"You killed my father!" Joktan blurted.

Skeltar merely shrugged. "Perhaps," he replied carelessly. "If so, then he was just one of countless others. I'm sure it was nothing personal on my behalf. You must realize, Joktan. I've slain more men than the Black Plague."

"Aye, maybe so. But how many Watchers have you killed lately?"

His breath had returned, as had his strength, but Joktan continued to feign weakness in an effort to close the distance between himself and the sorcerer. Skeltar had his hands up in the air, as if preparing to launch another blast of power, but now he let them fall slowly as a dark frown settled over his urine-colored features. He moved thoughtfully toward the savage.

"Ah, yes!" he hissed. "Now it all makes sense! I must admit, I wasn't sure just how you fell into the picture, but now it's all perfectly clear."

"My father was a Watcher, and you trapped him, using me as bait," Joktan growled. "Then you sold me as a slave and slew him."

"Well, almost, but not quite," Skeltar sneered. "He's still alive, actually, although that little morsel of news will avail you nothing. The truth is, I wanted his blood. I thought it would give me immortality. As it turned out, his life force was too pure. It burned in my veins like fire, and instead of giving me life, it would have brought about my death."

He peered at Joktan from obsidian orbs that contained no apparent signs of humanity. "In my quest for immortality, I have traveled the entire world, but it has only been in the last few years that I've made my most startling discoveries. Your father told me much after I weakened him!"

"I have learned the origins of Sheba's bloodline. It was once very pure, but somehow it became polluted, and that blessed fact is what will make me live forever......once I've drained her of her blood!"

A sudden jolt from an upper level rocked the chamber, loosing more debris from the ceiling. Joktan used the commotion to move nearer ever so carefully, as bits of stone rained down about them.

"Why did you go through all these elaborate means just to enter the city? Why not use the tunnels that lead from your keep into the palace?"

"Because I couldn't!" Skeltar retorted. "They were constructed long ago by a witch. Some Elven bitch named Aradia," the wizard fairly spat the name out.

"Straltonia didn't even exist back then," he continued with a sinister laugh that almost turned Joktan's blood into ice. "Oh, I could probably explain the feminine powers of the Earth and Moons which she bound to her will, but your primitive brain would never understand such exalted concepts. Suffice it to say; very few men can pass through those tunnels without becoming hopelessly lost. There are some very unpleasant creatures that dwell in the lower pits. Xalton's women have no idea, believe you me! Yet they are protected, and men are not, unless they are closely guarded by a woman."

"Elliasha could have brought you through," Joktan offered, inching a little closer.

"She was a corpse," Skeltar laughed. "She had no true soul within her. Even if Elliasha could have brought me through, the other women would have killed me as I entered the king's chamber."

"There are other reasons as well, else I would have used the tunnels straight-away. At any rate, I needed Sheba, and I also needed the talisman which you possessed."

He pointed a withered finger at him accusingly. "You caused me a great deal of trouble by selling that thing to the innkeeper."

Joktan simply shrugged. He was almost close enough for a thrust....

Skeltar's hand flashed out, moving too fast for the savage's eyes to follow, and four blinding rays of electrical energy erupted from his fingertips.

The luminous glow struck Joktan's chest with all the power of a sledgehammer, and he staggered backwards as tendrils of lightening danced over his mail armor in brilliant hues of purple and blue. He'd never believed that pain could be so consuming. The arcane power forced the air out of his lungs, making breathing impossible, and his mouth worked instinctively, but to no avail. Sweat poured down his brow in salty rivulets, and he sank to the floor gasping like a fish plucked from a stream.

"Did you think I was too stupid to notice you moving in?" Skeltar hissed venomously. "Ha! You are truly more simple than I thought you to be."

Joktan sprawled upon the floor, gasping raggedly for breath as the wizard's burst of arcane energy crackled and slowly dissipated. Another mighty surge shook the chamber, and cracks spread out like spider-webs across the checkered marble floor. A massive chunk of stonework was torn loose somewhere in the darkness up above them, and it plunged to the floor with titanic force, in an explosion of rock and debris.

As more and more pieces of rock began to rain down, Skeltar hastened toward the door. Joktan tried to move, but the pain from the wizard's arcane power was still coursing through his body. It numbed his nerves, rendering his arms and legs unresponsive, and molten anger welled within him at the prospect of dying helplessly in this ancient forsaken tomb of rotted stone. He'd expected the mage to slay him outright, but now he saw him moving hastily toward the entrance. As he was about to make his exit, the wizard turned and sneered at the struggling savage.

"These tremors are made by Dhampir. He is rising from the Underworld, and will be here any moment! I would love to stay here longer….at least long enough to watch you die….. I'm sure I could have used your blood in some very worthwhile endeavors too! But alas, time does not permit. This chamber is about to collapse, and before your body regains its strength, you will be crushed to a bloody pulp. I will be sure to give Sheba your regards!"

"Thanks," Joktan glared at him bitterly, trying in vain to move his legs. The fingers of his right hand were still clamped firmly around his sword, though how he could never know, and the agony he felt was so excruciating that every ragged breath felt like a red-hot dagger was being thrust into his chest.

"Think nothing of it," the mage replied with mock sincerity. "It's the least I can do." The unnatural rattle in his voice made Joktan's flesh begin to crawl.

Skeltar turned away with a pompous smirk and disappeared into the passage, leaving Joktan alone to die upon the ruptured floor. He mentally willed his body to move as fist-sized chunks of falling stone brutally pelted him from above, but his muscles would not respond, and he felt his last remaining strength begin to fade.

Each shallow, gasping breath felt like he'd sucked in a living flame. It cruelly burned his dusty throat and seared his aching lungs. Then the room was swallowed up in blackness and his consciousness departed. His body went slack and limp, and the chamber crashed in around him like a tidal wave of jagged stone.

# 24

*I see them anxious in the dark,*
*Almond-shaped, obsidian eyes,*
*I know they wait to tear my flesh apart;*
*Just enough to keep me terrified.*
*I hear their claws rip at the floor,*
*Searching the circle for a door,*
*And when it finally breaks in here,*
*I'll be suffocated in my fear!*
*I called to what I did not know,*
*And something answered from below;*
*I feel its breath against my face;*
*Something unholy fills this place!*

----Excerpt from "Something Unholy"
by Azriel St. Michael

As Joktan disappeared through the temple doors, Sheba closed in upon her foe. She immediately sensed the soldier's apprehension, and instantly decided to take advantage of it.

"I don't want to kill you," Brutus told her. "Throw down your weapons!"

Sheba snorted derisively. "You *can't* kill me, dog! Why don't you throw down *your* weapons?"

"I can't do that."

"Then I'll just have to persuade you!" she snarled.

He didn't relish the idea of hurting a woman, much less slaying one, and her incredible beauty made his predicament all the more difficult. This was a woman he would love to bed. Perhaps after he knocked her senseless…..

Sheba's sword stroke was a gleaming flash of razor steel, delivered with all the strength and fury at her command. Brutus blocked the blow with the small shield on his left forearm, cursing as a shower of hot sparks stung his face. The power behind her attack sent a numbing shock wave up his arm and split the tiny shield almost in two.

The soldier staggered backwards, momentarily startled by the shear ferocity of the blow, but already her ax was streaking toward his head as Sheba lunged in with a wild scream. He parried the weapon, twisting to his right and taking another step back, stabbing at her with the steel spikes on his nearly riven shield. She was too close to avoid the thrust, and the spike drove deeply into her unprotected right thigh.

Sheba howled painfully as blood spurted from the wound. Brutus felt a triumphant thrill course through him and sought to rip the spike from her flesh. The struggle would be over even sooner than he'd expected! But he was not prepared for her next move.

Instead of retreating, the woman dropped both her sword and ax. She grasped the shield by the uppermost spike with her right hand. Her fingers gripped like talons, locking the soldier's arm against her thigh, and as he raised his sword she grasped his breastplate with her left hand. Bending at the knees, Sheba jerked his upper body down and forward at the same time. Brutus lost his balance and cried out in surprise as the warrioress suddenly rolled over backwards, violently pulling him with her. He pitched headfirst over the woman's lithe body, smashing into the stone steps as her momentum brought him crashing down.

His mouth struck the limestone stairs in a bloody crunch of shattered bone and teeth. Brutus' front lips split open as they smashed into the unyielding stone. His left arm, pinned to Sheba's thigh at an awkward angle, made a sickening sound as the bones in his forearm snapped and his shoulder was dislocated simultaneously. Sheba screamed as the spike was wrenched out of her thigh, and together they tumbled down over the steps of the temple.

The soldier's steel helm was knocked off of his head in the scuffle. It clattered down the steps with a hollow metal ring. His left arm was useless, and as agony shot through the torn ligaments in his shoulder, he tangled his fingers into her thick, red hair, attempting to smash Sheba's head against the steps.

She snarled like an enraged beast as his hand pulled at her hair. Her long fingernails raked strips of bloody flesh from his face, attempting to gouge out his eyes. Brutus roared murderously, his features quickly becoming a mangled, gory mess, and Sheba assailed him with a series of powerful kicks and punches. His armor protected him, however, from most of the woman's strikes.

She shrieked insanely with frustration as her fingers wrapped about the corded muscles of his throat. Her grip was unbreakable, and he sputtered, choking for air as she locked her slender legs around him and they tumbled further down the unforgiving stairs.

They landed abruptly on the cobblestone street below, and Brutus used his considerable weight to maneuver himself on top of her. Sheba still grasped his neck relentlessly, her fingers digging deeply into his skin, but Brutus ignored the terrible pain, ripping a long dagger from its scabbard upon his hip. Sheba growled angrily, knowing that if she released her hold she was done for, and her fingers tightened like an iron noose on the soldier's throat.

She saw the flash of steel as his dagger plunged towards her, and managed to raise an elbow to block the movement of his arm, then she let go of his neck with her right hand and grabbed the small shield on his useless left arm by the steel point that had pierced her thigh. Brutus tried in vain to pull his broken arm free, and gathering all her strength, she thrust at his damaged shoulder.

Sheba's terrific force drove the upper spike into the unprotected flesh between his neck and collarbone. The diamond tip went through completely, stopping only when it hit the armor plate on the soldier's back. Unbelievable pain shot through the soldier's body like a white-hot saber, and he twisted away instantly, screaming in anguish as a crimson fount poured down his polished breastplate.

She let go of the spike and clenched her fist, striking him full in the face with a stunning, well-aimed punch. He reeled backwards, stars dancing before his eyes, and Sheba rolled onto her left side. Bringing her right knee up to her chest, she kicked him away with and scrambled free. The warrioress jumped to her feet and stepped back, glaring maliciously at her foe, her ample breasts heaving from exertion under the brazen cups that scarcely restrained them.

Brutus staggered to his feet and stood before her, his dagger held tightly in a huge, bloody fist. Sheba instantly reached for a blade of her own. Her hand grasped only an empty sheath, and she realized that her dagger had been lost in the fray. Brutus laughed at her like a madman, his breath coming in labored gasps.

"Give up, she-devil!" he hissed, spitting broken teeth and blood. His grin was truly frightening to see, and Sheba circled him warily. "This could have been a lot easier, you know."

She said nothing, and as they continued circling each other, Brutus suddenly looked down at her leg and gasped in disbelief. *"It can't be.....!",* he started, his eyes bulging from their sockets. *"I stabbed you! I even saw the blood...!"*

Now it was Sheba's turn to laugh. "Fool!" she exclaimed. "You saw only a pretty face. You imagined to overpower me with ease, didn't you? And then what were your plans? To tie me down an rape me before handing me over to the lunatic you serve?"

"I thought to go easy on you, wench!" he snarled. "Now I see that I'm just going to have to kill you!"

"Come and get me then.....!"

Her words were cut off by the soldier's lunge. Sheba had misjudged him, thinking the man to be much weaker than he truly was, and she was caught off guard by the speed of his attack. She tried to turn her body to the side in an attempt to evade his thrust, but it was already too late. His dagger sheathed itself between her breasts, and she dropped to her knees like a stone tossed to the sea as he stepped away.

The pain she felt at that moment was more intense and bitter than any she had ever known, and her long locks fell spilled over her shoulders and onto the ground as she stared down in amazement at the worn leather grip and jeweled pommel protruding from her chest.

Brutus shook with wretched mirth as he stood in triumph before her.

*"Bitch!"* he yelled venomously. *"You're not so tough now, are you!"*

Sheba didn't hear him. The only sound her ears detected was that of her heart pounding like a drum, and as the soldier voiced his ire and spewed his wicked glee in dreadful tones, she slowly placed a pale hand on the hilt between her breasts. She could feel her life-blood spilling down her back, rilling in a scarlet stream upon over her rippled abdomen and shapely legs.

With her teeth clenched firmly in grim determination, she readied herself for one more burst of searing pain. Then as Brutus laughed insanely, she tore the dagger from her chest with an awful cry. The soldier heard the scream and his laughter grew even more extreme.

He didn't seem to notice as the wounded woman rose. There was purpose in her burning gaze, a malice born in realms unnamed. She clenched the dagger tightly, as endless reams of untold bloodlust thundered loudly in her ears. She felt the open, gaping wound between her shoulders close, and watched as the stream of crimson disappeared upon her breast.

Suddenly she leapt toward the exalting man, and the expression on his gruesome features instantly changed to one of horror. She held the blade low, then plunged it deep into his unprotected groin, then wrenched it free and held it lightly at his throat. The utter blinding agony Brutus felt was unimaginable, the pain so excruciating that he couldn't even voice a strangled scream.

Sheba's left hand closed upon his throat, then she jerked the blade back quickly and let it rattle to the street. Brutus felt his blood spilling down his neck, legs and chest, and she turned his head harshly, forcing him to look her in the eyes. What he beheld was indescribable, an emerald sea of broiling hate. It was the last image that his mortal eyes would ever see.

With a vicious growl, Sheba sealed her lips over the soldier's bleeding neck and feasted like a ravenous beast.

# 25

The air was filled with the sweet aroma of wisteria and honeysuckle. It hung thickly about like a natural incense, offered graciously to the gods by the very Earth Herself. There was the familiar rustle of a soft breeze feathering playfully through green summer leaves; it was accompanied by the rich scent of fresh tilled soil and the gentle laughter of a quiet brook splashing over smooth rounded stones.

Birds gave voice to cheerful songs, each different and unique, and in the distance a chorus of ravens called, in answer to an eagles piercing shriek. Then the darkness gave way to golden sunlight in radiant silken strands, and a peacefulness that was profoundly enthralling seemed to permeate the very fabric of his soul.

Amid this tranquil setting Joktan felt at once overwhelmed and confused. Never had he experienced a dream so vividly real, and while he struggled to determine if it was nothing more than simply an extraordinary illusion, his attention was inexplicably distracted by the shimmering, golden splendor before him. Slowly he became aware of what it was that he beheld, and he realized with a sudden start that it was not the sun itself which he was seeing, but rather the sun's rays being reflected off of golden yellow hair!

This shocking discovery did little to diminish his confusion, and as he tried to make sense of it, the radiance shifted and turned, causing Joktan's eyes to nearly popped out of his head in amazement. Now he beheld the most exquisite pair of breasts he'd ever seen! They were deeply tanned and abundantly proportioned. This was a most pleasant dream indeed! He stared as if in a trance, then reached out and touched them, curious as to whether or not they were merely a mirage, but to his surprise, they felt compellingly real in every way.

*"Look at my eyes, Joktan!"*

It was a feminine voice which spoke; one possessed by a strangely familiar musical quality. The sound of it caused him to raise his line of sight instantly, and he found himself staring deeply into Lamashtu's cerulean eyes. He felt his cheeks flush with embarrassment, but she appeared to be somewhat amused, judging from the smile that graced her full red lips.

"Is this a dream?" he asked, more to reassure himself than anything else.

"No, Joktan," she replied. "This is not a dream."

"Then it is a vision of some sort," he decided.

"It is no vision."

He frowned apprehensively. "Then what is going on? I don't understand."

"It's quite simple, really," Lamashtu laughed. "You're dead!"

"What….?" he started, then looked around. "Is that supposed to be some kind of joke?"

"No," she replied. "You are very truly dead. Right now your body is somewhere beneath the temple of Dhampir, buried in a pile of rubble and broken stone. I simply drew your spirit to me."

"How?" he asked skeptically.

"I'm a Goddess, Joktan!" she exclaimed. "I can do anything I please."

He glanced about at the idyllic scenery. His eyes moved to her legs, then traveled upward gradually. "So this is the afterlife?" he wondered aloud.

"Is it so bad?" Lamashtu questioned. "An eternity here….*with me?*"

Joktan shook his head. "No," he chuckled, grinning sheepishly. "I suppose a man could do much worse!"

"It has been ages since I last enjoyed the company of a consort," the Goddess whispered.

"Is that why you sent me on a fools quest?" he asked. "Simply to die, and then join you here?"

"No!" she snorted. "I need you to succeed. I merely drew you to me because you died. It's not your time, trust me! You must go back!"

She threw her arms around him, and he responded impulsively to her embrace. He could feel the warmth of her naked flesh pressed tight against him as her lips touched his. She kissed him deeply, and then suddenly blew into his mouth and shoved him over backwards. As his body struck the ground she cried out. "Get up, Joktan!"

# 26

Sheba swooned as drunken ecstasy coursed through her pale form, and as the bloodlust gradually subsided, she released her grip on the soldier's lifeless body. The corpse dropped limply at her feet, the mangled, twisted, wreckage that had once been Brutus. She stood for a long moment, until she was certain that the wounds which the man had inflicted upon her were completely healed.

Then she turned toward the temple once more and climbed the steps, retrieving her fallen weapons as she went. She paused to peer up at the massive gargoyles before throwing open the temple doors and stepping cautiously inside. She noted that the sight of those stone guardians made her feel strangely ill at ease, but she pushed the thought from her mind and moved ahead. There should have been numerous priests roaming the temple, and the fact that she saw none only served to magnify her growing anxiety.

As she entered the inner court, her heightened senses detected the approaching rustle of heavy fabric. She recognized at once the distinctive sound of thick robes brushing lightly over stone, and hastened to conceal herself in the shadows along the wall beside a brazen monstrous image. Peering carefully around the idol, she saw another such metal sculpture nearby, from which the furtive sound seemed to originate. She crouched low, about to move forward, when a dark robed figure suddenly emerged out of the bronze statue's belly.

Sheba hesitated, pressing herself against the cool metal surface of the idol, as the figure moved across the chamber, staring down at the marble floor. It stooped down and touched a runic symbol engraved there. She heard the grinding movement of stone on stone and watched curiously as a portion of the floor parted and an elongated object slowly rose into view.

To her eyes it looked like an altar, a megalithic block of solid smoky quartz that had been skillfully worked by some ancient craftsman. It bore mysterious looking scripts along the smoothly polished edges, and one end appeared to be slightly lower than the other, where a silver bracket, embellished in swirling designs and adorned with jewels, had been purposefully affixed. Within this fixture rested an ivory vessel that sculpted into the image of a human skull. The likeness was exacting, save for the fact that the container was many times larger than any human head could ever be.

Along the face of the altar's flat surface, long, deeply etched incisions led from the higher elevation to the ivory vessel. They were stained darkly, and boldly contrasted against the lighter translucent stone in which they had been carved. Sheba's eyes narrowed as she noticed the silver manacles and cuffs fastened securely atop the stone. This altar had been designed specifically for human sacrifice, and the deep grooves leading to the ivory vessel functioned as channels, through which the victim's blood would flow and be collected within the skull-shaped container at the lowest end.

The robed figure circled the altar, running his hands lightly over the crystalline surface, and for a brief second Sheba saw his face. She knew instantly that it was Skeltar, and sudden hatred flickered deeply in her emerald gaze. She crept forward unconsciously, her knuckles tensing whitely around the grip of her unsheathed sword, and suddenly the wizard spoke. His voice was a dry hiss, and his tone was most unpleasant.

"Come into the light, Daughter of Cihuacoatl!" he intoned.

She froze in her tracks, wondering how on earth he could have seen her, and Skeltar continued in answer to her unspoken question.

"I heard your thoughts," he stated. "Extreme emotions are the easiest to detect. It's no great feat, but that is something you already know."

Slowly she stood, sword held out before her, moving warily toward him. The wizard peered at her from beneath the thick concealment of his dark hood, and his grin was a horrific sight.

"I saw the mess you made in my keep," he sneered. "Impressive, I must say." His expression changed abruptly and his eyes burned like molten steel. "You have no such power here though, and that sword will be of no use whatsoever. You might as well put it away."

"I don't think so," Sheba snarled. "Come a little closer and I'll gladly test your claim!"

Skeltar glared wickedly. "Very well."

Suddenly he was standing beside her, and she let out a startled cry as his thin, skeletal hand closed tight about her arm. A jolt swept through her muscles and her hand released its hold upon the sword. She gasped in terror as a wave of numbing energy shot down her spine, and as her head began to swim, her vision blurred surely. Her knees sagged, and she dropped to the floor like a rag doll as darkness engulfed her senses. The last sound Sheba heard as she blacked out was the clang of her sword striking the stone floor, and Skeltar's lurid peels of malignant laughter.

# 27

When Joktan came to, he was already running down the dimly lighted passage. He wasn't sure just how he'd escaped from the collapsing subterranean chamber, nor how he'd managed to arrive so near the winding stairs leading up out of those ancient halls. His last memory was Lamashtu's kiss, and he wasn't even sure if that was real either. All he truly knew was that Skeltar had escaped him, and he cursed himself for being a fool as he dashed recklessly up the steps inside the brazen idol's belly.

A savage did not accept defeat with the same begrudging reluctance of civilized men. The wizard may have managed to thwart him for a moment, but he was as good as dead once the tribesman found him. As he burst into the inner court of Dhampir's temple, he felt the floor beneath his booted feet began to swell, and he skidded to a halt as his eyes absorbed the scene before him.

Skeltar stood before an altar that had not been there before, his arms spread wide within the loose folds of his dark robe. Sheba lay starkly naked upon the crystalline stone, her arms stretched out over her head. Her wrists and ankles strained against silver clamps that held her fast upon the altar. Her large breasts heaved as she struggled furiously to free herself, but her desperate efforts were utterly useless.

The wizard bellowed unholy incantations in some ancient forbidden tongue, and Joktan's eye narrowed into thin slits of burning hate as he glanced toward the lofty ceiling.

Suspended there by thick chains was a bronze grill, roughly the same length and width of the altar below. From it protruded hundreds of long, pointed spikes, the purpose of which was immediately clear. This madman sought to impale Sheba, collecting her blood in the ivory vessel for use in some foul rite of godless perversion.

As Skeltar chanted, his voice rose in volume. The savage noticed instantly that the spiked grill had already begun to descend, being lowered with slow and steady deliberation.

His gaze searched the chamber for the mechanism by which the grill was controlled, and presently he spied a series of iron levers mounted upon the opposite wall. This caused him great concern, for while he needed to free Sheba, he also had no desire to be in close quarters with the mage. The electrical assault he'd suffered earlier was still vivid in his mind. He still wasn't certain if his vision of Lamashtu had been real of imagined, but he was of no mind to find out.

A sudden tremor shook the chamber, and Skeltar's incantation rose in pitch and frenzied fervor. Joktan stalked forward, moving as silent as a ghost, but he'd taken only a few short steps when another mighty jolt rocked the temple from below. The marble floor became a spiders-web of cracks and fissures, and he lurched unsteadily. He regained his balance quickly as the quaking subsided, but to his dismay the mage had seen him. Skeltar howled bitterly as he stared at the tribesman with hellish rage.

*"You!"* he screamed. *"You should be dead!"*

"I was," the savage answered with a spiteful growl. "Now it's your turn!"

Skeltar ignored the comment. "Did you like my Witch-fire?"

"I loved it!" Joktan spat. "Made me feel all warm and tingly inside....just like you're going to feel when this blade cuts through your innards!"

"Not likely!" the sorcerer condescended. "Do you recognize this?" He held up the talisman that Joktan had sold to the innkeeper Paltro in Luxantia.

The savage made no reply, except to grip his sword more tightly.

"This time I'll be sure to send your soul to Hell!" Skeltar declared. "I'm not without generosity, however. I'll be sending your whore along as well......to keep you company!"

Joktan cast a furtive glance toward the spiked grill. It was now several feet from Sheba's supine form. He knew that in a few minutes she'd be a bloody pincushion if he didn't do something fast.

Skeltar noticed his gaze, and his eyes shifted briefly in Sheba's direction. It was only for a split second, but it was all the time the tribesman needed. He sprang like a tiger, leaping at the sorcerer with a barbaric cry. His sword slashed through the air even before his feet touched the ground, but at that moment the chamber shook violently and the wizard was knocked off his feet. He went sprawling across the floor with a startled shriek.

It was the only thing that saved Skeltar's skull from being hacked in two by Joktan's blade. The tribesman's sword cut empty air where the mage had stood an instant before, and he too lost his footing as he came down upon the heaving, shattered floor.

He slipped on the ruptured tile, and his broadsword was jarred from his grasp by the impact, sliding hopelessly out of reach. No sooner did he regain his feet than the chamber erupted in thunderous chaos. The marble floor burst asunder as if from some titanic subsurface pressure, sending massive chunks of splintered stone and rubble high into the air.

Stained glass fell from the domed roof, and black smoke issued forth from gaping fissures as if from the bowels of Hell itself. The air was filled with a sulfurous, rotten, stench. It was at once noxious and nauseating, and Joktan's eyes burned from the acidic fumes. The spiked grill jerked and halted in it's decent, a mere foot above Sheba's naked form. It creaked on the rusted chain from which it hung, swaying ominously from side to side.

Now a yawning open pit dominated the space that had been the center of the chamber floor, spewing a column of broiling smoke and ash, and from this billowing haze lunged the most dreadful creature that Joktan had ever seen. He looked at the wizard, whose expression was now one of uncertainty. It was clear that Skeltar had not anticipated these events. Slowly the mage rose to confront the hideous demon that stood before them, its awful body and features wreathed in dense clouds of vaporous smog.

Its slavering maw displayed rows of dreadful, lengthy teeth as it vented its wrath. Its very flesh appeared to Joktan like plates of blackened steel as it peered about the ruined chamber intently. Dhampir's gaze passed over him with hardly a concern, then came to rest squarely upon the sorcerer.

As it stared at the wizard the demon's visage took on an indescribably fearsome aspect, and Joktan recognized the intent behind that hellish look. It was one of vengeance, and of undisguised malice. For the moment he felt thankful that he was not the one on whom that terrible gaze was affixed, but he also knew things would quickly change once the demon had satisfied it's current unholy desires.

The savage cast his eyes about the room, looking for his sword. He spotted it lying a few feet away amid a pile of dust and debris, and moved warily towards it, praying to the gods that his actions would go unnoticed. Sheba was still fastened securely to the crystalline altar. It was located behind the demon, obscured by smoke and dust, but soon she would be noticed. It was just a matter of time, and Joktan shuddered as the words of Nischoaz echoed in his mind. *We all want her....*

"The mighty sorcerer Skeltar!" the demon roared. "We meet again."

"I have summoned you this night, Dhampir," the wizard intoned, "to release your legions upon this city. Let them feast on human flesh and blood!"

"Oh, I will!" Dhampir sneered. "Make no mistake about that!"

The mage noted the demon's hostile intent and raised a withered hand. Within it he held a wand made of hazel-wood, inscribed with arcane symbols, while in the other he held a black magician's ritual iron sword.

"You will submit yourself to me, demon of the abyss!" he cried. "Remember, I have but to speak a word, and you shall be banished to your abode in the underworld for ever!"

"Try it, mage!" Dhampir dared him. "See what good it does you!"

Joktan stooped hastily and grasped his sword, then looked about suspiciously, thinking that surely they would have heard the rasp of steel on stone, but the demon and the wizard stood staring at each other. Their focus on each other was such that it excluded everything else within the room. The savage saw his opportunity and began to edge his way toward Sheba.....

"Get back!" Skeltar gestured with his sword and screamed an ancient incantation, and a bolt of brilliant light shot out from the blade, striking the demon in the chest. A resounding clap of thunder accompanied it, but if it was designed to repel the demon, it failed miserably indeed.

Dhampir charged at him, and in the next instant the wizard was lifted off of his feet to dangle helplessly from the demon's dreadful talons. The mage screamed arcane words of power, blasphemous and obscene, but Dhampir voiced his evil mirth with malignant joyous glee.

"I have power over you....by the....name of....." Skeltar started, but the horror cut him off.

"You cannot hurt me, mortal!" he roared deafeningly. "Where is your magick circle? Where are the supportive Elementals? Did you think yourself so powerful as to toy with one such as me, to bend me to your will without some true form of protection?"

Dhampir's laughter roared in the wizard's face. "You were wrong in Luxantia! I am no incubus or minor minion of the eternal abyss, but I played the part and you bought it like a fool! A wizard, of all people, should have known such things, but you did not."

"Let me go!" the mage demanded, but the demon continued without pause.

"From what source did you think my priests derived their power? I am a ruler, an ancient deity, which you shall soon discover while my servants torment your immortal soul!"

Skeltar struggled vainly in Dhampir's grip as Joktan jumped over a jagged crack in the floor and moved ever closer to Sheba's side. He suspected that he would be next on the demon's agenda, and he knew without a doubt that Sheba definitely was.

"I saw how you enjoyed the way I played with your little apprentice," the demon continued. "I could do the same to you, but that would be much too easy! If I kill you now, there will be nothing left to torment, save for your soul." He lifted the sorcerer slightly higher and peered into his eyes. *"And I have an extensive collection of those already!"*

Skeltar slashed at the demon's arms with his thin-bladed sword, but his efforts were wasted. It had not been designed for cutting objects that exist in the material realm. Dhampir shook the wizard like a leaf in a storm, and the talisman he'd so coveted slipped from an inner pocket and clattered to the floor. The frail man wailed hysterically, which seemed to further please the demon.

"My, my!" Dhampir exclaimed. "This is undoubtedly the most emotion you've displayed in years! It is believed by some that tears heal the soul......but I wouldn't get my hopes up if I were you!"

The wizard knew that he was done for. He'd underestimated Dhampir, made a disastrous mistake, and his trepidation was monumental. Never had he known such fear. His black heart beat a frantic rhythm, and at once he understood.

There would be no escape.

He screamed a frustrated, vulgar curse, but his captor paid no heed.

"I was once a god!" the demon declared, "and even now I am no less! My priests have spent thousands of years, dedicated to ancient rites and rituals, the origins of which even their sages no longer recall. They followed those precepts diligently, ever careful to give me only enough blood to allow me to maintain my physical form for just a few moments at a time within your world."

"Then you came along, a meddling, pompous wizard, and in one night you gave me more blood than I'd drank in countless eons. In truth I owe you much for that........but then you sought to make me your slave," he growled.

"I think it only fitting that you serve me instead."

Skeltar felt a sudden surge of hope swell within his breast. "I knew the legends!" he sputtered. "I gave you a pathway into the mortal world were once you ruled in blood. I even helped you destroy the ones that kept you in bondage in the abyss. No other priest or wizard dared to do such things......*yet I did!*"

"Of course!" the demon replied. "But only to make me your minion!"

"I made a .....mistake," Skeltar admitted in pleading tones. "Spare me now, and you will have the benefit of my magick!"

"I have no need of your sorcery. I have more power in my phallus than what you will ever possess! But perhaps I will spare you though......for the moment. It would be a shame to let you die so quickly."

"I agree!" the mage enthused. "You won't regret it!"

"No, I'm sure I won't!" Dhampir agreed. "This is what I shall do...."

The sorcerer's heart was pounding erratically in his chest. His mind raced, and he was so caught up in his own frantic thoughts that he did not even hear the ancient god that spoke to him. All he needed was enough time to retrieve the thorn he'd taken from Dhampir's phallus in Luxantia. With that he could cast a powerful spell upon him, without having to risk a face-to-face confrontation. All his carefully laid plans were now ruined, but perhaps he could yet salvage what he'd lost.....

"I'll permit you to live until you no longer amuse me," Dhampir continued. "With a tongue that cannot speak words of power, and lips that cannot form them. I will give you hands which are incapable of writing sacred signs, eyes that see only in darkness, and a form which even my legions from the Underworld shall look up with contempt!"

Joktan knelt at Sheba's side and spoke to her in lowered tones. "This is the second time I have found you naked and restrained," he commented, attempting feebly to lighten her mood. "It must be some sort of omen…."

"It is a sign that I'll be dead if you do not hurry up!" she gasped angrily. "This is not the place for your games!"

"Maybe later?" he suggested impishly, his eyes traveling quickly over her splendid form.

"Oh!" she growled, her beautiful features red with exasperation. "You are incorrigible!"

Joktan grinned, then tried opening the clasps that held her imprisoned upon the altar, but they would not budge. His gaze swept the chamber, and came to rest upon the rows of levers on the opposite wall. One had been struck by flying debris, and a stone shard the size of his fist was wedged between the lever and the mechanism it controlled. He surmised that this was why the grill had not yet fallen, and that perhaps one of the other levers would open the silver clasps on Sheba's wrists and ankles.

Knowing he had little time, Joktan began working his way toward the levers, trying his best to do so without bringing himself into the demon's line of sight. He would have to negotiate several gaping ruptures in the floor to reach the device, but there was no other visible alternative.

Meanwhile, Dhampir threw the wizard to the floor. From one of the demon's misshapen hands a green, slimy substance oozed, and he hurled it at the mage as he struggled to rise. Skeltar screamed horribly, and his dark robes fell away. He stood mortified, unclothed and trembling.

For a brief moment, he was a skeletal, twisted wraith. Then his flesh began to sag in drooping folds and drip onto the floor like melted wax, revealing in ghastly hues the underlying musculature, sinew, and bone.

From these skinless appendages and bones now sprouted coarse, sparse hair. Each black strand grew nearly two feet in length, while his fingers and toes slowly webbed themselves together. A corner of the mage's mouth split grotesquely across his cheek, transforming his disfigured features into a hellish abomination. His lips turned black and bulged with brownish, festering tumors, accenting a nightmarish maw. From it a thick, ocher tinted tongue lolled dripping a sickly, yellow puss.

The perversity of this mutation caused Skeltar unimaginable pain. He howled unintelligible sounds as a bulbous growth swelled out between his shoulders, forcing his upper body into a discomfiting, hunched position. The wizard's legs bowed outwards, and his arms lengthened unnaturally, until the parts of his hands that should have been his knuckles nearly scraped against the floor. His bitumen eyes became massive, obsidian orbs, protruding from wide, bony sockets with garish effect.

Dhampir's mirth was murderously insane as he watched Skeltar take an awkward, halting step. So horribly had the nails on his toes curved and spiraled that each step was utter agony. The mage looked down at his hands and moaned in anguish. They were four times their normal size and beaver-like, with tiny grayish claws sticking out of the webbed flesh were his fingertips might once have been. He covered his head and cowered beside a piece of ruined stonework, sobbing pitiful tears of sorrow. The salty fluid streamed down his wretched face from giant, wrinkled lids.

A host of feelings swarmed unbidden within the wizard's defeated soul, and for the first time in his life he knew what it was like to feel remorse. He understood the terrible pangs of self-loathing and regret. And he realized with absolute clarity that every despicable act he'd ever committed had been but a stepping-stone along the dark path which had led him to this appalling moment. He was weak and powerless, doomed to live at the mercy of a vile, heartless master, and he wept in bitter despair.

Joktan cleared the last bottomless crevasse with a running jump, landing roughly on his hands and knees upon the other side. Scrambling to his feet instantly, he didn't even notice the deep gashes on his legs, inflicted by the jagged shards of broken stone upon the floor.

A furtive glance told him Dhampir was still busily engaged with Skeltar. He rushed over to the lever mechanism upon the wall. Each iron arm was the thickness of his sword blade, and exasperation gripped him as he stared at the machine, bewildered.

There were nine levers in total, and they were all identical. He could find no marks or symbols that might give him a clue as to which one would free Sheba from her restraints, save for the lever that had been jammed by a chunk of fallen stone. He knew he must decide quickly, but which one should he choose?

Just then Dhampir turned away from his victim, convulsing with wicked mirth. Through the haze that roiling up from the open chasm he spotted Joktan along the wall a short distance away, and the interest painted upon his ugly face was sinister indeed. The demon roared mightily, a grim display of pointed teeth and deadly fangs, and the savage knew that his time for decisions had suddenly expired. He must make his choice, and do so now!

To her credit, Sheba lay upon the altar as silent as a ghost, and as Dhampir moved toward Joktan, the tribesman uttered an angry curse and placed his hand upon the nearest lever. Now he was the focus of the demon's attention.

It had been inevitable all along, but he'd hoped to have more time before the conflict began in earnest. Perhaps the devil wouldn't notice Sheba at all. He didn't want to think about what would happen to the woman if Dhampir saw her. As long as he could keep the foul horror occupied, she still had at least a slim chance of survival.

Joktan felt his heart beating faster. He saw the evil glare upon the demon's horrible features as it drew ever closer. Venomous drool dripped from it's menacing jaws, and the savage's right hand tensed upon the grip of Avatare while the other tightened on the knurled, rusty lever.

"Mithra, let this be the one!" he muttered, perspiration dotting his forehead.

He pulled the iron arm down firmly. Without warning, the huge marble tile beneath his feet suddenly dropped away into nothingness. A bottomless, black abyss opened to receive him, and Joktan felt his stomach turn as he plunged inexorably downwards.

# 28

Outside the entrance to the temple of Dhampir, the megalithic gargoyles began to tremble. At first the vibration was hardly noticeable, but the intensity quickly grew, and within minutes they shook as though rocked by a violent tremor. From somewhere deep inside of those gaping mouths, a subtle rushing sound escaped. It was accompanied by a loathsome stench and the distinctive, pungent reek of burning brimstone.

The strange noise grew in volume, and a vaporous green smoke wafted from each gargoyle's giant mouth. Soon the haze became a column, rushing out forcefully as if propelled by volcanic pressure.

Suddenly the smoke disappeared, and the terrible maws erupted from with a horde of hellish creatures bursting into the air. To those unfortunate observers that might of chanced upon the scene, it appeared as though the great stone beasts were spewing forth the nameless parasites that infest the darkest bowels of the infernal abyss. Few would ever live to testify that such appearances were, in fact, the awful reality.

The black legions of Dhampir streamed down the temple steps and into the city streets. Their numbers were incalculable, their aspects a hideous mockery of man, beast, insect and demon. Some resembled the locust horde that had ravished Luxantia, but they were few in number amid this uncountable host of angry horrors.

There were creatures in this blood-starved sea with leathery, bat-like wings, mutations with spidery legs and scorpion tails. Venomous slaver dripped in sticky strands from grinning mouths that brimmed with curving tusks and twisted teeth, and there were others as well....too terrible to describe....some of which were as large as a full grown man. They spilled out into Zebulon's streets in a mindless frenzy, an endless rush of blackened forms all desperate for human blood.

Dhampir's minions scaled the plaster walls of the city's buildings with eager haste. They poured in through doors and windows, an unstoppable swarm, like foaming waves sweeping over a floundering ship ravaged by a violent storm.

Merchants, nobles and commoners alike fell screaming beneath the onslaught, and a million phosphoric eyes gleamed with unholy madness as the residents of Zebulon were torn limb from limb in a bloody triumph of butchery and death. The demons preyed upon men, women, children and beast without discretion, and theirs was a gory feast of mutilated flesh. Many victims yet lived while the merciless creatures ripped strips of bloody meat from their ruined bodies.

That night upon the walls, soldiers fell in droves before the relentless assault of Kawisu's nameless horde. Their faces were tortured masks of unspeakable horror as they were buried under the crushing frenzy of a thousand shrieking devils. Fanged jaws opened widely to receive the fallen men, and the last breaths of Straltonia's finest soldiers were hurled against the gods in agonizing convulsions.

Cassius rallied his troops about him, and together they faced their nameless foes with brutal determination. They fought the demons back time and time again, but each counter attack or momentary victory was won at the cost of countless lives.

The parapets were soaked in a slippery mess of blood and demonic gore. Scores of infantry lost their footing and plummeted screaming to their deaths from the heights of the walls, and the short-lived cries of dead and dying became forever lost amid the cruel, screeching horde as it swept inexorably forward.

Not since the days of the Goblin Wars and Therion of old....that ancient mage of fabled myth and legend....had the civilized people of the world fought against such a hellish, bloodthirsty army. The carnage was extreme, the massacre indescribable, and the number of innocent lives lost that night was beyond reckoning.

Fires roared to brilliant life throughout the entire city, as people slowly realized that a flaming brand or torch could keep the demons well at bay. King Xalton gazed out from the pinnacle of Skeltar's keep, his features marked by grief and dismay, as the mightiest city of Straltonia gradually fell in utter ruin.

And somewhere close by....within the same fortress....another wizard fought a battle of his own against a demonic foe, and his daughter stood by his side embroiled in a desperate struggle with a huge, black hound from Hell....

# 29

Joktan cursed vehemently as he held onto the iron lever with a vise-like grip. He dangled inside a rectangular hole that plunged down eerily into nothingness. The lever squeaked and moved downwards in it's slot on the mechanism, until it had traveled as far down as it could go, and his hand slipped slowly down the knurled grip toward the end of the rusted bar. He realized with horror that only a few brief seconds remained before he lost his grasp completely.

Sheba felt a thrill of relief as the silver clamps around her wrists snapped open. She sat up instantly, only to see that the manacles about her ankles were still locked in place. She looked over at her clothes and weapons. They'd been tossed into a heap on the floor nearby, obviously by Skeltar when he'd placed her upon the altar. Try as she might, there was no way to reach them. She was still helplessly imprisoned unless she could find a way to free her feet.

Dhampir rushed at Joktan, and one of his dreadful hands swept out, plucking him from his tenuous hold upon the lever. The demon held him up for inspection, seemingly unconcerned about the bared yard of steel in his clenched fist, and the savage nearly wretched as the horror's breath assailed him.

There were numerous cuts and scrapes all over the tribesman's battered body. Several gashes were quite deep, and although he paid them little heed, they yet bled sufficiently to be of concern. As Joktan's blood ran down over his bruised flesh, Dhampir's nostrils flared and sniffed the air.

His tongue flicked out like a serpents, tasting the crimson flow, and instantly the demon's dreadful teeth clicked together. His lips fluttered as the dark Lord snorted in sudden surprise. Joktan was sprayed with slimy filth, and he hastily wiped at his face with his hand. The demon snarled and licked again, his horrible tongue moving with slow and deliberate strokes over the savage's bruised flesh, then he stared at him, his eyes wide in startled recognition. Without warning, Dhampir angrily hurled the tribesman to the floor.

The sheer force of the impact should have killed him outright, but as luck would have it, the creature that had once been Skeltar happened to be cowering nearby, and it was he who broke Joktan's fall with a pitiful cry. Even so, the savage's breath was knocked out, and he struggled to his feet, gasping for air. The demon leapt toward him, infuriated beyond belief, and the savage raised his sword, staggering to meet him.

"What trickery is this!" Dhampir stooped down to roar at him. "How is it that my ancient consort's blood flows through your veins?"

Joktan glared at the fiend, gripping Avatare in both fists, his ivory fangs gleaming whitely in a terrible grimace. "I drank her blood!" he replied tersely. "Now come close that I might spill yours and be done with it!"

"With what?" the demon scorned, "that tiny little toothpick?"

He frowned at the diminutive figure before him. "So tell me then, mortal, does Lamashtu yet haunt the ancient groves? Does she remember my name? What did she tell you about me?"

"I did not come here to have discourse with you," Joktan retorted. "I've come only to slay the wretch that once was Shamash."

"Do not call me by that name, fool!" the demon bellowed.

"What you are called matters little," the savage responded. "Go back to the abyss, or I shall gut where you stand!"

"Ha! I am immortal!" Dhampir laughed. "Has my wayward wife deceived you into believing that you can actually slay me? Take a look at the wizard behind you! He had magick to protect him, and to what avail?"

The demon paused to scrutinize him closely. "You I find most curious, however. It is no ordinary thing to drink the blood of a Goddess. She must be fond of you indeed! But who is she really? A mere phantom of the waste lands, haunting places long forgotten." He sneered luridly.

"She is but an ancient Queen no longer remembered….a goddess bereft of worshippers." His laughter was painful to hear, and a terrible sight to see.

"Her memory has faded from the minds of men. Now she is weak and powerless....yet I grow ever stronger! If she has set you against me, which she undoubtedly has, be assured that you will fail. No mortal can kill a god. Bow down before me, and your death will be quick and painless."

"I killed Kawisu, and Nischoaz before him," Joktan declared grimly. "Both of them boasted endlessly....just like you. Both of them claimed to be immortal, a boast you bellow as well." He twirled his sword and spat derisively at the demon's feet.

"In the end they bled like any other common foe, and I sent them back to the pits of Hell that spawned them. As for the manner of *my* death, that will be of my own choosing."

"You are mistaken!" Dhampir replied. "In truth it makes little difference to me, though. I will feast upon your flesh regardless."

The savage steeled himself for battle as the demon moved closer. "Tell me, where I can find Lamashtu?"

Joktan merely shrugged. "You figure it out, if you are such a powerful god." He whipped his sword through the air purposefully, and the silver glow lit up along his blade as he took a step forward, his jaw set firmly in determination.

"You will answer my questions as I desire!" the demon advised him menacingly. "I am the new ruler of the Earth! No other can save you now."

"I have no ruler and need no one to save me," the tribesman snarled. "By this sword I will save myself! I have no fear of you, for you are an abomination, and your time has ended."

"I can crush you like an eggshell!"

"Perhaps," Joktan replied dryly. "But I'm prepared to die, if need be. Are you?"

Dhampir was furious. He roared his anger deafeningly, and in that instant Joktan lunged like a striking cobra. His move was lightening, his sword a silver blur; and the demon had no time to react before the razor edge cut deeply into the inner side of his black, glistening thigh. The powerful slash opened a mighty wound, slicing to the very bone, and Dhampir howled in bitter agony. Even as he vented his rage, Joktan struck again and again. Avatare flashed about him, a steel whirlwind of gleaming vengeance, and the demon leaped away to glare at him insanely.

Dhampir's awful tail whirled through the air like a gigantic whip. He charged at Joktan while lashing out at him with the fearsome appendage, narrowly missing his head. It smashed into the floor around him with blinding speed and brutal force. The savage cursed, expertly dodging each titanic blow, then struck out at the monster with all his strength.

Dhampir's four arms were a nightmare of talons and gargantuan fists. Joktan thrust at the demon's belly, and the tip of his blade sank into steel-like flesh as though it were made merely of clay. He moved in closer as the horror shrieked, to jam his yard-long blade further into the creature's guts, but a well-aimed strike sent him suddenly sprawling across the chamber floor, his sword torn from his hands.

He grabbed desperately for a handhold as he slipped over the lip of a gaping fissure, then his fingers caught the jagged broken stone, and he held on for dear life. Joktan muttered vulgar oaths and pulled himself to safety, just as the razor edge of the demon's tail lashed out, carving a chunk of stone out of the floor beside him. He rolled to his left, then sprang to his feet and dove to retrieve his blade while Dhampir spun to meet him, his eyes broiling with hellish hate.

A horrible claw ripped through his mail tunic and tore a bloody furrow down his back. The savage ducked and swerved away, searing pain lancing up his spine. Never had he fought a foe so large and fleet of foot. Joktan's primitive reflexes were like those of a tiger, his agility and speed far exceeding that of most ordinary men. Yet compared to the demon's incredible dexterity, his responses seemed sluggishly slow, and he stumbled momentarily as the dark Lord swept towards him, screaming his unholy ire.

A frantic headlong leap brought him within inches of his fallen sword. He snatched it up and rolled, slashing wildly in defense. Two of the demon's misshapen hands groped at him amid the rubble, and the blade sheered through inhuman flesh and bone with a sickening, yet satisfying crunch.

Dhampir howled and cursed vehemently, spewing molten slaver. It struck the marble floor and burst instantly into flame, and the behemoth's tail slashed and thrust as if it had taken on a life of it's own.

Joktan jumped sideways to avoid a burning burst of preternatural flame, and one of the demon's talons tore painfully at his mailed chest. The steel link armor fell away as blood welled in the wound, and the tribesman felt his primordial instincts swell within his breast. An all-consuming anger filled his soul with animalistic ferocity. It was a rage no civilized man could ever imagine, let alone possess, and one which the demon could not have possibly expected to confront.

*"Why won't you just die!"* Dhampir snarled.

"You first!" Joktan retorted. Then he cried out. "Lamashtu!"

Dhampir's tail struck as if out of nowhere. The flat side of it caught the savage on the side of the head, a devastating blow that sent him reeling to his knees. Before he could move Dhampir smote him again, smashing Joktan to the floor with such force that for a brief moment his vision blurred and stars danced before his eyes. The demon moved in on him with deadly intent, his razor edged tail poised for an impaling thrust, when suddenly a feminine voice caused him to freeze in mid stride. It could not be heard by anyone else within the room, but Dhampir recognized it instantly. The voice spoke telepathically in an ancient, long forgotten tongue, a language no man had ever known, nor likely ever would.

# 30

"I see you!"

"Lamashtu?" the demon whispered, staring wildly about the chamber. "Where are you!"

"Where do you think?" came her gentle laughter.

"You are looking at me through the Face of Death," the demon surmised. "How predictable you are….too scared to show your face, even after all these years!"

"The last time I did that you tried to kill me," she reminded him softly. "I fear nothing has changed."

"I am the new ruler of this mortal world!" he declared proudly. "Do you think you can hide from me for ever?"

"Hide from you?" she queried. "I've never secreted myself away from anyone, least of all you! But you've been in the Underworld, skulking there for centuries."

"Remember the days of old?" he regressed, choosing to ignore her remark. "There was nothing withheld from us then…."

"Yet you lusted for more."

"Join me and we shall be great again!" the demon cried out. "Be my bride once more!"

*"Never!"*

Dhampir went into a frightful rage upon hearing her refusal. His eyes burned like molten lava, and flames of living fire kindled about his feet.

*"Bitch!"* he shouted. "I shall hunt you down, to the ends of the earth, if need be! I will capture you, and break you with my will. You shall beg for mercy, and in the end I will tear you to pieces upon your own sacred altar and feast upon your soul!"

"You are no god, Dhampir!" she sneered contemptuously. *"You never were!* Even from the first you were a devil, in that black stone you call a heart. It just took a while for your true nature to be revealed. But you are no more divine than the pigs which grovel at your vile and bloody altars."

"You were always such a pompous whore!" he snarled venomously. "Once I've finished with your toy here, I'll teach you your proper place!" He turned on Joktan suddenly, vomiting molten brimstone, and the savage's reflexes were greatly taxed in avoiding the searing blaze of demonic spew.

"How far you have fallen, Shamash!" the Goddess lamented tenderly.

The demon ceased its assault abruptly, seeking to cover his ears with nightmarish hands. *"Silence! I don't need your lectures anymore!"*

"Your glory was once brighter than all the stars in the heavens," she continued. "How I loved you then, even more than my own life! But you cared little about the depths of my feelings, and now at last, I cannot even pity you. What once was beautiful is now repugnant. Once my love for you blossomed anew each dawn within my breast, like the most exquisite crimson rose kissed by morning's silver dew."

Her voice hardened to an iron edge. "That love was burned to ashes in the fires of your hate. Oh! How I've wept bitter Ages for you, Shamash....*but now I weep for you no more.*"

From deep within the demon's awful throat a terrible sound escaped. He vented his indignation against the very Gods of heaven, and the chamber was shaken violently by the magnitude of his wrath. He screamed obscenities so profane as to make even the minions of Hell itself shudder in terror, and Joktan rose to his feet, Avatare gleaming like a bolt of jeweled lightening from his clenched and knotted fists.

"I built a weapon to destroy you, My Love," Lamashtu's voice rang clear and bright as a crystal bell.

"Then you are a greater fool than I thought you to be!" the demon growled. "No weapon will ever harm me!"

Just then Joktan lunged at the demon with all his might. His blade swung swift in a shimmering arc that smote Dhampir behind one knee. The steel sank through the devil's flesh with ease, severing muscles and tendons like dry, withered twigs. The demon howled in startled fury as the savage's sword smashed through the massive bones of his thickly corded leg. His putrid blood gushed out in an oily fountain of brackish filth. Dhampir stared at the unsightly wound with disbelieving eyes.

"It burns!" he shrieked, as though he'd never felt such pain before.

The dark Lord lurched forward uncertainly, and Joktan struck once more. This time his sword sheered away the demon's enormous phallus in a single up-handed sweep, sending the hideous organ flying across the chamber in a spray of unearthly gore.

The nightmare staggered painfully, his hellish features twisted in excruciating agony and grief. He screamed curses in a thousand different tongues and voices all at once, in the most unimaginable and blasphemous of tones.

Lamashtu's sardonic laughter reverberated within his head, a chorus of loving and cruel mirth which only a goddess could ever know and truly express. Her laughter drove Dhampir beyond the brink of madness as it echoed inside his skull.

*"Avatare is the blade that slays you!"* Lamashtu's voice proclaimed. *"The tears you made me cry tempered the steel that you now feel!"*

Joktan bellowed barbaric wrath and smote the wretch again. His blade fell like a woodsman's ax upon one of the demon's horrible arms, and it clove through those mighty, ghastly thews in a single, brutal stroke. Dhampir slavered rabidly, screaming murderous hate. His mangled stump spurted vile, dark fluid that gave off an acrid stench, and his razor sharp tail whipped towards the tribesman with impossible speed.

Miraculously the savage evaded the swipe, then spun with a chilling cry. His sword came down upon the monstrous appendage, cleaving it in two. The severed end writhed upon the floor like a wounded serpent before slipping over the edge of a gaping fissure and becoming lost in the bottomless depths below.

The realization that he was doomed drove Dhampir into a frenzy of desperate  madness, but Joktan swarmed upon the beast with a bloodthirsty vengeance pounding  thunderously in his ears. His sword rose and fell like a sledgehammer on a blacksmith's anvil, and every rapid, titanic blow dealt his enemy another mortal wound. The chamber about him was covered in filth too gruesome to describe, and the demon's Hel-spawned life force began to stream in pungent torrents. Feebly Dhampir tried to swat the tribesman away, but every time a horrific gash was hewn into his hands or arms. He knew he was finished, there was no escape from the savage gone berserk, and he moaned and wailed in bitter defeat, attempting to drag himself to the lip of the bottomless hole in the middle of the floor.

Joktan rushed in with a vicious thrust, and his blade pierced through the demon's thickly muscled neck. Dhampir gurgled grotesquely, choking on his own unholy blood, and the savage wrenched his sword free from the devil with a guttural growl. Preternatural vital fluids rilled along his blade, and Joktan's chest heaved as he gasped for breath and raised his broadsword for one last and final blow.

He paused for a second to gather his strength, and Dhampir managed to turn his head enough to stare him in the eyes. It was a moment that seemed to last forever, and one which Joktan would never be able to forget as long as he lived. What he saw was the foulest depravity, so stark and utterly debasing that it defied all human comprehension. It was a malice so perverse that even his primordial subconscious mind was unable to defy it, and in an instant he felt his soul being gripped by an unspeakably evil hand. It was as though he was being swallowed up by a force more dark than the blackest bowels of sin. A tortured cry escaped his lips unbidden, and suddenly he tore his eyes away and turned his head.

His muscles tensed, his sword moved with every ounce of power in his aching thews, and the blade of Avatare struck the ancient god's neck with a splintering, solid thud. Dhampir's final scream ceased abruptly as his decapitated head fell away into the black abyss, and after a few last involuntary spasms, his carcass sprawled limp and lifeless at Joktan's feet.

An eerie silence filled the chamber, broken only by the savage's ragged breathing. Then tiny silver particles of brilliant light began to appear in the air about him. He stepped back uncertainly from the demon's gruesome corpse, and the flecks of light began to coalesce, swirling about the unearthly mass in a dazzling whirlwind of blinding radiance. Dhampir's headless body was lifted into the air by the whirling mass. It hung motionless for a moment, suspended above the black opening of the bottomless chasm. Then the light vanished abruptly, and the demon's remains plummeted downwards, dropping out of sight in the darkness of the pit like a stone cast into the sea.

Suddenly the ground began to tremble once more. The huge cracks which had split the chamber floor came together again in a choking cloud of dust, and the jagged lips of the great abyss closed together in a grinding and grating of stone and debris. Within moments the shaking subsided. It was almost impossible to tell that the fissures had ever existed at all.

A feminine voice echoed in the room as the sound of moving earth and stone subsided. Although the one who spoke could not be seen, Joktan instantly recognized the sound of Lamashtu's voice.

"The world is safe once more, Joktan," she intoned. "May the blade of Avatare serve you long and well! You are now it's rightful master."

"Thank-you," he accepted. "Will you not show your face?"

"Not within this house of ancient evil," she replied, "but we will meet again in the sacred circle of the standing stone, once your journey has been completed. Until then, know that my heart goes with you. I bid you farewell!"

The tribesman nodded. "Farewell," he whispered.

Joktan stood for a moment longer in silence, then he slung the demon's rotten blood from his long steel blade and slammed it into it's sheath, crossing the ruined floor to Sheba's side.

"You all right?" he asked, glancing quickly over her lithe, naked figure.

"What do you think?"

Joktan grinned. "I think I did all the fighting while you lounged here naked and watched!"

"I just didn't want to show you up!" she countered, her eyes sparkling. "Besides, you had already claimed those two. It would not have been proper for me to interfere."

Joktan ran his eyes over her unclothed body, and his lust was undisguised. "We've still got a little time left, if you want to….."

"Just get me out of here!" she cut him off. "Honestly! Is sex the only thing on your mind?"

"Fine, have it your way this time," he obliged, getting up and striding toward the lever mechanism with a dejected look upon his bloodstained face. "The next time you may not have a choice…."

"We still have an audience," she reminded him.

Joktan had forgotten about Skeltar during his struggle with Dhampir. He turned to see the poor wretch skulking a short distance away. His sword leapt into his bloody fist as he crossed the chamber floor, and there was no mistaking the intent in his azure gaze. As he drew nearer the wizard crouched low, covering his bare pate with gigantic hands. Joktan placed the edge of his blade against Skeltar's throat and forced him to raise his head, looking him in the eyes.

The mage trembled fearfully, and in that moment the savage realized what a pitiful sight he truly was. His hatred of the sorcerer was extreme, but there was nothing he could do to him now that would be worse than what Dhampir had done already. Killing him would be the most merciful thing any one could do.

Joktan had no desire to offer the mage such kindness.

"Slay me!" the wizard pleaded weakly. His voice was difficult to understand, on account of his deformed mouth and swollen lips. "Avenge your father's suffering at last!"

Joktan was tempted briefly, but he returned his broadsword to its scabbard with a spiteful growl.

"I've waited for this moment for a long time," he told the humiliated mage. "Many times I have dreamed of lopping off your miserable head."

"Then do it!"

The savage shook his head. "No," he decided, "I'll let you live. Not because I pity you, but because there would be no pleasure in it now. I deem my oath fulfilled."

He turned away, and the mage began to weep, his voice consumed in bitter sorrow.

Freeing Sheba, and gathering up her few belongings, they turned their backs on the wizard and left the temple. Behind them Skeltar's mournful cries echoed hauntingly as they went, and together they made their exit and strode out into the first gray light of dawn.

# 31

Outside the demonic army had faltered, then suddenly fell away. Their hellish bodies began to weaken and fall apart, and they screamed tormented, angry cries before convulsing in spasms and falling dead upon the ground. Those who fought them stared agape in startled disbelief, and for an instant Zebulon was shrouded in an anxious hush, silent as a dead man's grave.

Then a triumphant din rose into the night, as those who had survived the chaos rejoiced in victory. As darkness slowly faded, however, the morning's light revealed a grisly scene.

The streets and walls were strewn with the carcasses of the dead. Everywhere lay mutilated corpses, in darkly colored pools of coagulated blood. Fires that had broken out during the fray yet burned throughout the city, and black smoke rose toward the heavens in great, billowing columns. The city's inhabitants had suffered sorely; of the thousands that had lived here just hours before, only a few hundred now survived. Heartbroken laments for the dead and dying drifted plaintively through the streets, where the few remaining soldiers separated the lifeless bodies of men and demons into gory heaps.

A pavilion was erected in which to tend for the wounded, and within men were laid upon stretchers in rows from wall to wall. A seemingly endless stream of soldiers and commoners alike flooded the makeshift hospital, and soon a long line of people stood waiting outside the doors. Many survivors wandered aimlessly in shock, and the sickening stench that pervaded the streets was unbearable.

Runners were dispatched into the surrounding land to summon any who could lend their aid, yet conditions were such that many of the wounded died before they could be attended. Their bodies were quickly added to the growing heaps of rotting, nameless corpses, to be eventually hauled away on ox carts and burned en mass outside the city walls.

The palace guards had been hopelessly outnumbered and overwhelmed, and the opulent halls were now stained thickly with slimy mounds of decaying filth. It was impossible to believe that such unthinkable carnage had been wrought in so little time, yet the once proud city of Zebulon bore grim testimony to this incontrovertible fact.

It would take several days to quell the raging fires, and weeks to wash away the horrible evidence of such wholesale slaughter.

Even the secret passages had been invaded by some of the horde, but there they could not venture very far. The mysterious powers that protected the tunnels had slain the demons within minutes of entering the caverns, and those that managed to somehow survive it were subsequently killed by King Xalton's women.

Even here the battle had been won at great cost, however. Scarcely half of his Elite Guards survived the subterranean fray, and in the coming years it would be decided that the tunnels should be sealed up and abandoned. As much as they provided a means of escape in times of trouble, they could still provide would-be assassins with a clandestine entrance into the very heart of the palace.

In the annals of Straltonian history, this night would be recorded for future generations to remember. It would prove to be one of their darkest moments, a deeply furrowed scar upon the proud brow of civilization, and one which the passing of centuries could never fully erase.

# 32

"Bandits," Joktan growled.

It had been over a week since leaving the ruined city of Zebulon behind, and they were now riding south along the western bank of the Tsargul River. The pair had agreed to accompany Chia and a handful of her companions back to the scene of their ill-fated battle against the saurgs. The king's elite warriors were returning to retrieve the bodies of their fallen comrades, for the women's sense of duty extended equally to each other as well as to the king. The remains of their friends were to be taken back to Zebulon, where they would receive a proper and honorable burial, before being interred within the precincts of the Royal Tombs.

Thus far, there had been no sign of danger along the way, and the journey had been most enjoyable indeed. From here, Joktan and Sheba would turn south, passing through the kingdoms of Gershom and Lagash on their way toward the far-away land of Lothair. This morning, however, the party had spied a small band of mounted men moving steadily towards them, and now they were just a short distance away. As the two groups converged, the intent of the newcomers became obvious at once.

The bandits swept towards them confidently, like a starving pack of hyenas upon a gazelle. They had superiority of numbers, and these plains were their domain. They were killers, thieves and reavers, condemned felons one and all. They exchanged scarred and cruel grins, then cheered like jackals and dove in for an easy kill.

Fate, however, had other plans for this day.

Joktan drew his sword as the women flanked him and drove his horse ahead with reckless speed. He slammed into the midst of the bandits like a raging tidal wave upon the rocky shore, his blade carving a shining silver path of death about him in every direction.

His horse smashed into them with such jarring force that three of the villains were hurled off of their mounts with startled cries. Several of the villains nearly halted in their tracks when they caught sight of the women, but they were quickly spurred into action as the beauties attacked with brutal fury.

A sudden cloud of brown dust choked the air around them as the fight commenced in earnest, and Joktan was thrown from the saddle as his mount collided violently with a hastily raised spear. The barbed, steel point was intended for him, but instead pierced his horse's chest. It was driven in mercilessly by the shear momentum of the tribesman's charge, and the poor beast let out a painful bellow as it fell kicking upon the sun-baked loam.

Joktan was on his feet as soon as he struck the dirt, snarling like a rabid lion, his leg muscles tensed, ready to pounce upon the nearest foe. From the haze a bandit appeared before him, brandishing a long, curving swalta with a bloodthirsty, desperate cry.

Joktan rushed recklessly to meet him, his blade raised high for a powerful blow, and another bandit joined his foe. He could hear Chia and her companions close by, and through the chaos he saw Sheba's ax rise and fall with furious abandon. The savage's long canines bared in a vicious, throaty growl. He twirled his sword like a windmill, then held it out lightly before him, eagerly inviting his foes to come and meet their deaths.

One man obliged, swinging his curved blade in a wide, horizontal sweep. The maneuver was intended to sever the tribesman's neck from his head, but he evaded it with nimble ease.

Joktan was a savage picture of barbaric, primordial rage. His uncivilized nature swelled to the forefront, as the animal inside was released and lustfully seized control. These bandits were a dangerous lot indeed, but they had all been born in kingdoms which had become civilized long ago, in an era when Joktan's ancestors still roasted their foes upon wooden spits and gnawed their charred flesh from dripping bones. He was in his element, and his heart beat out a dirge of death as he faced these dirty rouges with dreadful glee.

The bandit had pitched his full strength behind that sweeping blow, but now his sword passed harmlessly, cleaving only the empty air where an instant before a man had been. He staggered awkwardly for a mere second, off balance and over-extended.

Joktan swarmed in, his sword raised high for a devastating downward stroke, and a fire kindled in his eyes that turned the villain's heart to ice within his chest. His visage was a frightening grimace of murderous intent, and in that brief and frenzied moment the bandit chanced to gaze into his azure eyes.

In the savage's molten stare he saw the reaper's ghastly grin, and he knew then that this was the last thing he'd ever see.

For an instant time stood still.

He caught a glimpse of sunlight through the haze. The wind danced amid the grasses, the Tsargul River shimmered cool and deep. He suddenly wished that he were far away, somewhere safe and secure from this unreal scene, and he wondered how it was that he had ever became a wanted man. He knew his mother had loved him once....perhaps she was still alive....and he remembered being carefree long ago, before he'd raped and butchered his neighbor's wife.

Then his eyes brimmed wide with horror, his scream frozen upon dry, dusty lips, as time resumed its usual gait.

He sucked his last breath in.

There was no chance for surrender....no time to even blink....as Joktan roared insanely behind a yard of razor steel. The blade gleamed with thirsty vengeance, like a thunderbolt hurled from boiling skies, and it streaked unerringly in a silver blur toward the bandit's unprotected skull.....

# TO BE CONTINUED

www.ingramcontent.com/pod-product-compliance
Lightning Source LLC
Chambersburg PA
CBHW051831020726
47502CB00005B/1738